She was sexier than he'd expected, the kind of woman who was hot and didn't know it

Annie looked Sam up and down. "You deep-sixed my background check, and I want to know why."

He was used to being polished with the ladies, in control, on top...or whatever position suited him. "I don't have to explain anything to you."

She glared at him. Given her Hillary Clinton suit, she probably thought men could actually ignore her body and take her seriously. "How long did it take you to do my background check? A week? A day?"

He wasn't going to admit fifteen minutes. "You didn't pass the screen." What was wrong with him? He tried to sound firm. Annie Raye represented everything a man wanted. Spunky, pretty, with a cute little figure all wrapped up in that virginal package that said home cooking and flowered sheets...

Dear Reader,

When it comes to gambling, the casinos drain me dry every time. I have such bad luck that even standing near someone makes them lose. Now when my husband wants to gamble, I am relegated to waiting in our room. All those hours spent watching the in-room movies (including *Ocean's Eleven*) got me wondering what it would feel like to be able to beat the house at its own game. But those stories had been done, so I decided to take a new slant on beating the house.

Enter Annie Raye, a whiz at numbers and a blackjack phenomenon. At the tender age of twelve, she beat everyone who was anyone—and then disappeared, attempting to reclaim a bit of normalcy. Fourteen years later she's back in Vegas and still trying to rebuild a respectable life. Except one person seems to be standing in her way: tall, gorgeous and oh-so-hard-to-get-rid-of Sam Knight. Together they help each other learn that sometimes you have to accept your past to be comfortable with who you are. But before they learn to count on love, there are odds to be calculated and games to be played....

I hope you enjoy Annie and Sam's story. I love to hear from readers, either through my Web site, www.MelindaCurtis.com, or through regular mail at P.O. Box 150, Denair, CA 95316.

Happy reading!

Melinda Curtis

COUNT ON LOVE
Melinda Curtis

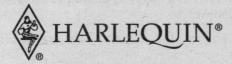

TORONTO • NEW YORK • LONDON
AMSTERDAM • PARIS • SYDNEY • HAMBURG
STOCKHOLM • ATHENS • TOKYO • MILAN • MADRID
PRAGUE • WARSAW • BUDAPEST • AUCKLAND

ISBN-13: 978-0-373-71448-3
ISBN-10:   0-373-71448-3

COUNT ON LOVE

Printed in U.S.A.

ABOUT THE AUTHOR

Melinda Curtis lives in Northern California with her husband, three kids, two Labradors, two cats and a circle of friendly neighbors who eagerly weigh in on everything from the best way to cut your lawn to the best haircut for a fourth grader—just what good friends are for!

Books by Melinda Curtis

HARLEQUIN SUPERROMANCE

1109–MICHAEL'S FATHER
1187–GETTING MARRIED AGAIN
1241–THE FAMILY MAN
1301–EXPECTANT FATHER
1340–BACK TO EDEN
1380–ONCE UPON A CHRISTMAS
     "The Night Before Christmas"
1416–THE BEST-KEPT SECRET

Don't miss any of our special offers. Write to us at the following address for information on our newest releases.

Harlequin Reader Service
U.S.: 3010 Walden Ave., P.O. Box 1325, Buffalo, NY 14269
Canadian: P.O. Box 609, Fort Erie, Ont. L2A 5X3

To my family, who never seem able to remember we have trash cans and dirty clothes hampers (no, the counter/floor won't do), who always wait until the last minute to complete assignments and lesson plans (which need something they assume I can miraculously produce from thin air) and who are my biggest fans. Love you guys!

To Calvin and Hobbs, who remind me it's break time by dropping a slobber-covered ball on my bare feet. Even writers need exercise!

To Anna Stewart, Susan Floyd and Sigal Kremer for listening, reading and occasionally admitting that my writing shows talent. The next bottle of wine is on me!

And to Dad. I hope I have your courage, big heart and gumption when I'm eighty-one!

PROLOGUE

"I'LL SEE YOUR five hundred and raise you five hundred." Vince's grin was infuriatingly superior. He thought he was going to win. What a *jamook.*

Aldo rolled his cigar from one side of his mouth to the other, studying his grandson from behind a poker face he'd perfected more than fifty years ago, his bland expression giving no hint as to his cards or his irritation. All Aldo's efforts to groom his heir seemed to be wasted.

You'd think by twenty-seven my grandson would have learned.

Aldo peered beneath the rim of his trifocals at his remaining chips. Vince hadn't planned this well, raising the stakes to the point where the boy had to risk it all.

His fingers shaking with age, Aldo selected five one-hundred-dollar chips with the Sicilian Casino's gold-and-black logo from one of his many stacks, and tossed them in.

"Call."

With a flourish, Vince snapped his cards onto the green felt. Everything he did was loud and flashy, drawing attention when subtlety was called for. "Two pair. Kings and tens."

Angling his head, Aldo glanced at his cards once more before fanning them gently in a row on the table. "Full house." He hadn't lost the touch. The same touch that had earned him the money to bankroll the Sicilian, one of the most opulent casinos on the Las Vegas Strip. He'd bought it over fifty years ago when he'd decided, with Rosalie's help, which side of the law he wanted to be on. Definitely, the right side.

Vince's face contorted. He was a good-looking young man when he wasn't upset about something.

Aldo estimated his grandson had lost about five thousand dollars. That was as good a reason as any to be upset, particularly since it was close to a quarter of the salary Aldo overpaid him each month. Aldo wasn't going to tell Vince what he'd lost was all going to charity. What was the point? He wouldn't believe him, anyway.

Vince stood, kicking his chair back in the process.

It took more than that to make Aldo nervous, but Paulo took one step toward the table from his post near the door.

"I'll see you tomorrow," Aldo said calmly. "Same time. Blackjack." For the past month, Aldo had insisted they gamble every night. He'd hoped that the card games would help mend the rift that had developed between them these past few months. Only they seemed to be doing the opposite. Perhaps a new approach was required.

"You won't always beat me." Vince scowled, his dark gaze centered on the pile of chips. "No one plays blackjack anymore. It's an old man's game."

"You'd rather I fronted you the money to play in the World Series of Poker, with gimmicks and too much left to chance." Aldo shook his head. "Blackjack is about beating the house, not another player."

"And you're the house." Vince raised his black eyes to meet Aldo's ever-watchful stare. "You're beatable. A little girl fleeced you. And she was only twelve."

"She had skill. Only a fool would side-bet against her." Aldo hid his annoyance. "She quit the game a winner." *Che peccato.* What a shame that episode had turned out so badly.

Muttering a curse, Vince stormed out of Aldo's penthouse suite. Long after the heavy door slammed, Aldo sat pondering what he was going to do with his grandson. He had never felt so alone.

When he finally moved, Aldo's legs were unsteady. They always were at the end of the day. Too many years pounding the casino floor. Too much regret in his old age. Aldo walked across the thick Oriental carpet to the bedroom, his knees giving out completely when he caught sight of his beautiful Rosalie.

He would have collapsed if not for Paulo's quick, steadying grip. His bodyguard half carried Aldo across the room, easing him gently into a chair next to Rosalie's hospital bed and the legion of machines that kept her alive. The private nurse on duty slipped discreetly out the door.

Aldo enveloped his wife's cool, frail hand in both of his. "I don't know what more I can do, *cara mia.*" And then he bent his head and prayed.

CHAPTER ONE

IT WAS LIKE SOME small-town parade back home. Men, children, women carrying babies—everyone was smiling and singing as they passed the young American soldiers on a pitted street in Baghdad.

Trying to find relief in the shade of the awning above the bank entrance, Sam found himself humming along to their tune. Anything to distract himself from the oppressive heat.

"Gun! Shooter!" It was Vince. Clearly panicked.

Sam lifted his M16 and—

Sat bolt upright in bed. In Las Vegas. Drenched in sweat.

He peeled off his T-shirt as his cell phone rang. Sam checked the caller ID before answering. The call originated from the Sicilian Casino. Assuming it must be Vince, he answered, "Knight, here," while he pressed his palm to his damp forehead, hoping to ease the ache behind his eyes.

"Hungover again?" Aldo Patrizio's cold voice penetrated through his headache.

Half a beer could only account for the bad taste in

his mouth, but Sam didn't correct his friend's grandfather. The call itself was unusual enough. "You wanted something?"

"I've got a job for you. There's a group of card counters becoming more bothersome at small places up and down the Strip. I need you to find them."

Cardsharps, or counters, kept track of the cards played in blackjack and increased their odds of winning by calculating the odds of cards coming into play. Casino managers considered playing by a system cheating. Sam thought being smart was fair, but who was he to judge when there was a paycheck involved? If only it wasn't Vince's grandfather asking.

"And don't tell me you already have work. You could do those background checks in your sleep," Patrizio added.

So much for that excuse. "Mr. Patrizio—"

"If you provide me with their names I'll make it worth your while." The older man named an attractive figure that would boost Sam's sagging bank account. It was a fee nearly triple what Sam might have charged. There was more going on here than a request for services.

His jaw tensed. "Why me?"

Aldo's laughter grated on Sam's nerves. "If you're anything like your father, you're good at locating people. Call Sabatinni to confirm it's them and I'll take care of the rest."

Rick Sabatinni was a retired cardsharp who consulted with the casinos. Sam had done some surveillance on Sabatinni's wife—now ex—last winter, and still had his number. Of course, a man like Aldo Patrizio would know about that. The old man knew just about everything that went down in Vegas.

"Vince isn't going to like this." Sam was still toying with the idea of turning the casino owner down. Vince Patrizio wasn't exactly on the best of terms with his grandfather and, having served with Vince in Iraq, Sam was protective of the younger man.

"He'll like it a lot better than if I had hired you to follow him. Having *family* hire someone to investigate you is low, don't you think?" Mr. Patrizio disconnected.

So the old man knew Vince had hired Sam to look into his activities... This did not bode well. Sam stumbled the few feet from his bed to his kitchen and swallowed more than the recommended dose of aspirin. At a rumbling beneath him, he squinted out the window, to see Vince backing his spanking-new black Porsche out of the garage.

Sam measured coffee, poured water and leaned against the counter while he waited for his first cup, waiting to feel the peace his Spartan garage apartment, uncluttered by reminders of his past, usually provided. Nada. Getting out of the job would be next to impossible. The trouble was Mr. Patrizio was setting Sam up.

His cell phone rang again, but it was his sister, and Sam let it go to voice mail. Restless, he paced the twenty steps from the kitchen to the front door, only pausing when his phone beeped to indicate there was a new message. One of several from his sister Sam wouldn't pick up.

The stack of job applicants for Slotto Gaming Machines sat next to his computer on a round kitchen table, waiting for Sam's approval. He really should get them done today so he could get paid. Plus it was the perfect excuse not to troll the casinos for Mr. Patrizio's card counters. He opened the first folder.

Annie Raye. The name conjured up innocence and sunshine. Sam disliked her already. He sat at the table and logged on to his computer. Raye was her maiden name, but apparently she'd ping-ponged from Ms. Raye to Mrs. Jones and back to Ms. Raye.

Her driving record and credit history were clean. It would be a waste of time to check for a criminal record, but Sam did it anyway. While the computer chugged through several databases, he got himself a cup of coffee. He should just rubber stamp Annie Raye's application so she could get that exciting finance director job at Slotto's. Conducting a complete search was a waste of his time. He'd been doing background checks for Slotto's for months and he'd never found information to recommend not hiring anyone.

Sam sat back down, looked at the search results and nearly dropped his coffee mug.

ANNIE TURNED EAST AND headed toward the apartment complex her dad said he was living in now. Located near the airport, it wasn't the nicest area, but Annie and her daughter needed a place to stay until her first paycheck came in.

"One, two, three green traffic lights ahead." Maddy

crooned softly from the backseat. "One, two, three, four red cars. Why are there so many red cars?"

Because it was Sin City—the desert metropolis where dreams were made and broken—and red cars symbolized the flashiness of risk and stupidity. Annie's knuckles whitened on the cracked steering wheel as traffic slowed to a halt, leaving her stranded midintersection two blocks from her destination. Horns honked as the green light turned yellow, then red. The jaywalkers jogged out of the way and Annie pressed on the accelerator.

"Big black cars. One, two-o-o!" Maddy wailed, kicking at the front seat. "You're going too fast, Mommy. I can't count."

"Maddy, when we get to Grandpa's house, could you stop counting out loud?" Annie's first priority upon moving back to Vegas was to find a babysitter. For now, she'd have to make do with her dad while she stopped by Slotto Gaming Machines to sign the paperwork before starting her new job. She wouldn't trust her dad with Maddy for more than an hour, two max. Not that he wouldn't keep her safe, but Brett Raye had a way of presenting gambling as a fun, exciting lifestyle.

"No, Mommy," Maddy said. "I love to count."

Annie struggled to keep her voice calm. "Grandpa doesn't like it when people count."

"Why not?"

Think fast, Annie. The last thing she needed was for her dad to discover her daughter's talents and mold them in ways that would scar poor Maddy for life.

"Because…he can't count and it makes him sad to hear other people do it."

"I can teach him, Mommy. I have good numbers."

"Yes, you do, but Grandpa is too old to learn." If he knew Maddy had skill, he'd be up to his old tricks faster than Annie could say boo.

"Okay." Maddy sounded reluctant.

Annie turned into the Harvard Arms, an apartment complex aspiring to be a dump with its faded rock-and-cactus garden, cracked windows and peeling paint. The 1992 Toyota she'd paid eight hundred dollars for when they repossessed her Mercedes looked like the newest vehicle in the lot. Annie parked and let the car idle, reluctant to get out.

"Is this where Grandpa lives?" Maddy asked.

"We can't stay here." Annie's stomach soured. This was no place for her little girl. Why couldn't she get a break?

"Is that Grandpa? He has whiskers."

Sure enough, Brett trundled down the concrete steps from the second story with a huge smile on his gaunt, wrinkled face. His wavy hair was gray and sparse. The years hadn't been kind. He looked far older than fifty-five.

"Annie!" He opened her car door, leaving her no choice but to turn off the engine and get out.

Her father grabbed her so tight that Annie felt his breath hitch, as if he might cry. Maybe she'd been wrong to keep her distance all these years…. Her doubt dissipated as her father held her at arm's length with that half grin he always used to give her just before he announced his latest scheme.

No. Annie had had enough of scheming men.

Her dad released her and opened the rear door, leaning in to see his granddaughter better. "And this must be Maddy. With those blond curls and bright blue eyes, you're as beautiful as your mother was at your age." Then her father ruined it by adding, "Do you play cards, Maddy?"

"No." Annie gave him a scathing look. "No cards." When his face fell, she had no trouble remembering why she'd kept her distance for six years. She took a deep breath. "Let me look at your place. If it's fine, I'll only be gone an hour or two." She unbuckled Maddy from her car seat. "I hope your bathroom is sanitary."

"It's not the Taj Majal, but it's clean, I swear." He led them upstairs, smiling in a way that made Annie realize how much this visit meant to him.

To her dismay, she noticed Maddy's lips moving as she climbed. She was counting the number of stairs to the top. Annie placed her finger briefly on her daughter's mouth and the little girl pressed her lips together.

"Did you lose the house, Dad?" Annie knew she shouldn't have bought it for him. She'd hoped her father would have changed. He was probably still hanging out with the same crowd of "could-have-beens" who wagered every nickel on the flip of a card and didn't seem to care where they lived, what they lost or if they had enough to retire on.

"This is only temporary." He looked up as a jumbo jet barnstormed Harvard Arms on its way to land at McCarran International Airport and shrugged apologetically. "You get used to that."

"SORRY, I GOT BACKLOGGED, Carl." Sam set the stack of candidate files on the man's desk. Carl Nunes, Slotto's director of human resources, stared at Sam, who stood like a kid in the principal's office awaiting sentencing.

"It's all right. We haven't gotten the drug testing results back for most of these, anyway." The fluorescent lighting glinted off Carl's bald head as he turned the pile around with his short, plump fingers. "I hadn't realized your stack had gotten so large."

Like hell he hadn't. But Sam knew when to keep quiet. He turned away, pretending to admire the photos of Carl's family on a bookshelf by the door. The older man had three girls with toothy grins. Sam swallowed and sat in one of Carl's plastic visitor chairs, his back to the bookshelf.

"My practice is more demanding now." Sam had spent the early part of the week out at Lake Mead with his WaveRunner, practicing jumps.

"Good for you. We'll always be here for you, Sam…as long as you're here for us."

As hints went, it wasn't very subtle. Sam mumbled something reassuring and stared at his boots. Background checks were a lucrative business Vince had gotten him into after their stint in the war. Too bad Sam had to deal with Mr. College Graduate, I'm-better-than-you types.

If he took that job for Mr. Patrizio—

"Any surprises?"

This was where Sam usually said no, unfolded his invoice, handed it to Carl and bolted for the exit. Carl was so used to the routine that he was already hefting the files onto the credenza behind him.

Sam leaned forward with a creak of plastic. "Actually, there's a problem with one."

Carl's pale forehead wrinkled. "What kind of problem?"

"Annie Raye. She's got an arrest record."

"Annie? There must be some mistake." Carl didn't need to search for Annie's file. Sam had kept it on top of the stack. "Everyone loves her. I already approved her moving expenses."

Damn if Carl didn't sound like the forgiving type. "She was arrested for embezzling. I think that makes her a bad choice as your new finance director." Sam pulled the invoice out of his pocket, smoothed out the creases and set it on Carl's fake-wood desktop. "Should I pick up more files from Winona on my way out?"

"YOU HAVE THREE DOORS in this house." Maddy looked up with big, blue unblinking eyes from the ball of Play-Doh she was rolling. Her short blond hair curled around her ears with a wildness reminiscent of Annie's at that age.

"Have you started school?" Brett asked, unable to stop smiling. His granddaughter was as sharp as a tack.

"I went for thirty-three days before we left to come

here. I was in Mrs. Guichard's kindergarten class. We had twenty-one chairs in room sixteen." She fluffed up her cotton dress before studying him again as if he were a lab specimen. "You have a lot of whiskers. So many I don't think I could count them all." Maddy reached up and touched his stubbled cheek, her fingers soft and warm.

Brett chuckled. He could listen to her talk all day. And if he played his cards right, he'd be able to. "I bet you learned a lot in room sixteen." And taught her teacher a thing or two.

Maddy nodded. "We learned about numbers and counting. How come I haven't seen you before?"

Brett swallowed past a lump in his throat. "You lived so far away."

"We have eight houses on our street. You never came to visit, even at Christmas. I would remember."

Annie hadn't wanted him to come. He'd only visited her once after she'd been married. Brett might have screwed up his relationship with Annie, but he wasn't going to make the same mistake twice. "The important thing is that you're here now."

His cell phone chimed.

"Where are you? I went by your house and you weren't there." Ernie's anger vibrated through the phone.

Brett rented cheap, furnished apartments close to the Strip when he was working. He paid cash for the temporary space and registered under a different name. He'd been living in this dump for nearly a week. Being a career cardsharp was hard. If a casino identified him he'd be out of the game for good—banned with the aid of a security program that identified his features for the larger casinos, and a newsletter distributed to the smaller gaming houses.

"I needed a day off." Brett tried to sound casual. He and his friends had just ten more days to raise twenty thousand dollars. He didn't have time to sit and fiddle with Play-Doh, but he couldn't let this opportunity with Maddy and Annie pass, either.

"Grandpa, I need yours." Maddy stretched out her hand and waved it. He'd been helping her make a string of Play-Doh pearls on the coffee table.

"Who's there with you?"

"No one." Brett handed Maddy the dough ball and went into the bedroom, closing the door behind him. "It's the TV."

"*Grandpa?*" In the ensuing silence, Brett hoped he'd lost the connection. "She came back, didn't she?"

"No." Brett denied it too quickly. He'd wanted to ask Annie to help the moment she arrived, but she'd made it clear she disapproved of anything to do with cards. He clutched the small cell phone tighter. Although they could use her help, Brett didn't want to risk losing her again. "Annie quit, remember? She won't help us."

"You shouldn't assume anything. Chauncey needs this."

Brett snapped the cell phone closed and returned to the living room. Chauncey might need money, but Brett needed his daughter back in his life. It was selfish of him to have wanted to see Annie again and to meet his granddaughter, foolish to think they could try to build a relationship when he'd agreed to such high stakes.

"How about an ice cream?"

"Isn't Mommy going to be home soon?"

But Brett didn't answer. He was too busy grabbing his car keys.

"I *FAILED* MY BACKGROUND check?" Annie's fingers were so numb from clasping her hands together, it was hard to believe it was a balmy eighty-degree October day.

"Annie, the committee made its final review of your application." Carl paused to clear his throat. "Unfortunately, we've decided to pursue another candidate because of this blip in your background check."

"What?" She barely had enough breath in her lungs to question the decision. "You said the job was mine. I packed up and moved."

"I'm sorry. We'll reimburse your expenses, but we can't offer you the job." His voice had lost its usual warmth and he wouldn't look her in the eye.

The shock of losing something she'd thought was hers, had based so many life-changing decisions on and looked forward to, left Annie speechless. She'd sold everything of value Frank hadn't already pawned or the courts hadn't taken, and left Los Angeles with two hundred dollars and barely enough possessions to fill two suitcases. She'd thought she couldn't sink any lower.

"You're a qualified individual," Carl was saying, when Annie's mind was capable of comprehending. "I'm sure you'll find something else soon."

"There must be some mistake. May I see the report, please?" At least then she'd know why she'd failed. But really, there was only one reason not to hire her. She suspected she hadn't run far enough away from Frank and the mess he'd made of her life.

"We don't give out that information." But Annie noticed a company logo on a piece of paper on top of a file with her name on the tab—an invoice from Sam Knight Investigations.

When she arrived, there'd been a tall man outside waiting for Winona to give him something. He'd had thick black hair and a face with features that probably inspired plenty of female fantasies, despite the gaunt look in his eyes, rumpled khakis and a well-worn polo shirt. He'd looked like an unscrupulous private investigator standing at the edge of a sea of sad gray cubicles. The secretary may have even called him Sam.

"I need this job, Carl. I can do good things for Slotto." Annie smoothed her skirt and tried to compose herself, tried to sound like the qualified, un-ruffled businesswoman she'd been before Frank was arrested. "If there's been a mistake, you'd still hire me, right?"

"Of course, if there's been a mistake—"

"I'm sure there has been." Standing, Annie cut Carl off. She was just desperate enough to face Sam Knight and get the truth out of him. If only he hadn't left yet…

SAM PULLED A HOT DOG from the warming rack at the 7-Eleven across the street from Slotto, feeling pretty damn good about the morning.

"You've got a lot of explaining to do, buster," a woman next to him said. Sam had been called much worse than buster by more threatening babes, but this taunt threw him for a loop. The woman looked like a petite Swedish schoolteacher. Short ruffled blond hair, boring if well-filled suit, plenty of leg, pearls around her neck. Just the right combination of good girl and sex appeal.

Sam turned his back on her and filled a soda cup with ice.

She sidled closer to him, invading his personal space, whispering as if what she had to say was for his ears only. "You're a disgrace to…to…the private investigator profession…and men in general."

Wait a minute. He remembered seeing her in the reception area of Slotto. "Lady—"

"My name is Annie Raye. Ring any bells?"

She was sexier than he'd expected, the kind of woman who was hot and didn't know it. He disliked her all over again. "How did you…? What are you…?" *Smooth, Knight.* He filled his cup with Pepsi.

Annie looked him up and down. "You deep-sixed my background check and I want to know why."

He used to be polished with the ladies, in control, on top…or whatever position suited him. But that was before Iraq. "I don't have to explain anything to you."

She glared at him. Given her Hilary Clinton suit, she

probably thought men could actually ignore her well-proportioned body and take her seriously. "How long did it take you to do my background check? A week? A day?"

He wasn't going to admit fifteen minutes. But it had been one of the most enjoyable fifteen minutes he'd spent in a long time.

"That's what I thought. You should spend more time getting the answers right. Now, call up Carl Nunes and let's straighten this mess out."

"You didn't pass the screen," Sam said lamely. What was wrong with him? He tried to sound firm. "There is no recount, no redo, no make goods. Not for embezzlers."

"My husband..." Her cheeks lost some of their color. "My *ex*-husband is the crook. I was booked on suspicion, but no charges were ever filed against me. Didn't your so-called background check pick that up? There's no reason Slotto shouldn't hire me." Annie glowered at him, but the look was ruined by the bedroom huskiness of her voice as she whispered, "In fact, it's illegal for you to even use that information against me."

"It's illegal in California, but we're much more lenient in Nevada, sweetheart."

She made a huffing noise. "That's not a good enough reason, *darling*."

He stared at her a moment, then cleared his throat. "How about this? Your father is a professional gambler, and probably a petty crook who hasn't yet been caught scamming tourists." There was no way Annie Raye could work in any field even remotely connected to gambling when her father made his less-than-successful living playing cards.

"Slotto doesn't want to hire my dad." She pushed out her lower lip, which was pink, plump and tempting.

Annie Raye represented everything a man wanted. Spunky, pretty with a cute little figure—all wrapped up in that virginal package that said home-cooking and flowered sheets. No wonder Carl Nunes had been fooled. But she couldn't put one over on Sam.

He finally came to his senses and headed to the cashier.

Annie lacked the bravado to stand in his way, but she doggedly trailed after him. "I packed everything I own in my car, left at five this morning and drove four hours to get here. And do you know why?"

"No, and I don't care. Go peddle your résumé somewhere else. I need breakfast."

"A hot dog and a soda? No wonder you look like a truck ran you over."

His hot dog was no longer hot. Wearily, Sam turned back to her. "You might get better results explaining all this to Carl or a reporter. Maybe Slotto is the type of company that would hire you just to escape bad press. Of course, you'd have to be willing to bare your soul and your past. But, hey, Vegas loves gamblers, right?" He found himself caught in her vivid blue gaze. There was more than anger in her eyes. There was fear, as well.

Sam may not have discovered all the skeletons in Annie Raye's closet.

CHAPTER TWO

WHY COULDN'T SAM KNIGHT have been an old, cig-
arette-smoking P.I. Annie could easily charm?
Instead, he was intimidatingly tall, with long limbs
that outpaced and outreached a height-challenged
woman like herself. His haunted green eyes hid a
stubborn streak Annie hadn't been able to break. And
she didn't want to acknowledge the solid curve of his
biceps beneath the short sleeves of his shirt or the way
her heart ka-thumped when his studied gaze roved
beyond her face.

With one eye on Sam's big black truck in front of
her, Annie dug her phone out of her purse and called
her dad. "May I speak to Maddy?"

"We're doing fine, honey. How are things with you
on the job?"

"Fine," she lied. It wouldn't be a lie when she convinced Sam to change his mind. "Is that…are you in a
car?" Annie had to accelerate to keep up with Sam
through a yellow light. "I forbid you to take Maddy to a
card game." Her father knew nothing about parental
limits.

"We're just going for ice cream. No cards for this little girl. I promise. Ain't that right, puddin'?"

Annie's heart lurched. He used to call her that. Back then she'd adored her dad and couldn't wait to do whatever he asked. "Let me talk to Maddy."

"I can't turn this girl into a cardsharp in one afternoon, Annie," he said, as if reading her mind. "And I'm not going to try. Here, talk to her."

"Mommy, we're going for ice cream." Maddy's excitement bubbled through the cell phone.

"Is everything okay, sweetie?"

"Yes, Mommy. We're having fun. Grandpa borrowed a car seat from the lady who lives under him."

Her dad said something Annie didn't catch.

"Grandpa says I can hold the cell phone and call you anytime, okay?"

He knew just how to reassure Annie that everything was all right. How she wished she could believe him. "That's great, sweetie. Tell Grandpa I'll be another hour, maybe two."

"Bye, Mommy!" And Maddy hung up just like an independent teenager. Annie wanted to call her back just so she could hear her five-year-old's voice.

"DO I HAVE TO CALL the cops?" Sam demanded when he'd started up the stairs to his garage apartment and realized he had company.

Annie Raye walked up to him with her suit jacket buttoned up to her neck as if she was ready for a business meeting. "All I want is a chance to prove to you that I'm dependable."

Sam's cell phone rang. He checked the display but didn't recognize the local number, and picked up.

"Sam? It's Tiny Marquez. Aldo Patrizio said I should call. One of those card players just walked in. I'd throw him out but I need proof before I lay a finger on him." Casinos had been sued for heavy-handed treatment of suspected counters. That's why independent houses relied on third parties to I.D. and detain sharps.

So much for the small hope that he could wheedle his way out of Mr. Patrizio's job. If Sam didn't deliver those card counters' identities his own name would soon be worth nothing in Vegas.

"I'm there." Sam disconnected the call and then dialed Rick Sabatinni. When the retired gambler answered, Sam turned away from Annie, lowered his voice and quickly explained the situation.

"A group of card counters?" Sabatinni asked, an odd note in his voice.

"Yeah, why?"

"I'll call you back."

Swearing, Sam flipped his phone closed and clipped it to his belt. Something wasn't right.

Tiny Marquez ran a small casino at the outskirts of the Strip. Vince had told Sam that his grandfather sometimes helped out the mom-and-pop casinos in the area. Sam had no idea why. What with running the Sicilian and taking care of his wife, Mr. Patrizio seemed to have his hands full.

"Where are you going?" Annie sidled between Sam and his truck. "We haven't settled this."

Sam refused to look at her, especially her legs. He didn't like the way Mr. Patrizio had boxed him in, or the way Annie was trying to do the same. "I've got business," Sam snapped. He closed the distance between them by one step.

She didn't budge. "What about my job?"

"You're trying my patience," he warned, taking another step. Another two and he'd be able to touch her.

"Look, I'm nonthreatening. I'll work for a trial period." Annie smiled and tilted her head, trying to capture his gaze. With a face like that she could easily con people into believing she was the upstanding citizen she would've appeared to be, if it weren't for the arrest record. "Carl Nunes said all it would take for him to hire me is your approval. I'll disappear if you give it to me."

"Not happening." Sam tried Sabatinni's number again. Still no answer. This time he left a message. "Knight, here. Meet me ASAP at Tiny House of Cards."

As he took another step forward, Annie ran to her wreck of a car, leaving a hint of strawberries in the air. His blood pressure soared. It had been too long since he'd been around a woman like her...the woman she appeared to be.

"What?" she asked, holding the car door open when she noticed Sam staring. "I'm leaving just like you asked." She smiled as if they were best buds.

He wasn't falling for that act.

"Are you working on a case?" she asked too casually.

Sam grunted.

"Can you tell me about it?"

"No." Then he was in his truck and gunning it down the street, all thoughts of strawberry scent and blond hair left far behind.

Until he hopped out of his truck at Tiny House of Cards.

"I'm intrigued by what you do," a familiar voice said behind him.

Annie Raye.

"Go away." Sam clenched his cell phone before redialing Sabatinni. No answer, and his car wasn't in the lot. He'd probably chosen today to come out of retirement, and was in some blackjack tournament. Why else would he blow Sam and Mr. Patrizio off? Sam swore and wished the professional gambler bad luck times five.

"A girl's allowed to go where she wants. And right now, I want a drink." Annie pointed at the small casino. "In here." Then she sauntered in as if she was going to a PTA meeting, leaving Sam no choice but to follow.

Sam and Annie ended up standing together inside the entrance to Tiny's, near the obligatory row of slot machines. Four of the seven machines were occupied, and the cacophony of beeping and music annoyed him already. From where they stood they could see a lone player at the blackjack table, his face barely visible across the smoky lounge.

From behind the long, curving bar, Tiny, a huge, cue ball-headed Hispanic, gave Sam a slight nod, followed by a significant glance in the direction of the card table. Tiny was probably expecting Sam to be fully prepared. Without Sabatinni, this was going to be a royal waste of time.

As they walked deeper into the lounge, Sam cataloged the distinguishing features of the blackjack player. He wore a nice pair of khakis and a high-end bowling shirt at odds with his scraggly appearance. His frizzy salt-and-pepper hair was pulled back in a thin ponytail. Mirrored sunglasses with large tortoiseshell rims hid his eyes and much of his face. A shaggy gray mustache sprouted near a liver-colored growth the size of a malted milk ball below his left nostril. As disguises went, it was minimal but effective. The growth alone would keep most attention politely away from his other facial features. Most people wouldn't look anyone disfigured directly in the face, making recall of the details of his or her appearance difficult.

"What are we here for?" Annie trotted to keep up with him.

"None of your business. This isn't going down as planned. If I were you, I'd leave before Tiny gets angry." Slowing, Sam indicated with a nod who Tiny was. He'd met the proprietor a few months ago at a back room card game at the Sicilian, after which Tiny had knocked out the man who cleaned him out. With one punch. "I'm going to have to talk fast. Why don't you go on home to California?"

"And miss all the fun? Nah."

Weighing in at about three hundred pounds and in desperate need of anger management therapy, Tiny wasn't someone Sam wanted to piss off. He hoped Tiny wasn't losing enough money to pound his frustration out on Sam. Wouldn't that cap the day?

Annie looked worriedly at the large proprietor, at the blackjack table, and then back to Sam. She rubbed a hand over her stomach, as if she wasn't feeling well. "Does Tiny have a gun?"

"Guys like him don't need guns."

"You're joking, right?" she asked, her blue eyes looming large in her pale face as she caught Sam's arm.

"Ah, no. When you've got fists as big as ham hocks, guns aren't nearly as scary. Tiny expects results, not excuses. Excuses just make him mad. And when he's mad…"

Still holding Sam, Annie's eyes darted to the player. "Is he counting? Is that why you're here?"

"A rocket scientist in the making. Very good. My expert resource is a no-show, so the best I can do is make this guy nervous and follow him to try and find out who he is." Sam raked a hand through his hair. Worst case? Tiny would pulverize him and spread the word that Sam was worthless. Soon even Carl wouldn't give him background checks. "This isn't going to be pretty. Really. Why don't you wait outside?"

Biting her lip, Annie stared at Tiny, then the player, then Tiny. Her face was nearly chalk-white now. She turned back toward the door, mumbling something Sam didn't catch.

"Are you okay?" Was it too much to hope that the gambler would get up and leave?

Annie spun back. "Do you have twenty dollars?"

"What?" Did she want ringside seats? Oh, yeah. She'd come in for a drink, probably a nonalcoholic iced tea, just another attempt to make Sam believe she didn't have a crafty bone in her body. "If you need a drink that bad, I'll stop at the liquor store on the way home. I'll need an ice pack by then anyway." But Sam took a twenty out of his wallet. "Get me a beer."

"Thanks." Instead of going to the bar, Annie walked over to the blackjack table and sat two seats away from the man. She placed the twenty-dollar bill on the felt and smiled as sweetly as a churchgoer at the dealer. The player took one look at her and began coughing on his cigar. Annie hopped off her bar stool and pounded his back like the squeaky-clean Good Samaritan she would have been if her dad wasn't addicted to risk and her ex hadn't been so fond of other people's money.

THE MAN SAM SUSPECTED OF being a card counter smelled oddly familiar, but it was hard to tell with the cyst on his face. Annie didn't want to embarrass him by looking too closely. The combination of cigar smoke and cheap cologne irritated her nostrils and turned her anxious stomach. She wiggled her nose and tried not to sneeze, sneaking a glance at the man as the dealer, a thin Hispanic woman with sharp, cast-iron features, flicked out cards.

Annie wouldn't have jumped into this if it hadn't looked like Tiny might clobber Sam. He might be a sloppy P.I., but no one deserved to be punished like that. Besides, saving him from a beating might just get her that job. Still, she couldn't look at her cards yet, couldn't look anywhere but at the green felt in front of her. Annie hadn't gone near a deck for more than fourteen years and might have lost her touch, might have forgotten what it took to count.

In her dreams.

When she was younger, she'd gained her father's approval by playing cards for him. She had a knack for numbers, was able to memorize telephone numbers, dollar amounts and cards played with an ease her father envied and bragged about in his little girl. Annie'd spent much of the summer between sixth and seventh grade in smoky back rooms beating card players as much as fifty years her senior. She'd hoped finally having money would make her mother as happy as it seemed to make her father. Unfortunately, her mom had seen things differently. She'd left that summer. Annie hadn't heard from her since.

Now, as she finally picked them up, the cards felt awkward in her sweaty hands, as if she might drop them at any moment. Why had she jumped in like this? She had no idea when the dealer had last shuffled, and you couldn't start counting cards midgame.

Her mother's pearls around her neck were like a choke chain. Was Sam wondering how to get the two of them out of the Tiny House of Cards? Thinking about leaving without her? Or waiting for her to show her stuff? Sam didn't care that she had a little girl to provide for, that she'd been fired when she and Frank were first arrested. Annie wasn't getting any child support checks from Frank. If she wanted to eat, she was going to have to get a grip, get a job and get on with her life.

Two tens came reassuringly into focus. A solid hand. Ignoring Sam, Tiny, the smelly man at the table and the all-too-familiar atmosphere around her, Annie concentrated on the game.

SAM COULDN'T BELIEVE IT. What was Annie thinking? For all she knew, this guy was dangerous. But dragging her away now would only tip him off and make it that much harder to nail him when Sabatinni got here. If Sabatinni ever showed. Maybe Sam should call Vince to see if he knew where Sabatinni was.

But Vince would only get annoyed that he was working for his grandfather, so Sam retreated to the end of the long curvy bar, where he could observe Annie without turning. He signaled Tiny for a beer, and to occupy himself, he kept hitting Redial on his cell phone until someone called him.

"Knight, here."

"Hey, it's Vince. What's up?"

This was where Sam admitted he was working for Vince's grandfather—albeit reluctantly—and Vince, who was about the only friend Sam had left in the world, washed his hands of him.

"I'm working." Sam glanced over at Annie.

"Want to get a beer tonight at Tassels?"

Vince was obsessively suspicious that the manager of Tassels Galore and his grandfather had conspired to arrange the hit-and-run that had put his grandmother into a coma, despite Sam's inability to prove anything.

Since Vince was younger than him, Sam often found himself in the awkward position of being the voice of reason. "Maybe we could go somewhere else—"

"She'll make a mistake," Vince interrupted. "And I'll be there." He hung up before Sam could protest again.

The beer came and did nothing for Sam's nerves. Normally, the adrenaline rush of intense situations calmed him, focused his mental energy on the job at hand. But he didn't know anything about the man puffing on a cigar two feet from Annie. Was he a cool gambler or a paranoid cheat? Was Annie in danger? And what was Vince going to do when he found out about this?

Annie peeled off her jacket, revealing skimpy lace and a lot of bare skin.

It's been far too long since I had sex.

Sam took another sip of his beer and tried to observe the action without letting his mind wander.

He was far enough away that he couldn't make out the exact cards on the table, but he could see whether the players won or lost, and catch their expressions. The man kept his eyes on the cards the entire time, but still managed to sneak sideways glances at a fidgety Annie.

Jealousy he had no right to tingled in Sam's veins.

Maybe he should rescind that background check and let Carl deal with her. Annie Raye was turning out to be nothing but trouble.

He needed Sabatinni. Sam started dialing through his contact list. Somebody must know where Sabatinni was.

ANNIE STIFLED HER WORRY as she won another hand. The table held a four-dollar minimum bet. The object of her scrutiny was betting ten to fifteen dollars a hand, while Annie was sticking to four dollars. So far, they'd both won just as much as they'd lost, and the dealer hadn't shuffled. Annie hadn't seen anything to make her think the guy was counting cards. She was starting to believe that she wouldn't be able to spot him if he was.

The dealer's top card was a two. Annie glanced at her cards again, an amateur's habit. They wouldn't change. She had a ten and a nine this time. "I'll stay."

The smelly man must have liked his hand, too. He waved the dealer off, eyes glued to the dealer's cards.

The dealer turned over her remaining card. An eight. Adding to her two, it gave the dealer ten points. Not good from where Annie sat. At ten, a face card or ace would beat her hand. So far Annie hadn't seen too many high cards played, so they were due.

The dealer snapped out another two with barely a change in her expression. Twelve points. Then a four. Sixteen points. Annie tightened her grip on her cards. This was getting better for her and the man who shared the table. The dealer couldn't hold until seventeen. She had to give herself another card, and she flipped over…a six. Twenty-two.

The nickname for blackjack wasn't "twenty-one" for nothing. You couldn't accumulate more than twenty-one points. The house had lost, which meant that the players doubled their money as soon as they proved to the dealer they had twenty-one points or less.

Annie wiped her palms on her skirt and watched the man reveal his cards. A nine and a seven. Any combination from twelve to sixteen was a stiff hand, one that would require taking a chance on another card. Not a smart bet, yet he'd come up a winner this round. That didn't mean he wasn't counting. Card counters often lost a little or made intentional mistakes to throw off any suspicions and to reassess the probabilities of the cards.

"If you see a lot of high cards come out—tens, face cards or aces—and you've lost count, start betting low," her father had often said as he snapped cards onto their rickety kitchen table. "Chances are, a lot of low cards will be dealt, and low cards can kill you in blackjack. On the other hand, if you see a lot of low cards being dealt, bet big. That means the big cards are coming out and you're due for a win." He'd tugged one of her pigtails gently. "But you don't lose track, do you, puddin'?"

Since Annie had sat down, there had been only seven significant high cards dealt. If this guy knew anything about gambling, he'd increase his bet. If he'd been counting cards and calculating probabilities, he'd start firing chips onto the table.

After a quick glance around, the dealer looked sourly at the deck, probably trying to decide if she should shuffle or deal another hand. If she shuffled, the odds favored the house, because the card counter would have to start a new tally. With a put-upon sigh, she chose not to shuffle. The hair on the back of Annie's neck prickled.

Annie's eight dollars in chips still sat in the betting area. The other player bumped his bet to an uncharacteristic forty. Annie cast a worried glance at Sam. Though she didn't think what this guy was doing was wrong, she had to signal Sam so that Tiny's fist wouldn't end up in his face, and she'd get that job at Slotto.

But what would happen to this man if she did finger him? Annie couldn't repress the memory of fists pummeling her father's flesh, accented by her own terrified screams. She'd vowed to never let her gambling skills be responsible for someone else's welfare again.

Staring into his beer, Sam took no notice of Annie. His lips were moving. Was he singing? No. Talking on his cell phone. Tiny's dark eyes, on the other hand, bored into Annie, a shot glass barely visible in his fist.

The dealer flicked cards out onto the table. Annie didn't touch hers. She willed Sam to look at her, but he didn't as much as glance her way to settle her nerves.

"Taking one?" the older woman asked, her voice raspy. It was the first time she'd spoken since Annie had sat down.

"What? Oh, sorry. I need a drink," Annie mumbled,

stalling as she looked at her cards for the first time. A jack and an ace, twenty-one in a natural hand that was unbeatable. The ace could count as one or eleven. Annie flipped her cards faceup. She didn't need to play anymore.

The dealer stacked eight dollars in chips in front of Annie. The remaining player chewed on his cigar and brushed his cards across the felt to indicate he wanted another one. The dealer snapped out a seven. He laid his cards down. No smile, no frown. Cool as an ice cube. Annie could remember playing with that kind of composure when she was twelve and thought she was invincible. At twenty-six, she knew every decision came with a risk and a price.

She shot another nervous look Sam's way. From here he looked gorgeous, the trace of sadness in his eyes not evident. He gave no sign that he was aware of her predicament. She was on her own. Next time she'd pick a man who was a good protector and good father material.

Next time? Annie's breath came in near panicked pants. She couldn't wait for a next time. Maddy's toothy grin came to mind, a calming beacon. Annie inhaled deeply.

The dealer had an eight showing, and flicked her hole card over. A six, giving her a stiff fourteen. The rules dictated she had to take another card, and she snapped one down. Another eight. Once again she was busted.

The guy beside Annie turned over his two original

cards with a puff of smoke from his cigar. A seven and a five added to the seven dealt him gave nineteen. He gathered up his chips, tossed one to the dealer and headed to the cashier window.

Annie slipped her jacket on, collected her winnings and followed him, curious as to how much he'd won. She tried to stand unobtrusively behind him in the cashier's line, but had to step closer to hear the attendant count out his money. A quick glance showed her Sam was still engrossed in his call.

"One, two, three, four, five, six, seven, eight hundred and eighty-five dollars."

That much? He'd either been slipping his winnings into his pockets or he'd started out with a lot of chips. Only fifty dollars in chips had been out on the green felt. He hadn't bragged or otherwise given away in the least the fact that he'd won and won big. Only disciplined pros gambled like that. They had to be if they wanted to remain inconspicuous. Occasional players couldn't keep their good fortune to themselves. At a larger casino with extensive video cameras and pit bosses, the man's image would have been compared to a bank of known card counters and if a match was made, he'd be escorted out soon after his next win. The gambler certainly knew casino limits.

Moving quickly, he stepped back, almost on top of Annie. She scrambled out of the way and dropped some of her chips.

"Excuse me," she said as she crouched to pick them up, avoiding looking into his eyes.

His penny loafers paused too close in front of her face. She just knew that he knew that she knew what he'd been doing. At any moment, Annie expected him to drag her up by her hair and use her for a shield as he made his escape, or knock her aside so that she wouldn't follow him.

As if she had the courage to stop him. Annie's heart hammered. She crouched, frozen.

The brown loafers shifted, then quickly moved away.

Annie sighed and stood, knees spongy with relief, forcing herself not to turn around to see where the man had gone. That was Sam's job.

She poured her chips out to the cashier, who frowned at the obvious breach in protocol.

"Sorry," Annie said with an apologetic smile, helping the woman stack the chips.

CHAPTER THREE

ANNIE THRUST THIRTY-SIX dollars at Sam, who was still huddled over his beer with the cell phone glued to his ear. At the other end of the bar, the cashier who'd handled Annie's chips whispered in Tiny's ear.

"I need you," he said, before hanging up and pushing her hand away with a frown. Obviously, she'd interrupted him making a hot date. "What did you think you were doing out there?"

"What did I…" For the love of Pete. "I thought I was helping you out." What did he *think* she was doing? Annie tossed the bills he'd refused on the scarred, dark wood bar.

Sam leaned closer, as if sharing a secret. "He could have made you."

It didn't matter that Annie's own imagination had tumbled in similar directions just moments ago. What had Sam done about his fears? Nothing. Never mind that he had broad shoulders made for defending others. He was only interested in protecting his tush, not hers. "Well, the least you could do is back me up if you thought he was such a threat."

"I never left the room."

Annie rolled her eyes. "Did you even notice he's gone? What do I need to do to get your attention, bare my breasts?" She had been stripped of her prospects, classified as an unacceptable employee and given the heebie-jeebies by a professional gambler. Events had pushed her beyond the rules of propriety she'd conditioned herself to live by.

"*Que pasa,* Knight?" a deep voice boomed from the other side of the bar. Tiny filled the space behind the counter. "Was the guy a cheat or just lucky?" He cracked his knuckles just by squeezing his hands into fists.

"We can't say for sure," Sam said at the same time Annie declared, "Oh, yeah."

The two of them exchanged frustrated glances.

Sam recovered first. "This is Annie Raye, my card-counting expert."

She arched a brow at Sam before extending a hand across the bar, to be swallowed in Tiny's giant one. "Nice to meet you."

The man's shadowy eyes looked her up and down, then up and down again with a glance meant to put her in her place. And then he scowled. "Wait a minute. Brett Raye's daughter?"

The way Tiny said it, as if he'd heard of her before, made Annie queasy. By now her name should have meant nothing. Which could only mean one thing.

Dad.

Why couldn't he let her reputation fade?

"You've heard of her?" Sam asked, looking slightly perplexed.

Annie started to sweat again.

"Brett Raye isn't welcome here." Staring in the area of Annie's cleavage, Tiny rolled his tongue around in his mouth as if searching for some bit of food he'd missed at lunchtime, to make room for a bit of Annie. "And after today—"

"He's a player," Annie interrupted, fighting the urge to slump her shoulders and hide behind Sam. Instead, she buttoned her jacket up to her neck, even though the combination of pearls and material nearly choked her. She wasn't a woman men stared at like that, or someone who got tossed out of casinos. At least not anymore. "Isn't that what you wanted to know?"

"Is he better than you?" Tiny asked.

Sam's laugh came out in a sharp burst of disbelief, unexpectedly refueling Annie's temper.

"Mr. Tiny, I don't gamble for a living," she stated, refusing to look at Sam. What did he find so amusing? "Besides, it's not a point of being better than anybody. Professional gamblers know which dealers they can beat and what days they work. They know which house managers will toss them out right away and which will let them get by. They may play thirty minutes one day and then not play for as many as five days. They stop playing before the amount they win attracts unwanted attention. They're inconspicuously efficient."

Tiny looked over at his blackjack dealer, who was

leaning against the table and studying her nails. "Are you saying Yolanda ain't doin' her job?"

"No, no, no." Of all the things she'd said, Tiny had to focus in on the one negative he could most easily deal with. Annie didn't want to get the older dealer fired. This was just as much Tiny's fault as Yolanda's since he'd made the counter.

Tiny eyed the bills on the bar. "How much did you win?"

"Just sixteen dollars."

He shook his head. "In less than ten minutes, betting the minimum. I'd fire her ass if she weren't my old lady's aunt."

"Here," Annie scooped up the pile of bills. "Take the sixteen back. It'll cover Sam's beer and a tip for you and Yolanda." She handed Sam his twenty. "Thanks for spotting me."

Tiny squinted at her. "Is she for real?"

"Down to her blond roots," Sam said unhappily, pushing away his nearly untouched beer.

Was it any wonder Sam annoyed Annie?

"Maybe I should hire me a blonde." Tiny gazed out at his bored dealer.

"Yolanda is doing the best she can," Annie said. "She just needs more training."

"Tell me about this guy," Sam said, ignoring Annie. "Have you seen him before?"

"I don't know about him specifically. They look like everyone else who gambles down here—older, worn-out. Me and the other houses, we want these guys gone. We called Aldo for advice and he said you were the go-to guy."

"We can deter them from frequenting your card tables by making sure they don't feel welcome, making it harder to win against your dealers," Annie suggested. "You don't just want to end the current problem, but also protect yourself against future gamers."

Sam's frown was fleeting as he glanced sideways at Annie. "Can I get a copy of the security tape of the parking lot? I'll run a search on his plates. We might get lucky and find out he has an outstanding warrant. If so, he'll disappear."

"My camera system's on the blink. Shouldn't you be following him?"

Sam went on to reassure Tiny of his skills in finding the card counter again. The casino owner didn't seem impressed.

Able to recognize a brush-off when she was given one, Annie slipped from the bar stool with a sigh. "Thanks for helping, Annie," she muttered as she walked out the door. "That job at Slotto is going to be yours. Don't you worry."

But it was hard not to when it seemed neither of the men noticed her leave.

"THAT WAS A GREAT ACT in there. You had Tiny eating out of your hand." Sam took Annie by the arm when he caught up to her outside. The afternoon sun warmed his skin. "It would have helped if you didn't overpromise on that training piece. I can't deliver on that."

"I've got somewhere I need to be." She extricated her arm and flipped open her cell phone, then hesitated.

Hesitation. Most un-Annielike.

She closed her phone and made a beeline for her decrepit Toyota. Giving up wasn't like her, either.

Sam walked alongside and still she said nothing. Normally, he let a woman in a snit stay that way as long as it didn't interfere with his plans. His agenda for the rest of the day included trolling some of the other small casinos to see if the card counter was going to stretch his streak. If Annie wanted to stew about something, Sam didn't care in the least. It was time to say goodbye.

"You all right?" he asked instead.

"Peachy."

Translation? Take a hike.

Sam should be happy. Annie wasn't going to follow him. So, this was it. He was almost disappointed. "Thanks for your help. As bluffs go, yours was first-class. You nearly had me believing you could spot a card counter." He pulled forty dollars out of his wallet.

She spun on him, late-afternoon sunlight glinting off her curls. "You thought I was bluffing?"

She might have a shady past, but he'd met a lot of gamblers since he'd arrived in Vegas, and she didn't fit the mold in the slightest. "Yeah, why do you think I didn't follow the guy when he left?"

"Oh, I don't know. Laziness? Incompetence? You spent more time on the phone than watching the game." She snatched the twenties from his hand. "Your pity money is insulting. You know what I wanted."

Sam made sure Annie knew he'd watched her tuck the bills into her purse. "Just the fact that you're going off the deep end without much provocation tells me you couldn't handle the stress of working at Slotto."

"You have no idea what went on in there, do you? If you change your mind about that background check, let me know." Annie slid into her seat and shut him out.

"GRANDPA'S PHONE." Maddy answered with practiced ease, as if she were his receptionist. No doubt she'd heard her mother take several business calls. Maddy stretched her arm to hand Brett the now ice-cream-sticky phone from the backseat. "It's for you."

"They sent Sam Knight." Ernie sounded rattled.

Brett had known the Vegas casino community would respond to their card-counting venture quickly. He slowed to a stop at a red light. "He's good."

"We haven't gone into the Sicilian. Or any of the other major houses."

"I thought we'd have more time." And that they'd send someone less well connected. Sam Knight worked for Vince Patrizio. Brett and Vince shared a past that Brett preferred not to revisit.

"It gets worse."

"Can I talk again?" Maddy waved her hand in the air at Brett's shoulder, talking louder than the voice in the tiny speaker pressed to his ear.

"Not just yet, puddin'. Say again, Ernie."

"Annie was with him."

"My…" Brett's voice cracked. "*My* Annie?"

"Police!" Maddy shrieked, turning her face away from the black-and-white cruiser that had stopped next to them. She kicked frantically against his seat.

With a curse, Brett closed the phone and tossed it onto the empty passenger seat. The officer looked over and Brett tried to smile, while watching Maddy out of the corner of his eye. She was still screaming as if the devil himself had pulled up beside them.

"What's wrong, puddin'?"

"He's got a gun," she wailed, chocolate-ice-cream-spotted hands over her eyes. "Don't shoot!"

Brett spun in his seat and bit back a curse. His no-account former son-in-law had been arrested while driving Maddy somewhere. When Annie had casually mentioned that detail, Brett had had no idea what effect the incident had had on his granddaughter.

The light turned green and the police car took off.

"He's gone, puddin'."

A symphony of honking arose behind them.

Maddy cracked open her eyes, releasing a large tear. Her lower lip trembled as she let out a ragged gasp.

"Police are here to protect us," Brett said. Unable to ignore all the honking, he turned around and drove. There would be time to wonder about Annie later. Right now his granddaughter needed him.

"No guns. No guns," Maddy chanted, hiccuping.

"YOU DIDN'T HAVE TO BUY groceries," Annie's dad said when he opened the door to her that afternoon.

"I bought meat and vegetables." She avoided looking Brett in the eye in case he could tell just by glancing at her that she'd played again after all these years. Annie hurried to set the bags down on the counter. "And milk."

Her father laughed self-consciously. "I guess you're right. Can't raise a child on peanut butter and crackers, can you?"

Instead of pointing out that that was exactly how she'd been raised, Annie swept Maddy into her arms. "I hope you didn't eat too much ice cream."

Her daughter hugged her tightly. "We—"

"We had one scoop," Brett interrupted.

With one arm around Annie's shoulders, Maddy looked at her grandfather and grinned. "The music was loud. I had to dance."

"Sometimes you've gotta dance," he crooned, doing a little jig.

Sliding to the floor, Maddy giggled and then grabbed her plastic princess dress-up shoes. She swayed and clacked the heels together like a tambourine, creating an uneven beat.

"Are you feeling all right?" Annie asked. Her father didn't dance.

"Right as rain." He reached for Maddy, who came willingly into his arms. "I'm a grandpa, you know."

The sight of the two of them, so happy and at ease, only made Annie feel more alone. She'd been that girl once. Annie sidled around the dancing pair into the small kitchenette. The day had been full of too many ups and downs. She'd done well at the casino and had been irrationally disappointed that Sam hadn't offered to call Carl Nunes on the spot…or to offer Annie the card-counting-expert job. At this point, even temporary employment had its allure.

Who was she kidding? She'd be a fool to want to get tied up with Sam.

"How did the job go, Annie?"

Oh, it went, all right. Annie froze in the middle of putting milk in the refrigerator, staring inside as if searching for something. The light was burned out and the top shelf was cracked and covered with duct tape. She'd come full circle.

"I'm not sure the job is going to work out," she said, as casually as she could manage through her tight throat. She'd graduated early from high school and breezed through the University of Nevada, Las Vegas, on an academic scholarship. How had she become such a failure?

"That's too bad." Her dad deposited a giggling Maddy on the boxy brown burlap couch. "You'll find something you like in no time, though. You always did manage to get yourself out of a bind quicker than most."

Not knowing what to say, Annie just stared at her father, noting a funny-colored smudge near his nose. Ice cream? He twitched under her scrutiny and turned away.

"Well, quicker than me, anyway," he said sheepishly.

There was too much water under the bridge for Annie to correct him. Still, guilt had a way of loosening lips. "I thought it might be nice to have spaghetti."

"Just like old times." He grinned over his shoulder and the smudge fell from his left cheek.

Maddy laughed and bounced on the couch. "Grandpa didn't get all the Play-Doh off his face."

There were two open canisters of Play-Doh and several doughy strings of pearls on the scarred coffee table. Annie shouldn't have worried about Brett. He was throwing himself into the role of grandpa without any of the ulterior motives she'd expected.

"Come on, Grandpa." Maddy held out a small hand. "Let's make an elephant."

Obedient as a love-struck puppy, he sat on the couch and pulled the five-year-old close to him. Unexpectedly, Annie blinked back tears. How she'd loved to do things with him as a child. He'd been her best friend. Losing that closeness had been the hardest part about refusing to play cards for him. And much as she'd wanted to find that with Frank, Annie realized now that her marriage had been lacking many things, most importantly, trust.

"How is she?" Vince asked, without greeting Aldo as he entered the bedroom. The maids who scrubbed toilets had better manners than this *cafone*.

"The same." Always the same. In a coma. He walked out of the room, giving Vince some time alone with his grandmother.

"Of course." Vince always sounded as if Rosalie's condition was Aldo's fault.

The day nurse came only as far as the doorway.

"Is that a Picasso?" Vince asked when he joined Aldo scant minutes later.

"Come in. Sit down." Aldo shuffled the deck. Keeping his hands busy made the shaking less noticeable. He did not like to appear weak in front of Vince.

His grandson didn't sit until Paulo pulled out a chair at the table. Aldo spoke three languages fluently—English, French and his native Italian. Vince only understood the language of a bully. He was becoming more like his father every day.

Once he was seated, Aldo nodded to the painting on the wall. "*Le Rêve* by Picasso."

"The portrait of his mistress?" Vince angled around for a better look. He and Rosalie shared a passion for art that Aldo never completely understood.

"Of his love," Aldo corrected. He'd gotten the painting for Rosalie. She would enjoy it once she awoke.

"How much did that set us back?"

It was on loan from Steve Wynn, the Bellagio owner, in exchange for a large charitable donation, but Aldo wasn't going to admit he didn't have deep enough pockets to purchase such a prize. "Not nearly as much as it's worth."

His grandson laughed, the sound grating along Aldo's bent spine. "You've still got it, old man."

Part of Aldo preened at the compliment. It was rare since his grandson had returned from the war that the two of them exchanged anything other than sharp words. Sometimes Aldo wished for a better relationship with him, and sometimes—

"I don't feel like playing tonight," Vince said. "I've got places to be."

Sometimes Aldo thought he'd be better off alone with Rosalie. "I don't ask for much from you, Vince, except these games."

"You ask more than that."

"I suppose the beauty pageant rehearsal downstairs has something to do with this."

A grin unfurled on Vince's dark face. "I'd hate to disappoint the ladies."

"So, you'll play at being a celebrity. Only you'll end up like your father, living in a trailer park in Florida with a gold-digging former showgirl. Hard work pays off, not gambling and skirt chasing." Aldo didn't care if Vince's wife had left him. A married man honored his vows.

"Regretting sending that P.I. after me when I ran away as a kid?"

Aldo slapped the cards onto the table. "I may have been the only one in the family who did not. Your father was glad to see you go." It was the blackjack game all those years ago that had led to his family's unraveling. Aldo's son, Nick, had overreacted to the situation. They'd all paid a price back then, but he and Vince had found common ground. Or so he'd thought. Now they'd come to this—trading insults like schoolboys.

"And now Dad's in Florida, waiting to come back."

"Waiting for me to die, you mean," Aldo growled. "I won't give what I've built to anyone who's not willing to work for it." Nick would benefit very little from Aldo's passing. And Vince—

"You won't be able to control us from the grave."

"*Che brutta.*" How ugly Vince was. Disappointment froze Aldo in his chair. How had two generations of Patrizios become such schmucks? Three, if you counted how coarse Aldo himself had become.

Vince laughed off the insult, but his parting smile wasn't happy and didn't reassure Aldo that things would turn out well for any of them.

"I think I'll retire, Paulo." Aldo shuffled toward his bedroom, where he could face his bleak future alone with Rosalie.

STUPID. THAT'S WHAT SAM WAS.

Stupid for following Annie after she'd left him at Tiny's. Stupid for lurking in the produce aisle while she selected zucchini and grapes. Stupid for tailing her to this run-down apartment complex where someone had let her in to the second-story apartment. And the stupidest mistake of all was him driving all the way home, only to come back, climb the shaky stairs, stand on the stoop and contemplate knocking on her door.

Sam was used to following hunches, but this was crazy. Annie wasn't the answer to his problems on this case. She pretended to be a staid financial analyst from the tips of her heels to the curve of the pearls around her neck.

He didn't buy for a minute that she hadn't at least known her husband was a crook. And then there was the slick way she'd handled the situation at Tiny's. Obviously, some of her father's habits had rubbed off....

In the span of less than eight hours she'd tried to confuse Sam about who she really was, but he'd seen through the facade.

He hadn't heard a word from Sabatinni. Sam was in a bind. And from the looks of the shabby apartment block, so was Annie. Maybe she did have skills he could use, and since she wasn't Suzy Homemaker, he had no qualms about using them.

Sam rapped on the door.

"Can I help you?" The older man who opened it looked like he'd seen too many late nights in smoky bars. He had to be Brett Raye.

The furniture was dated, and the television was bolted to a stand as if this was a cheap hotel, but something smelled wonderful. Fast food was not being served for dinner. "I'm looking for Annie Raye."

Wiping her hands on a kitchen towel, Annie, barefoot and wearing only that little lace blouse over her skirt, appeared behind the old geezer. "Sam?" Her face brightened. "You called Carl Nunes?"

Much as he hated to clear that smile off her face, Sam had to shake his head.

That quick, he became unwelcome. "How did you find me? And what do you want?"

Sam stepped into the apartment with a grin. "A funny thing happened to me in the parking lot of Tiny's after you left."

The old man's mouth dropped open dramatically and he turned to Annie. "You were at a casino today?"

"Not now, Dad."

"But—"

"*Dad.*"

"I left enough messages in Sabatinni's voice mail that his box was full. And as I watched you pull out, I couldn't help but think—"

Annie raised her brows.

"—that you were just the expert I needed on this case." Sam waited.

She didn't disappoint. "Go on."

"Maybe we could work something out. You help me for a couple of days and then I help you with Carl." He didn't even care if she was bluffing about how much she understood card counting. As long as they found the group of cardsharps, Mr. Patrizio would be happy. And Vince? Sam would have to admit he'd taken the job, and hope his friend understood.

"This sounds an awful lot like blackmail," Brett said with an assessing look. "I don't think I like you."

"Let me handle this." Annie twirled the towel, as if about to swat someone with it. The woman had fire beneath her conservative exterior. "This is not an even exchange. My services are worth more than the price of a background check."

He bet they were. "I can offer you a cut if we identify this card counter and any accomplices. Enough to help you out."

Brett was making incomprehensible noises and working his mouth like a fish.

"How much are we talking here?" Annie cocked one eyebrow.

Damn, she was sharp.

A toilet flushed. A door opened. A little blond kid skipped into the room. "Is it dinner yet?"

Sam stepped back. His hands felt clammy and something unpleasant climbed up his throat. A jet roared alarmingly close overhead.

"Are you all right?" Annie had him by the arm in an instant. "Dad, help me get him to the couch."

"Who is he?" Brett demanded.

Sam didn't hear her answer. The little girl was floating in and out of his vision, blending and separating from images of a war-ravaged street. Shouting voices, dark robes and the barrel of a gun propped between the legs of a screaming toddler....

His feet dragged across the worn carpet until hands guided him to a sitting position. He chopped his head between his knees and gulped for air, fighting back images of a desert town and Iraqi insurgents, of bullets and... Someone pressed a glass into his hand and, keeping his eyes closed tight, Sam sucked the water down.

"She took me by surprise, is all." He waved in the direction of the kid, without opening his eyes. "Can she go somewhere else?"

"No." Annie's voice. Close. The smell of strawberries reached him, stimulating and calming at the same time. "She's my daughter. Maddy."

Deep breaths sent much-needed oxygen to Sam's numb limbs. Mucus dripped from his nose. His ears rang as the room spun at carpet level, which was all Sam dared look at. *A kid?* He had to get out of here.

"Are you all right? You're dripping buckets of sweat. Maddy, go soak this towel for me. Hurry."

"It's all right…" Sam slurred the words. "I'm outta here." But hands held him firmly in place.

"You're not going anywhere, buster. At this rate, you'll tumble down the stairs and break your neck. Then where would I be?" She ran something cool across his forehead and behind his neck, sending shivers down his spine, almost making him lose that hot dog he'd had for lunch.

Annie Raye kept touching him, and Sam couldn't have moved if he tried.

CHAPTER FOUR

"GET RID OF THIS GUY." Annie's dad took her by the arm and led her to the kitchen. "He's trouble."

Annie knew that ten ways from Sunday. Sam Knight sparked reactions in her that should be illegal, even in Nevada. "The man nearly collapsed. I'm not going to shove him out the door." Besides, he was getting her the job with Slotto.

"You always were a sucker for strays. I'll roll him out while you look the other way," her dad said, making a move toward the living room.

"Dad," Annie warned, tugging him back. "Help me finish dinner." The water was ready for steaming the zucchini, which she had yet to slice, and the bread still had to be buttered so she could broil it. She handed her dad a small tub of margarine and the loaf of bread, then peaked out.

"Would you feel better if I sang to you?" Maddy asked Sam, as he slouched on the sofa. Without waiting for him to answer, she burst into song. "Three blind mice. Three blind mice."

With his hands over his face, he groaned.

"See how they run. See how they run." Maddy was feeling the groove now. She popped out of her chair and began dancing while she sang.

"Maddy has showgirl potential," Brett said.

"She's a ham. Don't get any ideas. She'll grow out of it." Annie didn't know which was worse, him teaching her daughter how to gamble or how to wave a fan in front of her nonexistent bosom.

"She's so…loud." Her father grinned. "That's just what that P.I. deserves."

Annie stopped slicing to study Brett. "I never said he was a P.I."

"Didn't you?" he said innocently, spreading margarine over a slice of bread with the intensity of a brain surgeon.

"Dad," Annie whispered suspiciously, "has he been after you before?" Was Sam after him now?

"Before? No, no. I recognize the name, is all. Heard the scuttlebutt and such."

Annie went back to cutting zucchini. "What scuttlebutt?" Most likely it was about Sam and a showgirl…or several.

"Everyone knew his dad. He was a P.I., too, but he specialized in tracking teenage runaways here and in Phoenix," Brett said respectfully, shaking garlic salt on the bread. "I hear his son works a different side of the business."

Annie's radar went off and she set the knife down. "You're scared of him." Brett, unfortunately, lacked the gene that enabled him to heed fear.

"No." The word came out squeaky. He cleared his throat and repeated, "No. It's you I'm worried about, being with him."

"Why?" But he didn't answer, and Sam, who was trying to sit up during the second encore of Maddy's song, didn't look like a threat, not with his long limbs folded awkwardly on the small couch and his skin still a sickly shade of green. "I was at Tiny House of Cards today."

"I thought you swore off the habit." For all the trouble he'd given her earlier, he didn't seem surprised.

"One-a-penny, two-a-penny, hot cross buns." Maddy was running through all of her counting nursery rhymes, even though Sam hadn't opened his eyes.

"Don't joke, Dad. I had some business with Sam there."

"So you didn't go near the tables? You had no trouble resisting the urge to feel the texture of the cards in your hand?" He gave her a knowing smile.

"I left all that behind me." Bitterness crept into her tone. "You saw to that." Maddy started another counting song. Annie dropped zucchini into the small pot before adding, "Tiny knew you and…" She lowered her voice. "*Me.* I think he wanted to throw me out. Have you been telling stories again?"

"Come on, puddin'. Tiny only knows me by reputation." Brett tried to chuck her on the chin, but Annie ducked out of the way. "Why would I be telling that story?"

"Because you're the biggest gossip in Las Vegas."

"Some stories just get passed around. The little girl with pigtails who beat Aldo Patrizio has become something of a myth around here, but your name's been forgotten. Mine, unfortunately, hasn't."

Annie wanted to believe him. She wanted her life to be as normal and boring as everyone else's in suburbia. But even when she'd been married, Annie hadn't been able to blend into the woodwork.

"I know you find it hard to believe your old man, but I haven't told that story in a long time." He crossed his heart. "Now, how about we get rid of this snooper?"

"No way. I need him."

And, amazingly, Sam seemed to need her, too.

"IT SHOULD BE ME lying there." Holding Rosalie's hand, Aldo sat looking out toward the Strip. The Bellagio fountains were in midperformance.

He gazed down at his wife's pale, high cheekbones and aquiline nose. Rosalie had been from the neighborhood back in Queens. They'd grown up together. When she'd first arrived in Vegas, she'd sung in a nightclub for slave's wages and tips, and stayed with someone's grandmother. Girls like Rosalie were off-limits to young men such as Aldo. You could treat most women fast and loose, except ones from the neighborhood. Italian women got taken care of, with wedding bands.

"I have dreams, Aldo. Someday, I'm gonna own a bakery."

Aldo couldn't help laughing. With her sequined

dress nearly showing her goods, she didn't look like any baker he'd ever seen.

Her dark eyes flashed. "Don't you dare laugh, Aldo. You can achieve anything in America, but you'll only keep it if you come by it legitimately."

"I make money, bella. A lot of money." Aldo leaned closer, even though it was against the rules, and let his gaze wander down the V of her dress.

"You make dirty money and you know it." She pushed him back. "I won't marry anyone that might leave me for prison."

"Marry?"

"I have dreams, Aldo. I want to share them with someone. If you're not that someone…" She shrugged. "Well, there are plenty of men in Vegas."

"There were plenty of men in Queens, too, but you came out here, where there are too many women." He knew she'd come chasing after him when he'd left, but Aldo was a rising star in the family, and women would do amazing things to get his attention.

Rosalie scoffed. "I have something none of those other women will ever have." Unexpectedly, she grabbed hold of his tie and pulled him to her. Her kiss— their first—was light and sweet, as if she'd never kissed anyone before. Then she did something with her tongue that told Aldo her experience matched his. All too soon she released him and smoothed his tie without looking him in the eye. "I have the hunger to get what I want. Do you?"

Aldo watched her walk away, mesmerized by the

way her evening gown swayed around her curves, barely keeping himself from crawling after her.

Rosalie was the reason he'd severed all ties with the Mafia fifty-odd years ago. Without her, there would have been no Sicilian. Without Rosalie, Aldo would most likely have ended up in a shallow grave in the desert.

Thrill seekers rocketed up the Stratosphere. Aldo could imagine the riders' screams of fear and joy. So much had changed in Las Vegas since he and Rosalie had gotten married and started the casino. She'd gotten her bakery, all right. And a five-star restaurant.

And then eight months ago they'd been arguing on their way out to dinner. Aldo had held the door for Rosalie and paused to speak to one of his managers. His wife hadn't waited, and had been hit by a drunk speeding through their lot. She hadn't woken up since. The police had been unable to find the *strunsu* who did this to her.

"What would you say about our little Vince?" he asked. "That I should give him another chance?"

But Rosalie didn't answer. And Vince didn't seem to want another chance.

"DOES THAT MAN HAVE the flu?" Maddy asked, chasing noodles around her plate with her fork. Amazingly, her off-key songs had been a lifeline for Sam to cling to.

Still, he avoided looking at her. When he'd been sent over to Iraq, he'd been worried about coming back with all his body parts. He hadn't thought to worry about coming back with his mind intact. It was rare that he let himself be surprised by a child. Sam stayed away from where they tended to be. What few groceries he bought, he picked up at the corner convenience store in the middle of the night. Likewise, he frequented the twenty-four-hour Wal-Mart at midnight, when there was less of a chance of running into terror-inducing children.

"He's got a mental condition, puddin'," Brett Raye explained. "It's called being neurotic."

"I think you *meant* to say Sam has a *neurosis,*" Annie corrected. "In other words, Maddy, Mr. Knight gets scared in certain situations."

"I was not scared," Sam insisted. "I…I…" He wasn't going to tell them the truth. "I have the flu."

"The bathroom's back there." Out of the corner of his eye, Sam saw Maddy point. She was trying very hard to charm him. The little girl reminded him a lot of his niece, Tabitha. Or how he remembered his niece, the last time he'd seen her.

Sam kept his gaze on Annie. The food tasted like paste in his mouth. "This is good spaghetti. Thanks for having me over."

"Sam, before you passed out—"

"I didn't pass out."

"—you were about to tell me how much you'd be paying for my help on that job for Tiny."

The pounding resumed in Sam's head. All desire to work with Annie had disappeared when he'd learned she had a kid. Not that his inconvenient attraction to Annie had dissipated.

"I don't think working for *him* is wise," Brett noted.

Sam turned his head slowly Brett's way. "You got a problem with me?"

"Yeah. You're dangerous. You better not be carrying a *gun.*"

Annie made a strangled sound into her napkin.

"A gun?" Maddy leaned into Sam's line of vision, her voice high-pitched.

"I don't carry a gun and nobody's shot at me since Iraq," Sam said evenly, feeling sweat pop out on his forehead.

"Of course you carry a gun. You work for Vince Patrizio." Brett swung around to Annie. "Did you know that, Annie? You're asking for a job working for Vince Patrizio."

Annie's eyes widened.

Why would she care about Vince unless she was one of his many exes? Sam gave Brett what he hoped was his worst stare, which made his head feel as if it would fall off. "I can't tell you who I'm working for on this case, but it's *not* Vince Patrizio."

"You were a soldier? In the war?" Maddy was persistent, as if she knew he didn't want to see her and was determined to keep vying for his attention…although there was still a tremble in her voice. "Did you shoot anybody?"

Sam stood, his gaze carefully averted, as he willed his knees to lock. "Thanks for dinner."

Despite Annie's protests and the distracting pounding in his head, Sam made it down the stairs. He managed to navigate around the narrow rock garden to the parking lot. Miraculously, he was still standing when he reached for the door of his truck.

"Are you gonna be okay, mister?" Maddy asked in a small voice that seemed far too close.

Caught off guard, Sam turned abruptly to find the little girl on Annie's hip, her face inches from his.

And then the world spun into darkness.

THE SUBTLE SMELL of strawberries brought Sam around. The back of his head throbbed and odd parts of his hands and arms stung. He groaned but didn't open his eyes, not yet ready to know where he was.

"You could have told me you were scared of kids," Annie said.

"I'm not scared of kids." His throat was so dry the words had come out as a croak.

"Then my daughter's beauty must have swept you off your feet."

"It figures I'd be stalked by a smart-ass accountant." Had they taken him back to her apartment? No. It was too quiet.

"I gave up stalking you at Tiny's. You followed *me* home, remember?"

He heard a creak of leather, then something cool swept across his forehead. There had been no leather furniture in the small second-story apartment. Tentatively, Sam lifted a hand to his steering wheel.

"Can't drive without opening your eyes. Although I'm amazed you can see to drive above the collection of fast-food bags you've got in here."

Sam kept his eyes closed. If Annie's daughter was in the truck with them… "My effort to keep the planet green. Better in here than in a landfill."

Bags rustled on the floorboard. "Uh-huh. I sent Maddy upstairs with my dad after he helped me scrape you off the pavement. Kind of decent for a petty crook, don't you think?" She passed the cool rag over his face again. "So, where'd you get this phobia of yours?"

No way was he admitting anything. Sam cracked one eye open and stole a look at Annie. She handed him a bottle of water.

"You may as well tell me. I'm not going anywhere until you're ready to drive."

"I am ready to drive." Sam tried opening the other eye, and squinted against the streetlight. Pain lanced his eyes and he snapped them shut again.

"Uh-huh." She kept swabbing his face. "Thought so. That's why I took your keys."

"That's just not right." A man without his truck keys was emasculated.

"Now *you're* starting to annoy *me.*"

Sam successfully opened his eyes.

"The way I figure it, you were either traumatized as a child or really screwed up by the war. Now, I'm no expert, but you don't strike me as an abuse victim, so—"

"Spent a lot of time thinking about me, have you?" Sam shouldn't have been pleased.

"I spent ten minutes waiting for you to come around."

He turned his head to glare at her. Mistake. He lost his equilibrium and Annie had to push him back against the driver's seat. The heat from her delicate fingers penetrated his thin polo shirt.

"Now, if I were you, I'd be thinking how I could make a quick exit," she continued. "I'd be hoping that that ditzy blonde would forget the way I humbled myself and practically begged her to work for me in exchange for clearing the snafus in her background check."

Damn it. "I suppose you're going to tell me why that wouldn't work."

"I think you know I'll make your life really unpleasant if you take back your offer."

Sam's phone rang. *Please, God, let it be Sabatinni.* He fumbled with the phone clip at his belt until Annie grabbed the waistband of his pants with one hand and the phone with the other.

"Theresa." Annie must have read the cell phone display. "Girlfriend?"

"Sister," Sam growled. "Don't answer—"

But she already had. "Sam can't come to the phone right now. I'm Annie, his *assistant.* Can I help you?"

She sounded so sweet. Sam wanted to strangle her.

"He hasn't returned *any* of your calls? That's so unlike Sam."

He reached for the phone, but Annie pulled away. Now his sister was going to call more than ever.

"I'll tell him the girls are wondering if Uncle Sam is coming home for Christmas. Yes, yes. Uh-huh. Well, he has been busy. I'll let him know you called." Annie snapped his phone closed. "I take it the sight of your nieces sends you into a tailspin, too. Which must mean you only date single women…or you're living the life of a monk."

"I'm not celibate." A muscle ticked in Sam's jaw.

"Ahh, a pickup artist."

"Aren't divorced women men-haters?"

"Someday I hope to find a more worthy partner, a real family man. In the meantime—"

"Stay out of my business."

"I'm more than happy to keep our relationship strictly professional."

He gripped the steering wheel with one hand and thrust the other in her direction. "Hand. Over. My. Keys."

"Just as soon as you tell me what time we're starting tomorrow."

"I'll call you." Never.

Annie flipped open his cell phone and dialed a number. Instead of putting the device to her ear, she held it in the air so that Sam could hear the voice mail message when it rolled.

"Hi, you've reached Annie Raye. I'm not available right now. Please leave a message."

She closed the phone and handed it back to Sam. "Now you have my number and I have yours."

But he'd be damned if he was going to use it.

"Mommy, I'm scared." Maddy's voice was high with panic and right near Annie's ear.

Light from a streetlamp came through a break in the

curtains, illuminating the bedroom in her father's apartment.

"Mommy's here, pumpkin. Don't be afraid." Barely opening her eyes, Annie enveloped her daughter in a hug. The sheets on the bed were scratchy, with creases in them, as if they'd just been taken out of the package. That hadn't helped Annie fall asleep. Neither did the occasional plane coming in for a landing overhead, or the worries of an unemployed mother and what she should have said to Sam Knight. He was a self-centered heartbreaker and she shouldn't feel sorry for him just because he'd been emotionally scarred in the war. Single moms had no business giving a man like him a second thought. If only Maddy would snuggle close and fall back to sleep, perhaps Annie would be able to drift off, too.

"That man said people shot at him," the little girl whispered.

"Soldiers." And soldiers carried guns, just like the policemen who'd arrested Frank. "He doesn't carry a gun."

"But he came here. Inside."

"Sam doesn't carry a gun," Annie repeated, more awake now. "Not anymore. Besides, Grandpa is sleeping out on the couch. He won't let anyone get past him."

"Grandpa's old. I miss Daddy and I want my own bed," Maddy wailed, starting to cry.

The slim hope that she'd be able to drift back to sleep disappeared. Annie rubbed her daughter's back. Change was hard on everyone, especially little girls. "You need some fixin', girlo."

"I do-o-o."

After the worst of the crying subsided, Annie sat up and pushed the hair out of her eyes. "I hope Grandpa has some Band-Aids."

Maddy sniffed in agreement.

As silently as she could, so as not to disturb her father, Annie opened the bedroom door and crept down the short hallway to the bathroom. A quick perusal of the medicine cabinet revealed just what she needed, and gave her pause. He remembered.

"Trouble?" her dad asked, poking his head through the crack in the door.

"No," Annie said, putting the small, unopened box of Band-Aids behind her as unobtrusively as possible.

"Mommy, I need fixin'," Maddy pleaded in a thin voice.

Brett's smile was all-knowing. He'd done his share of fixing when Annie was young. "You can never have too many bandages around." He faded back into the shadows of the living room.

It shouldn't matter that he'd bought a box of Mickey Mouse Band-Aids. But it melted her heart all the same.

Annie left the light on in the bathroom and returned to Maddy, pulling her daughter into her lap. "Here's some courage." Annie kissed the back of her tiny hand.

"Keep courage safe, Mommy. Hurry." Maddy held out her hand and Annie pressed a Band-Aid over the place she'd kissed.

"And here's some love." Annie kissed Maddy's other hand and covered it with a Band-Aid. Then she kissed her forehead. "All fixed. Time to close those eyes and go back to sleep."

Maddy admired her Mickey Mouse bandages in the dim light. "Good thing Grandpa knows how to fix things, too."

Annie tucked her daughter back into bed, wishing that fixing her life could be as easy.

ONE HAND ON HIS BEER, Sam slouched in a darkened corner of Tassels Galore, one of the city's seedier strip joints. A nearly naked woman undulated on stage in heels twice the height of the ones Annie had worn. Damn it. Sam couldn't shake the image of a miniscule, buttoned-up blonde with a sassy mouth and brazen attitude.

"Tell me that's your first beer," Vince yelled above the music as, in slacks and a monogrammed shirt, he slid into a seat next to Sam and waved at the waitress. The table wobbled when Vince set his elbows on it.

"What are you, my mother?" Sam took a drink of the warm brew.

"I should be. You live with me."

Sam told him where to go, but his friend just laughed.

"Hey, it's not as if I have house privileges. I'm lucky to have running water and electricity. You definitely sold me a bill of goods when you offered me a place to stay," Sam said.

Vince snorted. "You couldn't get enough of the desert on the other side of the world." Something shifted in his gaze. He was always careful to skirt around the issue for Sam's sake. They'd served in the same unit, experienced the same triumphs and horrors. The war had created a bond between them that differences like wealth and college education couldn't shatter.

"Anyway," Vince said, running a hand through his short, dark hair. "Where's my beer?"

Knowing his friend was thinking about that day, Sam looked away, afraid his own expression was similarly bleak.

Lana Tisdale, the well-preserved manager of Tassels, flanked by her brawniest bartender, stood at a table where a pair of unruly drunks had tried too many times to cop a feel. One said something to Lana, something ugly, judging by the way her face contorted into hard lines. Since Sam had discovered Lana had sold the place to Mr. Patrizio, Vince insisted they meet here a few times a week.

Vince watched the scene with distaste and then turned back to Sam. "It's hard to decide who I feel sorrier for."

"She had nothing to do with your grandmother's accident."

Vince's face fell. "You just haven't found anything yet."

And all these months later it was doubtful Sam would.

"My grandfather is good at covering up scandals." There was something in Vince's past that made him unwilling to believe his grandfather's innocence. Since Sam knew Vince had been a teen runaway, he understood the suspicion. Whatever had caused his friend to run from his family in the first place was still ruling his life.

"He wasn't involved, either."

Vince snorted again. "He bought this place right after the accident. And he never said a word to me about it."

Lana moved behind the bar, as if she could feel Vince's animosity from across the room.

"Everything my grandfather says is designed to keep you in line. I want you to—"

"Keep looking. Yeah, yeah. I know."

"The truth will come out."

Sam was afraid the truth that was coming out tonight wasn't going to make his buddy any happier.

"Look at all that money out there." Vince's smile was forced as he watched men waving bills from their ringside seats. "If I could figure a way to license that, I could expand to every city in America."

"You want to franchise strip clubs? That's un-American." Sam pretended to be interested in the dollars being stuffed into the lingerie of the dancer currently on stage. The stripper didn't look in the eyes of the men manhandling her. A week ago that detachment would have appealed to Sam.

"Maybe that's what my grandfather has in mind. He says being American means making an honest buck."

"You rake in enough of those at the Sicilian. You've got the stingiest dealers and tightest slots on the Strip."

"The customers don't think so. Perception is a powerful tool." Taking his beer, Vince gave the scantily clad waitress a twenty and told her to keep the change, ignoring her approving appraisal of his office attire. Women of her ilk tended to ignore Vince's wedding band. But with an AWOL wife, Vince only considered himself married when it suited him. Tonight it suited him.

"On the topic of perception, you're probably going to take this wrong."

Vince's eyebrows slanted up, but he said nothing.

"You shouldn't. Take it wrong, that is." Damn, Sam sounded as stilted as a teenager asking for a job, a feeling compounded by the hole he'd just discovered in his polo shirt.

"If I had a sister I'd be worried that you'd gotten her pregnant," Vince said, testing the waters.

Sam sat up straighter and pushed the warm beer to the center of the table. "Your grandfather hired me to do a job."

Vince's jaw worked. "Let me guess. He offered you so much money you couldn't turn him down."

"There was that," Sam admitted morosely. "I tried to turn him down, but before I knew it I was caught up in the job. What could I do?"

"You could have said no."

"Yeah." Sam hadn't wanted to hurt Vince's feelings. When had he become such a soft touch? "But I'd be lying if I said the assignment didn't interest me." The assignment, not a pair of sparkling blue eyes.

"Go for it, then." His friend stood. "But once he has you on a leash he'll find a way to neuter you, too."

CHAPTER FIVE

"COFFEE?" Sam was waiting for Vince outside his friend's garage the next morning with a peace offering. They'd often shared weak instant coffee on their tour in Iraq. That's how they'd become friends. Other guys bonded over a smoke or a rare taste of contraband beer. Vince and Sam shared a different brew.

"Thanks." Looking every inch the next in line to run the Sicilian, in his dove-gray suit and power tie, Vince set his briefcase on the slab floor and accepted the travel mug Sam offered.

They sipped their coffee in silence. Sam pretended to be interested in the orderly workbench and shiny new tools Vince probably didn't know how to operate. Sam had never been in a garage without oil stains and cobwebs.

"I can't believe you're going to work for him," Vince said in a surprisingly calm voice, leaning his hip against the Porsche's fender.

Sam held his tongue, hoping that Vince had come to terms with his decision.

"My grandfather isn't to be trusted."

"I won't trust him."

"You will," Vince said miserably. "You're the trusting type."

Sam scoffed at the notion.

"And my grandfather can't stand anything he can't control."

"Including you, or so you think," Sam interjected, before Vince started to rant. "That wasn't the case when we were halfway around the world. He sent you care packages and daily e-mails. How many eighty-year-olds do you know who send e-mail?"

"That was before he fell in love with that woman at Tassels." Now it was Vince's turn to cast his gaze around the garage. Someday Vince might realize money and possessions wouldn't make him happy.

Sam lowered his voice. "You know your grandfather isn't in love with her. She lives with someone else." By all accounts, Lana Tisdale was crazy in love with her boyfriend, who was fighting cancer.

"No." Vince scowled. "Why would he buy Tassels unless he had some sick fascination with it?"

Sam knew he should let this go. Vince was a good guy if you got beyond the rash hotheadedness. "Your grandfather barely leaves the Sicilian. He's not the one who goes to Tassels every week." They were. If anyone had a sick fascination with Lana Tisdale, it was Vince, not his grandfather.

"I can see whose side you're on—the one who offers the most money. Are you going to charge me more now? Is that why you brought me coffee? To get more money out of me?" Vince slammed his mug on the workbench and snatched up his briefcase.

"You're not angry because of the money. You're angry because I'm working with your grandfather. Face it. You want to believe he's a decent guy. Instead of asking me to prove he's despicable, why don't you ask me to prove what a good man he is?"

Vince swung his briefcase over to the passenger seat and slid into the cocoon of chrome, wood trim and leather. "Go play in a park with some kids, will you? Remind yourself what a good guy you are."

"Of all the…" Sam would not go back to that day. "You think your grandfather puts up with your crap because he hates you? Are you afraid you're on some nonexistent hit list of his?" Sam took a quick step toward the car, blood roaring in his ears.

The younger man's answering obscenity was swallowed by the car door slamming shut. The Porsche's engine roared to life, and then tires squealed as Vince gunned it out of the garage and Sam fought the urge to hurl his coffee cup after his so-called friend.

DERELICT STORES lined the road several blocks behind the Strip. Brett flexed his fingers on the steering wheel. Lights on a pole ahead started a neon striptease. Tassels Galore.

Annie would kill him if he took Maddy inside, even this early in the morning.

"I like ice cream after breakfast," his granddaughter said, her lips rimmed with chocolate.

"You need a napkin, puddin'." Brett handed her one. They'd stopped at a 7-Eleven while he'd shored up his nerve.

Instead of driving past Tassels, Brett parked in the small lot in the shadow of the Sicilian and took stock. Cars in various states of disrepair and grandeur clustered together beneath the neon stripper on a pole. A decent crowd for a Wednesday morning.

He'd spent a lot of time here during his more successful runs. The women were beautiful, of course, but it was the manager, Lana, who intrigued him. Who'd intrigued a trio of friends—Brett, Ernie and Chauncey.

Brett had tossed and turned on the couch all night. He had an obligation to his friends, but Annie seemed determined to help Knight uncover their card-counting group so that she could be gainfully employed. If Brett told her what he and Ernie were doing, and why, she'd be mad, but she'd understand. Perhaps she'd even stop helping Knight. But wouldn't that guarantee she'd never get the job at Slotto? And then she'd blame Brett for ruining her life…again. And she'd be right.

As he got out of the car, Brett reminded himself this was just short-term. He helped Maddy out of the car, crossed the lot to the back entrance. His granddaughter skipped alongside him, waving her skirt from side to side, her sunny, short curls bouncing.

The noise assaulted them as soon as he opened the door: music blaring loudly enough to cause permanent damage to the eardrums. Maddy broke free of his grip and raced down the dark hallway toward the stage,

Brett following. The nearly all-male crowd roared in reaction to one of the dancers pouring water over herself as she gyrated in a tiny wading pool. Thank God she was wearing a bikini. And then her hands traced the luscious curves of her body before she shook her wet hair, spraying those at the edge of the stage and evoking another rumble of appreciation.

Maddy clapped. Red-faced, Brett led her back toward the office. Yet before they'd gone far, he saw Lana poised at the other end of the hall, as sultry and beautiful as ever with her white-blond hair swept up and her face carefully made up to disguise the effects of too many late nights.

Her head tilted toward Maddy, Lana walked toward them, her blue silk robe rustling. "You decided to show...*Grandpa.*"

Brett wanted to kill Ernie. Grandfathers were...well, not exactly viewed as sex machines. Not that he didn't adore his granddaughter. The humor in Lana's expression was a blow to his ego, that's all.

Maddy stared at Lana's silver high heels. "Are you a princess? Those are princess shoes."

The woman was seldom struck speechless. She crouched at Maddy's level, brushed the child's yellow-blond hair behind her ear and studied her face. Finally, she said, "No one's ever called me a princess before."

"But you're beautiful," Maddy said solemnly. "You have to be a princess."

Lana smiled and took her by the hand. "Do you like to play dress up?"

"Mommy and I dress up my dolls. I have three dolls. How many dolls do you have?"

"None. I thought you might like to try on some...*princess* clothes while your grandpa runs an errand." The melancholy smile Lana gave Brett would have stolen his heart if she hadn't been Chauncey's girl. She led them into the office that doubled as her bedroom and costume storeroom.

Pale as paste, Chauncey lay in a worn recliner, the scar outlining his left cheek barely visible. Brett could distinguish nearly every bone of his friend's six-foot skeletal frame. His green eyes, though faded and sunken, lit up when Brett introduced him to Maddy.

Uncharacteristically shy, the child tugged on Brett's pant leg until he leaned over. "Is he okay?" she whispered.

"He's been sick." The big C had nearly put him in his grave, and might still if Brett and Ernie didn't raise the money for his medical care. After nearly two years, the treatments had drained Chauncey's assets, and most of Lana's, too. "Believe it or not, this is the best he's looked in a long time."

The emaciated man waved at Maddy, rings glinting on four of his spindly fingers. The symbols of Chauncey's success were something none of his friends would let him sell.

"He's got lots of rings. Is he your prince?" Maddy glanced up at Lana, who was smiling at Chauncey. Brett's chest ached. What he wouldn't give for someone to look at him like that.

"He *is* my prince," the woman murmured.

"I'll let you wear one of my rings if you sit with me awhile." Chauncey slipped off a bulky gold ring and held it out. "I won this from a Russian in 1975."

With a coo of appreciation, Maddy slid the ring onto two fingers and held up her hand so it wouldn't fall off.

"Let's find you something to try on." Lana slid hangers holding brightly colored satin costumes across a bar bolted to the wall.

Ernie ambled in wearing one of his Tommy Bahama bowling shirts, this one sea-green with palm fronds—most touristy—and a pair of ratty blue jeans. But that wasn't why Brett's jaw dropped.

"What happened to your arms?" Chauncey's voice was weak but hadn't lost its customary rumble.

"Fake tattoo shirt." Ernie thrust out his arms. "It came in the mail yesterday all the way from London. They look real, don't they?" The long sleeves were flesh-colored and covered with tattoos. Since the material fit over Ernie's arms like a glove, at a casual glance it would look as if he had magnificent tattoos covering both forearms.

Maddy sidled in for a closer view, her hands falling to her sides. Chauncey's ring bounced across the linoleum.

"The cuffs at your wrists are a dead giveaway," Brett said, bending to pick it up. Otherwise the concept was interesting. Anything that diverted attention to their eccentricities, and away from their true identities, was useful and kept them in the casino longer. He handed Chauncey his ring, ignoring Maddy's pout.

"Lose the Tommy Bahama and pick up one of those Harley Davidson T-shirts," Chauncey said.

Lana walked around Ernie. "Leather wristbands." She'd spent years in Hollywood working in the wardrobe department and then in makeup. "A bandanna on your head and an earring."

"Fake, right?" Ernie tugged at an earlobe.

Lana chuckled. "Of course. Have you met Maddy?"

"Only on the phone," he said with a smile and a wink. He turned to Brett. "Are you working today? I know of four dealers on shift."

"Well, I've—"

"We'll watch her." Lana cut Brett off. "She'll be fine with us. We have lots of pretty clothes for her to try."

"Fix me up, then," he said.

After Lana sent Maddy with an armload of clothes behind the red Oriental screen that separated the office space from her bedroom, she went to work on Brett's face, applying a large, irregular birthmark that started on the bridge of his nose and ended at his jawline. Add dark-tinted glasses, with his hair tucked beneath an English driver cap, and he'd be unrecognizable to his own daughter, he decided, checking Lana's work in a mirror.

"How's Annie doing?" Ernie asked, snapping leather strips over the cuffs of his sleeves.

"She's good." Brett felt compelled to add, "She's applying for a legit job at Slotto."

Lana and Ernie exchanged glances, and the hair on the back of Brett's neck rose.

"Might be easier if we set her up in a game," Ernie said casually.

"She won't play." Brett rummaged in a plastic box for a pair of large, hideously outdated sunglasses.

"She played yesterday. Right next to me." Ernie tugged at a Harley-Davidson T-shirt that was a tad too tight across the chest.

"Let it go." Chauncey shifted and looked away. Brett knew what the man was thinking. Here they were, raising money for his treatment, and he was helpless to aid or stop them. "Others have offered to help."

"She won," Ernie added, bending over so Lana could tie a red bandanna on his head. "And she came in midgame."

"She came in with Knight," Brett pointed out. "What if you ask her to play and she doesn't want to help us?"

Everyone was staring at him now.

"Doesn't Knight work for Vince?" Chauncey asked.

"He says he's working for someone else." Brett put on the sunglasses, wishing it was that easy to hide from his friends.

"This smells of Aldo's doing," Ernie muttered, checking himself out in the mirror.

Reaching for Chauncey's hand, Lana perched on the arm of the recliner.

Ernie turned. "Why are you all looking so glum? If it is Aldo, it's the perfect opportunity. Annie beat him before. A guy like that doesn't forget. He'd probably be open to a rematch. We could clear enough on one game with him to complete Chauncey's treatment. One game."

"Or someone could be hurt," Brett said quietly, picking up a set of car keys from Lana's desk.

"Tah-dah!" Maddy clumped from behind the screen in red, sparkly high heels, a tiara and a red sequined minidress that came to her ankles.

"You look gorgeous," Lana said, but her tone lacked its earlier enthusiasm.

"I think we should ask her." Ernie picked up the conversation again. "With a few side bets—"

"No!" All eyes turned at Brett's shout. "I'll win the money. We don't need Annie." He pushed the glasses farther up his nose and practically ran out the back door.

"So you've seen a guy like that? Older, dark glasses, mustache, growth on his face?" Sam asked the dealer one more time, just to make sure.

"Honey, I've seen hundreds of old guys with tinted glasses and hideous facial features. This is Vegas. But this guy doesn't talk much and leaves generous tips. *That* I remember." The woman snapped her gum.

"When does he come in?"

"Last week he came in on Friday. Late morning. Just before the weekend started up."

Sam handed her a business card and a twenty. "Thanks again, Mildred. If one of them comes in, give me a call."

"Oh, I almost forgot. He has a slight limp. You can barely see it, but he dropped a couple of chips and I watched him walk away to make sure he was okay."

Sam had been to five casinos and had had no problem finding dealers who remembered someone partially fitting the description of the card player he and Annie had run into the day before. Two different builds, but always something unique about their features, and tinted glasses. Even though Sam still lacked concrete leads, he was more fired up than he'd been about anything since he'd returned stateside.

Blinking in the morning sunlight, he put on his sunglasses. It wasn't long before he was pulling out of the parking lot on his way to the next casino on his list, with a small vehicle a few car lengths behind him.

Annie.

She'd been keeping her distance, following, but not coming inside the casinos. It might have flattered him, except Sam knew she was only tailing him because she wanted that job at Slotto. She'd do anything to make herself useful and get back in his good graces. But there was no way Sam was using her, after making a fool of himself last night. Besides, she'd been raised by a con artist and married to an embezzler. She might amuse him with her amateur detective tricks, but she wasn't someone he'd ever be able to trust.

He smiled as he approached the Lucky Horse Casino without a glance Annie's way. Let her think she was following him undetected. He'd be able to shake her if he really wanted to.

In fact, she was getting too close. He needed to send her a message.

ANNIE REFUSED TO WORRY about what her father might be teaching Maddy while she shadowed Sam. She didn't have time for distractions. Why couldn't Sam just stop being so stubborn and let her help? Then maybe she'd get that Slotto job.

Standing outside the casino wearing what looked to be new blue jeans and a black polo, Sam didn't seem as burned out today. He smiled at an elderly couple coming out of the double doors, and they stopped to talk. Soon they were nodding and pointing inside.

Had he given them a description and they'd remembered something? Was one of the card counters in there?

As she'd done at each previous casino he'd visited, Annie dug her cell phone out of her purse, waiting for Sam to call. Of course, he wouldn't contact her right away. He'd wait until he confirmed that one of them was inside. She had a good feeling about this one.

Annie released her seat belt and grabbed the door handle, convinced that he needed her. The Lucky Horse Casino was larger than the other ones he'd been to this morning. It would take her awhile to find Sam if he called. Still, he'd be impressed that she'd gotten here so fast. If a cardsharp was inside, following Sam would pay off.

"Excuse me." Hopping out of the car, Annie put on her friendliest smile as she walked over to the same couple Sam had spoken to a minute ago. "I noticed you gave my husband directions while I parked the car."

"Yes, he told us to watch out for you. We sent him

on to the gift shop," the woman stated helpfully. "He was looking for a deck of cards. He mentioned something about learning to play blackjack."

No. Sam couldn't have seen her. Oh, heck. Of course he had. And he was trying to rub her nose in it. Annie wanted to kick something, preferably Sam's shin.

"Aren't you going in, dear?"

"I need to make a phone call first." Or at least come up with a plan so that Sam understood he couldn't get rid of her that easily.

"THE GUY'S HARMLESS." This dealer was trying very hard to make light of the card counter. She fit the profile of the other dealers he'd located who'd seen the card-sharps—middle-aged woman, no wedding ring.

"Does he tip well?"

"Better than most. Why all the fuss? He's nothing much in the scheme of things around here, and he's only been in twice lately."

Lately? "When's the last time you saw him?"

"A week ago."

"And he tips well?"

"Very well." Her smile was private.

Sam gave her his business card even though he knew she'd never call. He made a mental note of her name— Isabelle. The Lucky Horse topped his list for a stakeout.

Buoyed by his discovery, he made his exit, smiling.

Except Annie had turned the tables on him. She'd blocked him in. Her car and his truck made a perfect *T.*

Her car's hood was up, but there was no way anything could be wrong with it.

"Sam." Annie tried to appear amazed to see him, but Sam knew better. She looked so domestic in her form-fitting pink Tinkerbell T-shirt, white shorts and tennis shoes. "I'm having car trouble. I'm glad you came along."

He propped his hands on his hips and leaned over until they were nearly nose to nose. Close enough to kiss. "Move your car."

"I wish I could. It won't start." Annie blinked those baby blues without backing away. Didn't she have any sense of self-preservation? She dangled the keys in front of him. "Here. You try."

His desire to kiss Annie warred with the need to shake her until her teeth rattled. Sam took her keys.

"Why doesn't this seat slide back?" he grumbled, squeezing behind the steering wheel. He jammed the key in the ignition and cranked it. Not that he'd expected it to start.

"Not much on this car works except the engine." Annie dropped into the passenger seat, still trying to float that poor-helpless-me routine. "What's wrong with it?"

"Did you loosen the battery cables?"

"Did you offer me a job?"

"I'm too busy to play games with you." Looking straight ahead, Sam saw a man with a birthmark on his face, wearing dark glasses and an English driver cap, come out the door. The man headed in the direction of the parking lot.

Annie leaned forward. "Do you think—"

"It's one of them." He was sure of it.

This man wasn't as heavy as the gambler they'd run across in Tiny's. He wore black pants and a checkered shirt that hung off his thin shoulders, crossing the parking lot with a slightly uneven gait, as if one of his knees was gimpy. Sam wouldn't have noticed if the dealer hadn't said something about a limp. He'd probably been gambling at Isabelle's table before Sam came in.

The man climbed into a red car and backed out a little too quickly. He'd seen them.

Annie leaped out of the car before the man had a chance to drive off. She tightened the screws on top of the battery, closed the hood and jumped back in.

"What are you waiting for?" she demanded, trying unsuccessfully to close the door. It was stuck open. "Let's go."

She turned and the excitement in her blue eyes was almost palpable.

Sam reached across her, grabbed her door handle and yanked it closed. His shoulder brushed against the softness of her breasts as he returned to his cramped space behind the wheel. The car backfired and shuddered to life.

"Are you sure you're Annie Raye?" When he'd first opened her file he'd had a much different set of expectations, despite her arrest record.

"What?"

Sam concentrated on finding room for his elbows in her small car as he turned a tight corner. If he didn't, he'd touch her again. Her car had been designed for midgets. "You're supposed to be a numbers cruncher with a boring job, and except for the embezzler husband, a boring life." Not a woman who claimed to know her way around a blackjack table, or how to disable a vehicle."

"If I'm so boring, why don't I have the Slotto job?"

Why indeed. "I could call Carl this afternoon."

"Would you?"

Sam didn't want to. What was wrong with him?

He glanced at Annie. Yep, she was dressed just as he remembered—conservative T-shirt, housewife shorts and tennis shoes. So why was it he kept visualizing her in something low-cut, with sexy high heels?

"Sam?"

"I can't." His father had always told him to follow his instincts.

"Why not?"

Another turn. Another scrunching of elbows, less successful this time. Sam's right elbow skimmed Annie's shoulder, and he drifted into the other lane to a chorus of irritable drivers leaning on their horns.

"Because you're hiding something. You've packaged yourself to sell boring and predictable, but, lady, you are anything but that." Sam struggled to sound disapproving.

"There's nothing wrong with creating the right impression." Annie's voice lacked her usual bravado. He'd hit too close to home. "Don't you care what people think?"

"No. I know who I am and who I'm not." Sam didn't think Annie could say the same.

CHAPTER SIX

"YOU'RE WRONG. I'm boring and I want a boring job."
Annie rubbed her forehead. That hadn't come out right.
The big lug threw her off her game.

"Did you lose him?" she asked as they pulled onto
Las Vegas Boulevard a few minutes later.

"He's a couple cars ahead."

"The red one, right?" Annie sighed. It made no sense
that the gambler would come down to the Strip.

"What's wrong?"

The red-tiled roof of the Sicilian loomed ahead. Her
stomach did a quick flip-flop. She prayed that the man
wouldn't turn into the Sicilian's entryway. "Why would
he come to the Strip? To get stuck in traffic? Or to
gamble where they have the most sophisticated security
systems around? It's not like Tiny's or the Lucky Horse
where security is a pipe dream."

"Hey. Should I be taking that personally? Maybe
he's just trying to get across town."

"I'm sure a lot of people enjoy driving down the
most congested street in Vegas, loaded with diversions
and drunken tourists who occasionally step in front of
oncoming traffic."

The older model red sedan pulled into the Sicilian.

Not there. Of all the casinos in Vegas, why had the gambler picked the one Annie couldn't enter?

Sam slowed in front of the opulent building until the cars behind them started honking. Annie thought he wasn't going to follow the red car. It disappeared into the parking garage and Sam didn't slow down. But then he made the turn at the last minute. The air went out of Annie's lungs in a rush.

"Didn't want to risk him seeing us," Sam explained.

"Wouldn't want that. He might panic and take off," Annie managed to croak, ruing the fact that Sam wasn't as incompetent as she'd first thought.

They pulled into the parking garage and began circling upward.

"There he goes," Sam said, nodding in the direction of the casino entrance on the third level.

"Why don't I stay here?" Annie suggested weakly. There was no way she was going in there. She could still see Aldo Patrizio's face as her father lay beaten and bloody on the floor, as Aldo warned her to never set foot in here again unless she had a death wish. Annie definitely did not have a death wish.

Sam whipped the car into a compact space. "You wanted to be part of this. Here's your chance."

"Pass." She planned to huddle on the floorboard.

"Move, Annie. Now!" Sam barked, as if glaring at her wasn't enough.

She didn't trust herself to stand. "No."

"Why?"

She clenched her hands, trying to hide her fear. If she entered the Sicilian, she'd be in trouble. Her presence might even put Sam in danger. And Maddy. Who would take care of Maddy if something happened to her? Brett? "You were right. I was bluffing at Tiny's. I'd be no help to you in there."

"Hey." Some of the edge disappeared from Sam's tone. He was probably going to try to lure her with money or the promise of clearing her name with Slotto.

Annie didn't need money or a job that badly.

He clasped her shoulder and then moved downward, stroking her arm. Softly.

She closed her eyes. She didn't need sex, either. She never thought of sex anymore.

"Annie. Tell me what's got you spooked." Sam's voice was smooth as velvet as he turned her to face him. The narrow center console offered a slim barrier between them. He slid his hand back up to her shoulder, but his touch ignited heat much deeper inside.

It had been over a year since she'd been touched by a man, other than a firm handshake or her father's hug. Perhaps longer since Annie believed anyone other than Maddy truly cared what happened to her. That had to explain this sudden need to have Sam's arms around her, the urge to close the distance between them and draw on his strength. All she had to do was open her eyes, identify the annoyance and calculation in Sam's gaze and this warm, fuzzy, dangerous feeling would be vanquished. Open her eyes and destroy the illusion that Sam cared. Open her eyes and continue to face the world alone.

With effort, she searched his expression. There was no anger there, no irritation, only understanding. How could that be?

"I'm very experienced with panic attacks, Annie. Take a deep breath."

She couldn't have broken away from his gaze if she'd wanted to. They breathed in and out together.

"Everything's going to be all right." Sam's voice soothed her jangled nerves. He slid that hand back and forth across her shoulders. "Stay with me now."

Stay with me. How many times had Annie wished that she'd hear Frank say something like that to her? But he'd only been interested in trying to save himself.

"That's it. Look at me. Breathe. Look at me."

Annie was looking at Sam—at how his green eyes had deepened in color, at how his tempting mouth moved when he talked. She glanced back into his eyes as she leaned closer until their lips were almost touching, waiting to see his reaction, hoping she wouldn't find rejection.

Sam's eyes widened slightly before he closed the distance and covered her mouth with his. Then he wrapped his arms around her in a bruising embrace, until she couldn't breathe. Annie didn't care. Sam kissed her as if he couldn't last another minute without the taste of her, without touching her.

And she felt the same way.

SAM INHALED STRAWBERRIES as he kissed Annie. Sometime during the last few painful minutes of her panic attack, he'd realized that touching her wouldn't satisfy him.

Annie exploded in his arms, her hands under his shirt, heating Sam quicker than a practiced stripper.

He pulled back, capturing her hands. "Whoa, hold on. We're in a parking lot."

It took a moment for his words to sink in. Annie bumped back against the door and her cheeks bloomed deep red. "Don't do that again."

He laughed—how long had it been since he'd laughed?—and reached for her. "You kissed me."

"A mistake I'm not going to repeat. I want that job. This…this shouldn't have happened." She nearly fell out of the car in her haste to get away from him.

Sam followed at a more leisurely pace, tucking in his shirt. Then he took Annie's hand and led her toward the casino. "You think too much."

She tugged, but Sam wouldn't release her. He turned to face her and captured her other hand.

"Don't kiss me again," she warned, leaning back, unwittingly thrusting her Tinkerbell cleavage forward.

"Annie," he said in a low voice meant to calm her. "We'll attract less attention if we're not fighting as we go in."

"Oh." She frowned. "So you don't want to…" Her cheeks turned even redder.

Sam's body throbbed with an answer he was sure she didn't want to acknowledge. "Can we change the subject? Otherwise, I won't be able to walk unnoticed through the casino."

Annie cast her gaze downward and then began striding quickly.

In the direction of the casino.

For once, she was doing what he'd asked.

So why was he disappointed?

ANNIE WASN'T SURE if it was her fear or her desire that made her knees unsteady. She couldn't settle down, couldn't shake off the memory of Sam's lips on hers.

She wiped her mouth with one hand. Her other one was wrapped in Sam's. His grip was strong, but he wasn't strong enough to ward off an angry Aldo Patrizio. The midweek crowd ebbed and flowed around them, giving Annie a small measure of safety. The years had changed her appearance. Aldo's security men couldn't possibly recognize her. Could they?

The Sicilian was a gorgeous casino, painted the soft tan of fresh baked bread, with a red-tiled roof and blue faux shutters. Here, away from the heat and fumes of the traffic, richly colored, flowering vines and shrubs accented the building and cobblestone entries. As a child Annie had thought it was the most beautiful place she'd ever seen. So bright and colorful, so different from her own small, drab home. She'd wanted to live here.

It wasn't until Sam held the door for her and she stepped past him into the marble entry that her survival instinct kicked in again. She spun to face the door, away from the security cameras she had no doubt were pointed her way that very second.

"I can't do this."

"Come on. He's bound to be at the tables by now." With a firm yet gentle touch, Sam turned Annie back around. "He might have cut through and gone to another casino, in which case we've lost him."

Annie rubbed her forehead, trying to shield her face with her hand, fully expecting security to descend upon her at any moment. What would Sam think then?

He looked down at her. "Headache?"

She nodded, her head bent, concentrating on the soothing mandolin music as they walked past a small fountain.

"Keep your eyes open. If he's still here, he'll be on the main floor."

Annie went on the lookout, all right, but for security, not the gambler. He'd be a fool to try anything in Aldo's place, or any of the other major houses on the central Strip.

A blur of burgundy caught Annie's eye. A tall, broad-shouldered man strode confidently through the crowd toward them, the Sicilian logo emblazoned in gold on his breast pocket. Her heart stopped with a painful lurch. This was it. She shrank back behind Sam.

The security guard walked right past her without so much as a glance.

When Sam gripped her by the arm and pulled her back to his side, her heart started again.

"We'll talk about your problems with authority figures later."

"Like never," she said to herself.

Sam gave her a reproachful glance.

It didn't take them long to reach the edge of the tables, near a bank of rare coin-eating slot machines. Most slots at the larger houses only took plastic, but Aldo apparently had a retro thing going on in this section.

"See? You're doing great." Sam cupped her face and leaned over to whisper in Annie's ear, creating all the wrong sensations in all the wrong places. "We won't get too close. If we spot him and our man turns your way, look at something else as casually as you can. I'd rather follow him and find out who he is than risk losing him in the crowd if he knows he's being watched."

Annie repressed the shivers Sam's warm breath generated, the fear that her memories of the Sicilian brought back, and nodded. Her legs still felt wobbly as she searched for a checkered shirt and beige cap, not expecting to see the gambler.

But he hadn't left. Cap brim pulled down to the rim of his dark glasses, he was circling the blackjack tables, no doubt looking for a few smiling patrons being treated well by the dealer. That's what she'd do. But he'd already made one stupid mistake simply in targeting the Sicilian. Dealers here were better trained, players more closely monitored. Anyone suspected of counting cards to increase their odds of winning would be hauled into the inner corridors by security, photographed and escorted off the premises. With that birthmark of his, he'd be easy to spot the next time he tried to enter the place.

"What do we do now?" she asked Sam.

"Watch and wait." He nodded toward the tinted black half globes that hid video cameras jutting from the ceiling at regular intervals. Sam dug into his pocket. "Here. We can't just loiter. Get some quarters so we can play."

Shoulders hunched, Annie hurried off to the cashier. The line was long. When she returned, Sam was gone, but their man was still gambling.

"What now, Sam?" Annie mumbled, shaking her cup full of change. It was hard to believe she missed Sam's annoyingly steady presence. She could run out the door, but that might attract too much attention. What choice did she have but to play?

While she slowly fed her quarters into a slot machine, Annie glanced frequently across the casino to the blackjack tables. The card counter was losing, too. Annie hadn't expected that. Had she been wrong about him?

From her vantage point, Annie could see him handing over chips. Gamblers on either side of him won. He fidgeted and rolled his head from shoulder to shoulder, a move oddly reminiscent of the way her father relieved the tension. If the guy was smart, he'd tally his losses and give up. And if Sam hadn't shown up when he did, Annie would have to decide if she should follow him or not.

Her machine suddenly came alive and coughed up five hundred quarters.

"It's your lucky day, honey." A blue-haired woman

patted Annie's arm and gazed covetously at Annie's machine.

Annie glanced back to the gambler's table, but he was no longer there. Her eyes darted around the floor.

What was she going to tell Sam? She was a bust at this private investigator thing. Annie scooped up her quarters, but it quickly became clear they wouldn't all fit in her cup or her little purse.

"Looks like you could use another one of these." Tingles rippled down Annie's spine as a man offered her another large coin cup.

Slowly, fighting to keep her panic under control, Annie turned her head just enough to catch sight of a red birthmark beneath dark glasses.

SAM CONCEDED THE SICILIAN'S surveillance team was damn sharp. He sat on a leather chair in a stark back room in the casino, wondering which Patrizio had pulled him from the floor, hoping it was Vince. A summons by Mr. Patrizio might reveal his ulterior motive for choosing Sam, but some clients had a desire to micromanage their cases. Sam didn't work for that type of client. But Vince had warned him....

Two stocky men stood on either side of the only door, staring impassively down at him. Their gigantic arms and barrel chests had Sam trying to recall what he'd learned of peaceful negotiation tactics during his stint in the army, but he decided silence was his best option.

They continued to tower over him. The square-face

guy had asked him politely but firmly to accompany them, so he knew at least he wasn't mute. Sam had gone along, grateful that Annie was occupied elsewhere. After her skittish reaction to the Sicilian's security, the sight of two guards escorting Sam away might have caused another meltdown.

"I do have a schedule to keep, fellas." Sam needed to get back to Annie before she realized he was gone. Even if she kept her composure, she might do something foolish, like gamble next to their mark.

Mr. Patrizio opened the door. He wore an expensive suit and a frown that warned Sam to ignore the facial wrinkles, thick glasses and white hair. He might be old, but the Sicilian's founder wasn't to be taken lightly. The security guards parted to let Mr. Patrizio through, and then stepped back into their bookend positions.

"Mr. Knight, I thought our agreement was clear—find those cardsharps. And yet you're here on my casino floor… Gambling." Mr. Patrizio spoke precisely, his brows drawn down in annoyance. He had a reputation for being a royal pain in the ass if you didn't do things his way. "One might think you aren't earning your money."

"I have a few good leads." Sam wasn't sure if it was Mr. Patrizio's manner or his pride that made him reluctant to divulge the details. And then there was Annie's fear of the security guard. "I could have wrapped this up yesterday if Sabatinni had showed up like you promised."

"Sir, Sabatinni was seen gambling in Henderson yesterday." The other guard proved he also had a voice.

Mr. Patrizio's frown deepened. The fact that they knew where Sabatinni was when Sam hadn't been able to find him was unnerving and implied Sabatinni had decided he could make more money playing blackjack than consulting. Sam chose not to think about this latest development until later. "I found my own expert witness. From what I've gathered, these counters aren't hurting any one house specifically. Sure, they hit and run, but they win less than a thousand each time."

"I have a responsibility to the smaller casinos in the area. I help them with issues outside their expertise and they offer our coupon books exclusively to their players. Their staff recommends our hotel, nightclub acts and bars if anyone asks." Mr. Patrizio spoke carefully, his gaze steady.

"The business you generate from them has got to be small."

"Small adds up. Now please, Mr. Knight, I'm still waiting for your explanation of why you're here today."

There was no more getting around it. "I followed one of them here."

Mr. Patrizio scowled as if he couldn't believe a cardsharp would dare enter his casino. "Describe him." After Sam did, he turned and told his bookends to find him.

One of them disappeared through the doorway. Irrationally, Sam hoped the gambler had left. He may be working for Mr. Patrizio, but it was Sam's case.

"I want this taken care of by Monday. Is that clear?"

"I'll do my best." Sam wasn't getting nearly as much

grief as he suspected Vince got every day, but it still raised his hackles.

The guard poked his head back in. "The control room says there's no sign of him on the main floor, sir. Do you want us to keep looking?"

Annie was just stubborn enough to follow their guy alone, especially if he left the casino. The idea both pleased and worried him. "I'll take care of it." Sam shot up from his chair.

THE GAMBLER ESCORTED Annie out the front doors. Clutching two grande-size cups of quarters to her chest, she took a deep breath of fresh afternoon air. She was terrified and didn't dare look at him. If this was what she got for going into the Sicilian after all these years, she'd never go back again.

Annie finally found her voice. "Where are you taking me?"

Instead of answering, he just tightened his grip above her elbow and grumbled something about not being able to trust family.

With a shiver, Annie glanced around the crowded sidewalk, searching for Sam, a traffic cop or any burly man she could appeal to for help.

"Oh, for cryin' out loud, Annie, move your butt so we can talk."

Her feet cemented themselves to the sidewalk, and she turned to confront her kidnapper.

"*Dad?*" She peered past the dark oval lenses and splotchy birthmark, trying to see Brett's features.

Anger crushed the last of her fear. "Dad." An accusation.

Her father shushed her.

"You're one of the card counters? You scared the crap out of me." Annie yanked her arm away. "Where's Maddy? If you left her alone—"

"Maddy's fine. It's you I worry about, waltzing into the Sicilian. I came here because I knew you had sense enough *not* to follow me inside. Didn't I teach you anything?" He removed the beige English cap and tucked it into the back of his trousers beneath his shirt, producing a purple baseball hat and settling it on his head.

"Where's Maddy?"

"With a babysitter." He glanced at his watch. "I need to pick her up soon."

Annie's heart raced. "If anything happens to her—"

"She'll be fine." He pulled a handkerchief from a pocket and wiped the red stain on his face. It didn't completely disappear, but was much less noticeable.

"I should have known it was you at Tiny's." She glared at him, weighing the threat to Maddy against her need to get her baby back right now. "Except why would I have recognized you? You were *winning*."

"Puddin'," he said, smiling almost apologetically, "you won't believe me when I tell you, but once you left me and I didn't have to provide for anyone but myself, I found I could win pretty easily. But that wasn't me yesterday."

Annie just shook her head. "If Maddy isn't home by

the time I get there you'll have more to worry about than the Patrizios."

Brett pulled her over to the palm frond landscaping, out of the way of most foot traffic, and faced the casino, scanning the crowd coming out.

"You're in trouble." The nausea Annie had kept at bay in the Sicilian crept up her throat. The heavy cups weighed down her hands. "How could you leave her with strangers? She's just a baby."

"I tell you, she's fine. She's with my…oh, crap. He's coming." Brett wrapped his hand around Annie's arm again and urged her farther away from the Sicilian.

"Who?" She tried to look over her shoulder.

"Never mind." He quickened his pace. "Why do you ask so many questions? Hurry up. We're a team, remember?"

Annie did remember, and the kaleidoscope of memories had her digging her heels in. "No."

His gaze bored into her with more than a hint of betrayal. "I've got to do this, Annie. Don't go near the Sicilian again. Too many people in town know you. And don't trust that P.I." Her father turned and was swallowed by the crowd.

Annie stood frozen in place and remembered what it had been like that summer of her twelfth year. The thrill, the adrenaline rush, and eventually, the fear. Most girls her age spent their summers dreaming about boys, doodling hearts around initials and trying to dance the way kids did in music videos. Annie had spent that summer in private rooms at casinos like this one. She'd been an oddity. Someone every gambler shook his head at and swore he could outlast, until his chips were gone and she sat with stacks in front of her, basking in her father's smile.

Which would have been fine if Brett Raye hadn't underestimated the sting the Patrizios would feel at losing five hundred thousand dollars to a twelve-year-old with blond pigtails.

"Annie!" Sam was close, and she found herself shivering, swaying like a drunk on the sidewalk. "Annie!" He spun her around, grasping her shoulders with his strong hands.

Too many people know you're in town. Why would anyone care? Except Aldo.

Annie searched Sam's eyes with barely contained terror. She had to get to the apartment, find Maddy and leave Las Vegas. There must be somewhere else she could go…if only she had enough money to get there.

"What are you doing out here?" Sam asked. He craned his neck, scanning the throng in the direction her father had disappeared. "I thought I saw you with our guy."

Annie clutched the cups of quarters to her chest. Her father was making her choose again, as he had so many years ago. The choice should have been easy.

You can quit if you want, puddin'. But we can go far. There'd been a gleam in Brett's purple-and-black-rimmed eyes back then as he stared up at her from his hospital bed. Annie knew he didn't want to quit. Heck, she hadn't wanted to quit. The only time her father seemed to approve of her was when she was playing cards. But Annie had also known she couldn't have her dad's death on her hands.

She tossed a nervous glance over her shoulder at the Sicilian.

After the Patrizio incident, she and her father hadn't discussed Annie's retirement, just as they hadn't discussed Iris Raye's departure. In fact, they hadn't exchanged much more than pleasantries since. They'd bought a house in Henderson, a suburb of Las Vegas, set up a college fund for Annie with most of her winnings and lived like two strangers who had no interest in becoming friends....

Sam shook Annie's shoulders gently, and she fell against him in relief. "Hey, what's wrong?" he asked.

Everything. Her dad was in danger, apparently way out of his league again. She should help him, but there was Maddy to consider. Annie didn't know what to do. Much as she'd like to trust Sam, she couldn't. He was too observant for her to think this through now. And he was searching for her father.

"I...I followed him out here and got too close." Annie backed up a step. "I guess I should have left the private investigator stuff to you." She smiled weakly, unable to meet Sam's inquisitive gaze.

"I'm sorry." He enveloped her in his arms, careful not to spill the quarters. "My fault. I ran into trouble with casino security and it took me a while to straighten it out."

"Security?" Annie mumbled into Sam's chest as panic shook her composure once more.

With one long arm draped over her shoulder, he steered them in the direction of the parking garage, oblivious to her distress. "It's okay. I straightened everything out. Hey, you won." Sam covered one of her hands with his and shook the cup, making barely a rattle, it was so full. "You're lucky."

Annie managed a nod of agreement.

CHAPTER SEVEN

BRETT PUSHED THROUGH the crowds, circled the fountain at the Bellagio and crossed the street. Anyone could be following him—that P.I. or someone from the Sicilian.

He paused at the street corner and lingered, casually searching the crowd as if he was just stopping to take in the sights. No one paid him any mind. Only when Brett felt safe did he cut through the back of Bally's parking lot, taking a side street to an alley that came out near Tassels Galore. Hugging the corner of a neighboring bail bonds building, he scoped out the rear entrance.

"Brett Raye."

Hearing his name, Brett nearly collapsed. He looked back down the alley, which had been empty moments before.

"It's been a long time. I almost didn't recognize you in those glasses." Vince Patrizio sauntered toward him wearing a crisp white shirt with the sleeves rolled up, fine wool slacks and a tie. You would have thought he was coming out of the elevator at the Sicilian, not the back entrance of the bail bonds shop. How in the hell had Brett missed him in the crowd?

Brett's heart pounded furiously. He hadn't caught more than a glimpse of Vince in over a decade. He looked nothing like the cocky teenager who'd been eager to introduce himself to Brett before one of Annie's card games.

"How did you find me?" How many times had Brett imagined this encounter? And why were the words he'd planned to say suddenly elusive?

"Sam Knight came into the casino. My grandfather hired Sam to find some card counters. All I had to do was wait and see who Sam was following." Vince's slightly upturned lip indicated how pleased he was with himself.

Hot damn. Aldo had hired Sam. Brett's knees buckled so badly he had to lean against the warm cinder block wall. "I ducked inside to try and shake him. I'm not working on your turf. I lost every chip." Brett held up his hands as if Vince had a gun.

The younger Patrizio frowned. "Put your hands down."

Slowly, he lowered his arms. "What do you want?"

"I want to know why my grandfather is so intent on shutting you down."

Brett considered lying, but he owed Vince. "He hasn't been friendly toward card counters since…" Brett shrugged awkwardly. "I don't take it personally. It's business."

"But you think it's unfair."

"Lots of things happen in this world that aren't fair." Without meaning to, he shifted his weight, calling attention to his bum leg.

Vince noticed.

The apology he owed Vince stuck in Brett's throat. "People…people sometimes do things they shouldn't. Like take certain bets. Some of us accept it and move on."

There was no change in Vince's expression. He just kept studying him as if Brett held the answer to a most elusive question.

A shiny sedan with a stereo blaring rocketed into Tassels's lot, drawing Brett's attention away. When he turned back to Vince, he saw the younger man disappearing around the corner.

He'd waited years to say something to Vince, to take on his share of the blame. He'd blown his chance.

Brett crossed the lot and slipped inside Tassels, immediately assaulted by the pounding beat of the music. Rod Stewart was singing, wondering whether or not someone wanted his body. Brett knocked once before entering Lana's office where the music was blessedly muted.

He caught sight of Chauncey sleeping on the bed behind the Oriental screen. Brett would have liked to talk to him about Vince. He'd have to tell them about Aldo. *Aldo!* They were tap dancing around dynamite.

"Grandpa!" Maddy clumped toward him in oversize high heels and a sparkly Cleopatra headdress. "Those glasses are silly."

Brett yanked off the glasses and baseball hat, pulled

out the English cap from underneath his shirt and handed everything to Lana. He bent to hug Maddy.

"That's better," the little girl said, squeezing him tightly, unwittingly calming Brett's frazzled nerves. "I tried on twenty shoes, fifteen rings, twelve skirts and ten crowns." She patted the headdress. "What took you so long?"

"She was born to be a princess," Lana said in her lyrical voice, running her fingers through Maddy's now tamed hair.

"She looks like Shirley Temple." Brett frowned. Annie wouldn't be pleased. Correction: Annie wasn't pleased. This would send her over the edge. "It's time to go, puddin'."

Dutifully, his granddaughter began taking off Lana's things. Annie had raised a good girl.

"Trouble?" Lana asked, somehow knowing just by looking at him.

"It wasn't a good day to go out. I had to make a detour. Your car's at the Sicilian. Level three." He ignored Lana's sharp intake of breath and set the keys on her dresser, along with the wad of cash he'd won at the Lucky Horse before Knight came in.

Lana kept the beat-up vehicle in a small garage accessible through a door behind her desk, although she drove an Audi. Another precaution. One of Lana's girls had left the rough-idling red sedan in exchange for a loan. With video surveillance in parking lots nowadays, they couldn't be too careful, couldn't drive their own cars to play. Ernie had walked to the casinos he'd marked today.

"Ernie's not back yet. Perhaps you can swing by later. After dark." There was desperation in Lana's eyes as she handed him a makeup remover cloth to take the rest of the birthmark off his face, her fear of losing Chauncey almost tangible.

Brett had felt that way himself after he'd lost Annie. "Not tonight. We'll get the money, Lana, don't worry."

Her gaze darted toward the Oriental screen and she blinked rapidly before looking at him again. "Maddy was no problem. I'll watch her again if need be."

Brett merely smiled, knowing Annie wouldn't let that happen. This might be the last time he'd be able to hold his granddaughter.

"We appreciate what you're doing. Chauncey responds so well to this treatment. They say one more…."

"No one can say this will be the last treatment. If he needs another, we'll raise the money again." Brett had already dipped into his savings to help pay Chauncey's medical bills. If it meant prolonging the quality and length of his friend's life, Brett would find a way to get the money, even if he had to sell his own home next.

As if sensing the seriousness of the conversation, Maddy lay her head on Brett's shoulder.

"The P.I. is getting too close, isn't he?" Lana murmured.

"We'll be fine." Brett would make sure Annie and her P.I. stayed away.

Lana fingered one of Maddy's curls. "I worry about you and Ernie. It's one thing to play a bit for vacation money. The stakes are higher now. You can't go unnoticed forever. Wouldn't it be easier on everyone if Annie played?"

Just the opposite. Brett shook his head, unable to speak. Seeing Vince Patrizio seemed to have shriveled his brain cells.

"Think about it. We'd have a cushion and you could go back into retirement. It's just a game."

"That's what I thought fourteen years ago." Meeting her gaze, Brett hoped Lana could see the years of pain, the anguish over decisions he'd made that had hurt others, and the losses he'd suffered. From what Brett had heard, Vince had been emotionally scarred from the incident. He'd even run away. "I put everything on the line for money, but in the end everyone got hurt. *Everyone.* Are you willing to stand by and watch the fallout, knowing none of it would have happened if not for you?"

"I already am." Of course she was. Lana loved Chauncey and would sell her soul to the devil to save him. Hell, she already had.

Unable to stand firm in the face of Lana's courage anymore, Brett hitched Maddy higher in his arms. "Ready to go, puddin'?"

She grinned, lightening the pressure around his heart. "Wait until I tell Mommy what we did today."

Without a backward glance, Brett carried the child out the door. "Yes, about that…"

"THIS IS WHERE WE SAY goodbye," Annie announced miserably as Sam pulled her car in front of his parked truck. Her sweaty palms still clutched the cups filled with quarters. What if Maddy wasn't there when she got back to the apartment?

"Giving up? That's not like you."

"I need to get back to Maddy." Annie willed her feet to move. She should get out of the car, only if she left too soon Maddy might not be there. Annie couldn't bear that. Maybe if she sat a few minutes with Sam her father would have time to get home.

"So now your secret's out."

"What?"

"You have some kind of gambling phobia, don't you? You were hyperventilating in the car at the Sicilian's parking lot," Sam explained, flipping her key ring on his finger. "I recognized the signs…of the *flu*."

"I do not have a gambling phobia." Even now, the cards in the Lucky Horse Casino seemed to be calling her. If she played, she might earn enough money to leave town.

Sam reached out and brushed her cheek with his knuckles. "If it's not that," he said softly, "what is it you're afraid of?"

Annie had to stop herself from leaning into his touch. It would be so easy to rely on someone else for a change. But she'd tried that with Frank, and look where that got her—unemployed, reputation in a shambles, homeless. It wouldn't happen again. "I could ask you the same question."

"And I wouldn't answer, either." Sam opened the driver's door and eased his cramped left leg out. "I

promised Mr. Patrizio I'd track these guys down by
Sunday." Four days from now. Sam didn't sound as if
he was pleased.

Annie, on the other hand, almost passed out in alarm.
All Sam needed was a good look at her father when he
was out in one of his ridiculous disguises, and Aldo
Patrizio would know that Brett had gambled in the
Sicilian.

"What will you do when you find them?"

"Ask them to stop playing. The alternative is to give
their names to Mr. Patrizio and let him handle it.
They'll be banned from play in Vegas."

She could talk her father into stopping, at least until
Aldo's interest died down. "What does a Patrizio have
to do with card counters harassing casinos like the
Lucky Horse?" The more Annie knew about this, the
better chance she'd have of helping…plus advising her
dad on getting free of this mess.

"Mr. Patrizio watches out for the little guy. From
what I've heard he helps the smaller houses get a start
and stay in business. The Patrizios are a respected part
of the community."

Respected? That implied trustworthiness, honor,
morals. Annie blinked. "I need to go." Her body obeyed
instructions this time. She set the cups on the floorboard, opened the door and came around to the driver
side.

"I could still use you," he said as he stood.

"If they're moving into larger casinos, I'm not
interested."

Sam hesitated before handing Annie the keys, picking a hair from the front of her T-shirt and tossing it away.

It was all Annie could do not to gun her poor excuse for a car out of the parking lot on the way to her baby.

AFTER SAYING GOODBYE to Annie, Sam climbed into his truck to think. He was amazed that she had demons she was just as unwilling to talk about as he was. Marriage to an embezzler seemed to have left scars as deep as any Sam had from the war.

Yet Annie looked so buttoned-up and unflappable, as if everything about her life was perfect. She had that girl-next-door appeal that meant she was off-limits to Sam. The girl next door almost always wanted to settle down in the suburbs with two-point-five kids.

Normally, one was enough to keep Sam away.

But the woman could kiss. And, more importantly, she'd had a wavy, pepper-gray hair on her T-shirt.

Which meant she'd lied about losing that cardsharp.

Like it or not, Sam was going to have to break down Annie's barriers and uncover her secrets.

"WHY ARE YOU TRYING to get rid of the card counters?" Vince had waited until the rest of the executive committee left the boardroom, their Italian loafers hushed by the thick burgundy carpet.

Aldo waved off his secretary and took a good look at his grandson over the rim of his glasses.

"Do you…is it…because of me?" Finally, Vince met Aldo's gaze, looking more like the youngster who'd lost a side bet on his grandfather than the cold, cynical executive he'd become.

"Part of the reason," Aldo allowed. "Everything that goes on in Vegas affects our business."

Vince's eyes narrowed. "But you've turned down requests for help before. Someone must have dropped a name to catch your interest." He didn't say the name neither of them could forget.

"The names of those involved don't matter." At least, not to anyone but Aldo. "But if a certain someone were involved, he would know that I haven't forgotten." That he would never forget.

"So, you'll have Sam find these cardsharps and then what?"

"They'll learn not to trifle with casinos in Vegas." He'd make sure their names and faces were well known throughout the valley.

Vince stood without any of his usual grace. "Don't ask me to take care of them."

"You think I'd ask you…?" He didn't honestly believe… "When have I permitted—"

"When have you not?" Vince's hands were fisted at his side and his gaze burned with accusation. After a moment he gathered his pad and folders, and left.

Aldo fell into the high-backed leather chair and spun it slowly around so that he could stare out the window. Except he didn't see any of the Strip's grandeur.

Aldo heard the sound of flesh smacking flesh as he left the VIP room after losing to the little girl. He had thought nothing could penetrate his shame.

"How could you do it, Vince? Goddamn it, you don't have that kind of money." Nick, Aldo's only child, held his son by the shoulder, cocked his arm and hit Vince in the face. Again.

Vince's lip was already swollen and blood spurted out his nose.

"Stop!" Aldo wedged himself between his son and grandson. *"What are you doing?"*

"He lost half a million on that game." Nick's venom came out in a whisper. He was a hulking brute of a man accustomed to using his strength on the college football field and, if rumor was to be believed, in the seedier parts of Vegas in bare-fisted boxing matches.

"No one would bet with a boy," Aldo countered. *"We won't honor such a bet. It's illegal."*

"Like playing cards with a twelve-year-old?" Nick stepped back. Red-faced, he spun on his heel and returned to the VIP room.

Aldo offered Vince his handkerchief. At thirteen, the boy had already inherited his mother's height and was closing in on six feet tall. Aldo had to tilt his head to look into his grandson's face. In it there was no sign of tears, of shock.

The world shifted under Aldo's feet. *"This...this is not the first time he's hit you."* He wanted desperately to take Vince into his arms.

Vince ignored Aldo's realization. *"I made the bet. I'll honor it."*

For his grandson to have so much faith in his talents was heartwarming, but a bet with a thirteen-year-old

shouldn't have been made. "I'll take care of this. You go
upstairs to your grandmother. You'll stay with us for now."

Tears welled in Vince's eyes, but he blinked them
back. "You can take the money from my trust fund."

"You let me worry about this." And other things, like
cash drawers that had been short when Nick was in
charge of the casino floor, and the recent revelation that
Vince's trust fund was nearly empty.

The high-pitched scream of a young girl pierced
the hallway.

Then and now, everything he did seemed to make
things worse. Aldo pushed himself out of the chair.
How could a man love his flesh and blood so much and
yet be helpless to make them happy?

"Excuse me, sir. Lana Tisdale and an associate are
here to see you."

Aldo leaned against the window. If only he could go
back and start over.

"Sir, they don't have an appointment, but they insist.
Something about a woman named Annie Raye."

"MADDY? MADDY?" Annie pounded up the stairs to her
father's apartment, the wrought-iron railing warm from
the afternoon sun. She didn't know what kind of car her
father drove, so she couldn't tell if he was home or not.

Her dad opened the door. Maddy was dancing in the
living room, clapping the heels of her princess shoes
in time to a beat only she could hear. She looked
carefree and unscathed, if you ignored the fact that
someone had tamed her blond curls into tight ringlets

and put heavy makeup on her precious little face. Annie swept her daughter into her arms and clung to her as if she'd never let go again, despite the thick cloud of perfume that threatened to choke her.

"Mommy, too tight."

Annie eased up and turned on her dad. "Lipstick?"

Maddy drew her head off Annie's shoulder. "I played dress up today with a real princess. She made me a princess, too."

"She had fun," her dad said, all trace of the birth-mark gone from his cheek and nose. He'd changed into shorts and a white T-shirt. "She was probably the only one of us who did."

Annie sank onto the couch and pulled Maddy into her lap, trying not to lose her temper. "Do you know how worried I was?"

"I wouldn't have left her if I didn't think she was safe."

"You lied to me. I gave you permission to take care of her, not leave her with someone else."

"Mommy." Maddy put one hand on Annie's cheek as if to reassure her. "Don't fight."

Poor Maddy had witnessed too many arguments between her parents. Annie had to work enough saliva into her mouth to swallow before she could speak. "This won't happen again. We'll leave tonight."

"And go where? Back to L.A.? What about your job?"

One of her old friends from Los Angeles might take her in. "I'll work in McDonald's if I have to."

"And where will you put Maddy while you're at work? She's safe here."

"I'll find a place." Working for minimum wage wouldn't pay for decent day care, though.

"Don't give up yet. You don't want to put her with strangers."

"Like you didn't?"

"I left her with Chauncey. You remember Chauncey, don't you?" The steam seemed to blow out of him.

Annie did remember. Chauncey was one of Brett's oldest friends. She'd always had a soft spot in her heart for the tall man with a penchant for playing poker with flashy foreign tourists. He wore the rings he'd won over the years like trophies. "You expect me to believe Chauncey did this to her?"

"It was his girlfriend."

"I want to stay with Grandpa," Maddy wailed, her eyes filled with crocodile tears.

Annie was a breath short of telling her daughter that staying with Grandpa wasn't an option, when someone knocked on the door. Her dad nearly jumped out of his skin.

Annie raised one eyebrow. "Safe, huh?"

He peeked through the peephole and then threw open the door. "*You.*"

"I thought I'd treat you to dinner this time. I picked up burgers and fries." Sam didn't come in, probably couldn't without catching sight of Maddy and passing out. How could he live like that?

"I smell French fries." Maddy hopped out of Annie's lap and trotted to the door before she could stop her.

Holding out the fast food bag like a shield, Sam pitched forward against the door frame, lost his footing, overcorrected and banged his head against the door.

"I got the fries," Maddy cried, running to the table with the bag of food.

Eyes closed, Sam sprawled on the floor, his head against the doorjamb.

"He passed out again," her father grumbled.

"Finally," Annie said. "A man who's predictable."

"I DID NOT PASS OUT," Sam said, struggling to stand upright. It was true. He'd been expecting Maddy this time, but Annie's daughter was hell on his equilibrium. "I just lost my balance."

"There must be some medication you can go on, boy," Brett said taking him by the arm.

"It's called bachelorhood." With the older man's help, Sam made it as far as the couch.

"I thought we went our separate ways." Annie stood over him with her arms crossed.

"That was before I realized you lied."

"Mommy, why didn't he bring soda?"

Sam steadied himself on the burlap armrest. He couldn't decipher Annie's reaction to his accusation. And then she turned to Maddy. "We have milk with dinner. You know that."

"But, Mommy, French fries need soda."

"I'll get her milk, because I'm a good grandpa," Brett said, indicating that there were tensions in the household not caused by Sam.

Annie huffed at her dad.

Sam cleared his throat. "You played me."

"I…what? Has everyone lost their mind today?" There wasn't much room in the apartment to pace, which might have explained why Annie walked in a small circle, but didn't quite explain why she eyed him suspiciously. "When?"

"Outside the Sicilian. You weren't just following that card counter, you were talking to him."

Annie exchanged a look with her father, guilt written in marker over her face.

"I want to know why you talked to him and what you talked about."

"Is Mommy in trouble?"

Sam swallowed. "Not if she tells the truth."

"Mommy always tells the truth."

Sam wasn't so sure. The silence in the room was testament to Annie's secrets. He pressed his fingers to his temples.

"I knew him," Annie blurted, her cheeks pink. "The man we followed."

"Who is he?"

"Annie…" Brett murmured, clearly in on it, too.

She waved her father off. "I can't tell you that."

There was something more going on here than Annie recognizing the gambler. If Sam wasn't feeling so nauseous, he might have been able to pinpoint what was wrong. He slumped deeper against the hard couch cushions and rubbed his forehead.

"Are you okay?" she asked reluctantly.

"He needs fixing." Maddy passed in front of him on her way to the bathroom.

Sam's autofocus went on the blink again as the room spun. He dropped his head back and closed his eyes, fighting memories of a child's scream and blood that should never have been spilled.

"Maddy, don't do that," Annie said.

"But he needs fixing." The little girl's voice. Too close. "It's hard to be brave when you're broken."

Sam didn't dare open his eyes. Images flashed too quickly for more than fleeting impressions—guns, blood, another child's scream. He couldn't tell if the roaring in his ears was from the adrenaline rush or an airplane.

"You needs some courage." Small hands lifted one of his. Maddy pressed a kiss on the back of Sam's shaking hand, then put it into her lap and put something sticky over the warm, damp spot. "And something to keep it safe."

Sam couldn't breath, couldn't escape this torture. *I'm so sorry.*

"And here's some love 'cause you're not alone." Maddy kissed the back of Sam's other hand and covered it with something sticky as well. "All fixed. Now, come eat. Come on." She tugged at his arm.

Sam drew a shuddering breath, then another. Against his better judgment, he cracked open his eyes. Maddy wore a toothy grin outlined with red lipstick—a grin that would charm the socks off the boys in about ten years.

It had a different effect on Sam.

CHAPTER EIGHT

"IS HE DEAD?" Maddy asked, her eyes wide. "I didn't mean to do it."

Brett chuckled and swung his granddaughter into his arms. "You did just right. He's sleeping." At least Brett wasn't a total failure at parenting. His fixin' trick still endured. Aldo Patrizio's whipping boy was passed out on the couch.

"Now what do we do with him?" Annie put a damp washcloth on Sam's forehead. She was such a soft touch.

"We eat. Food's getting cold." Brett carried Maddy to the table. He doled out burgers and fries onto three paper plates before he deigned to acknowledge Annie's hands-on-hips incredulity. "A nap did him good the last time," Brett pointed out, sitting down to eat. There was nothing as disappointing as cold greasy food.

"He's following you," Annie murmured, drifting over to sit with them.

"If you don't get rid of him I'll just have to be more careful. But it would help if you'd get rid of him." She didn't need some weak-kneed pansy stringing her along.

"We can't stay with you. I can't let you drag Maddy into God knows where."

"I know where, Mommy. There were dancers and music and a big splash of water just like at Disneyland. Everyone clapped, didn't they, Grandpa?" Giggling, Maddy twirled an extra-long French fry in front of Brett and then ate it in petite bites.

"Yes, they did." He avoided Annie's reproachful stare.

"A strip club?" Annie lowered her voice to a deadly whisper. "That's worse than a card room. I thought you said she was with Chauncey."

"Lana and Chauncey live in the back of a strip club. I made sure she didn't see anything."

"While you were in the Sicilian? Now I know what kind of people you left her with."

"Hardworking girls." Brett took a bite of his now cold burger.

"They were pretty dancers," Maddy added dreamily.

He loved his granddaughter, but she wasn't helping.

"You see." Annie pointed at Maddy. "You see what a mess you've made."

Annie didn't know the half of it. Brett chose to remain silent.

"I don't want Maddy to have regrets before she turns thirteen."

"I was wondering how long it would take you to blame everything that's ever gone wrong with your life on me. Are you going to hang your bad marriage on me now, too? I told you Frank was a liar and a con artist the first time you brought him home."

"Like recognizes like."

"Don't fight." Pulling her lips into a pout, Maddy pressed her hands over her ears.

"Sorry," Brett murmured. "I just don't want you to do something you'll regret only to spite me." Like marry the first man to take an interest in her, despite the fact that Frank clearly didn't understand the difference between right and wrong.

It took Annie a moment to compose herself. "We're not talking about my choices. We're talking about you. You're not going back, right? Sam won't find you in some dive in the next four days, will he?"

"Your P.I. won't find me," Brett mumbled. He'd figure something out. "Can we talk like a normal family now?"

"We're not normal or anything I'd call a family."

Ouch. On two counts. "Someday you're going to realize that your talents make you special." Probably not the right thing to say when he didn't want Annie to use those talents, but her fixation with fitting in had to stop. "I'd take that over normal any day."

"Are you special?" Maddy piped. "What can you do, Mommy?"

"It's bath time and then bed for you, young lady," Annie said, and went to fill the tub, leaving her dinner half-eaten. She was good at avoidance. She'd been avoiding for years talking about what happened that night.

"I don't want to wash my hair. It's too pretty," Maddy said when her mom came to get her.

"Okay." Annie sounded worn-out.

Brett and Annie had been close when they gambled together. Maybe Annie needed to rediscover the fun of the game. Maybe she wanted to. Maybe that was the appeal of this P.I. She'd gone into casinos for the guy, which was more than she'd done for Brett or that loser husband of hers in the past fourteen years. Maybe having her play for Chauncey was the answer.

Brett pinched the bridge of his nose. Couldn't they just play for fun like they used to?

"ALL YOU NEED TO DO IS stop playing cards, and Sam will go away." While Maddy splashed away in the bathroom, Annie returned to the kitchenette to try to talk some sense into her dad. She kept her voice low so that Sam wouldn't hear. "I should have recognized Ernie playing at Tiny's yesterday. He always did wear that god-awful cologne. Who else is in on this? Chauncey? If I tell Sam you've stopped—"

"He'll want proof. *Names.* I'm not betraying my friends, and you aren't, either," her dad snapped. "If Knight wants to do the job, he'll have to do it on his own."

"He'll find you." Annie didn't think she could bear it. "I can prove it some other way, with that hat or that hideous growth Ernie had on his face. It was a fake, wasn't it?"

"You'd do this to me? Your own father?"

"I need that job at Slotto. It's a respectable living. I have to prove myself." No more speculating on the role

Annie had played in Frank's schemes. No more microscopic scrutiny of everything she said, everything she did and what she wore while doing it. "Haven't you heard of sacrificing yourself for the good of others? Maddy deserves a predictable life."

"Predictable?" Her dad rubbed his temple. "You sound like your mother. She worked in that bank and she was miserable. Every day the same old thing."

Which was exactly what Annie liked about working in finance—no surprises, no excitement. "What choice did you give her? She was trying to provide a good home for me. She held up her end of the stick."

"Oh, that explains why she left town with that Seabee based in Japan. And here I thought it was because she wanted to see the world without worrying about a mortgage or a college fund."

"Grow up." Annie's voice was no longer low. She was huffing like a kettle about to blow. "You know what I mean. You haven't held a legitimate job in your life."

"And look how happy I am." He had the nerve to smile, but then again, he was always smiling. Annie felt as if she hadn't smiled since she was twelve.

"I can see you've done really well for yourself." Annie looked pointedly around the apartment.

"There've been some bumps in the road, but that makes life interesting. Look me in the eye and tell me you didn't find that job in L.A. drudgery."

There was a brown stain on the tan linoleum at Annie's feet that required her immediate inspection.

"I didn't lose the house, Annie," Brett admitted when she didn't say anything.

"You didn't?" She couldn't tell whether to believe him or not.

He shook his head.

If he still had the house, he really had been doing well without her. That made Annie feel worse than thinking he'd sold it or lost it in some game. "I bet it's a wreck." She turned away.

"It's my home, puddin'. It looks a little different than when you saw it last. I had to give up on the grass and put in a rock garden. I gave her a fresh coat of paint last year."

Annie's forehead crinkled in confusion. "So, if you're such a dedicated home owner, what are you doing living here?"

"I stay in places like this when I play. If someone follows me here it's no big deal."

Oh, criminy. "I'm no longer convinced this is a safe place for Maddy. What if Aldo—"

Sam stirred.

Annie waited until she was sure he was still out cold. "Why is it so important that you play?" she whispered. "Do you need the money?"

"No. It's for a good cause." Her father tried to smile, but for once he couldn't pull it off.

That alone sent a tingle down Annie's spine. "You make it sound like a charity."

"That's because this time, it is." Brett put his hands on her shoulders, his expression drawn, serious. "All I need you to do is distract that P.I. for the next few days."

Annie shook her head adamantly. "I have a little girl. And this is Aldo we're talking about. I can't get involved, even that much."

"It's for Chauncey." Her father tightened his grip. "He's dying, Annie. We're raising money for an experimental treatment that's kept him alive these past few months. I'm not asking you to play. I'm asking you to buy us some time."

Chauncey had been sick for months and her father hadn't told her? Annie blinked. Maddy crooned in the bathtub. Of course. Annie couldn't have helped raise money. "And if I don't?"

"I'll have to end it quickly."

"With a high-stakes game." Annie looked him dead in the eye. "No. You can't be considering playing Aldo." She wanted to shout, but her words came out more like a whisper. Brett was older now, not nearly as strong as he had been. If anything happened—

"It's important enough to take that risk."

She couldn't escape her father's determined gaze, but she could reject the ugly memories that resurfaced. "No." But he was doing this for Chauncey, who'd helped her with her math homework and warned her about boys. For Chauncey, the most dependable of her father's friends.

Annie broke away and collapsed into a chair at the table, unable to take the anguish in Brett's eyes any longer. "Please don't let it come to that."

"Then help me."

"If you'd speak a little louder, I could make out more than every other word." Sam pushed himself upright, but he had one hand over his eyes, as if he wasn't yet ready to take on the world.

"What do you know about blackjack?" Annie's father asked Sam.

Brett was making nice to Sam? Something was up.

Annie had been about to escape to the bathroom under the guise of checking on Maddy. Instead, she ducked her head in, waved at Maddy, who was playing with her floating boats in the tub, and then dropped next to Sam on the couch.

"It's starter gambling," Sam was saying, holding his head. "You graduate from slots and go to blackjack before you move on to serious gaming."

Annie turned to him in disbelief. "So you think blackjack takes no skill?"

"All you need to know to play is stay when your cards add up to seventeen or higher," he answered, a hand still over his eyes.

"That's all?" Annie's cheeks heated, adding to her annoyance. "So if you make money at blackjack you're just a lucky idiot?"

"Pretty much."

Brett laughed. "I'll get the cards."

"Cards?" Sam opened his eyes.

"I hope you brought money," Annie said, standing. She'd never wanted to take someone to the cleaners so much. "Lots of it." He might kiss like a pro, but he wasn't very bright.

"Great. Your dad's going to fleece me? And what will this prove?"

"Dad's not playing," Annie said, watching Brett shuffle with all the panache of a professional dealer. For the first time in years she felt a jolt of anticipation, as if something fun was about to happen.

"But you have a gambling phobia." Eyebrows pulled down, forehead creased, Sam almost made Annie feel guilty.

Almost.

She helped him to the table. "What if I knew more?" she asked, ignoring what he'd said. She glanced up in time to see his rueful smile.

"Then I really couldn't recommend you for Slotto, could I?"

She'd have to try again somewhere else. Annie caught her father's eye. She owed it to Maddy to get another respectable job, but deep down Annie wished she could play cards the way she used to, and help Chauncey.

"ANNIE DESERVES BETTER than that Slotto job." Brett loaded a plastic dealing shoe with cards. Lots of cards.

"Her working at Slotto would be like unleashing Godzilla in the fisherman's village. Carl wouldn't know what hit him." Sam rubbed his bleary eyes while Annie made that little huffing noise she was so good at. "How many decks did you put in there?"

"Two." Brett stared at Sam as if he were a lesser breed. "You haven't been in Vegas long, have you?"

"Seven, eight months." Sam's head hurt, and all he

wanted to do was crawl into bed. But there was something going on here that he had to figure out.

"You put two decks in the shoe," Brett began patiently. "The less often a dealer has to shuffle, the more time can be spent playing and winning money for the house. The more decks, the poorer the odds for the player."

"Mommy, I'm getting out."

"Okay, pumpkin." Annie steadied Sam with a hand. "Look at me, Sam. That's it. Look only at me."

Everything about Annie was petite. She had a small, delicate face to go with her small, delicate hands. Sam's view of the room came into focus.

"Should I give you two some privacy or can I deal?" Brett's bushy eyebrows hung low over his eyelids.

"Dad."

"Can I deal?"

Annie leaned closer until Sam could see how long her lashes were, how they swept down over her blue eyes. "Deal."

"Ante up," Brett said. "I ain't got no chips. This is a real man's game."

"We'll keep a tally," Annie said, her warm hand still on Sam's arm. "So, if I lose, I qualify for the job at Slotto?"

"Has anyone ever pointed out your tendency toward one-track-mindedness?" There was no way he was recommending her for the Slotto job, because…

Sam frowned.

"A tally?" With a grumble about practicing without any stakes, Brett snapped the cards out on the table.

"If I can't get the job at Slotto I'm free to beat the pants off of you. I'm betting you can't win more than four of ten hands."

Sam didn't disagree with her. "How many will you win?"

"Oh, six or seven."

"That's my girl." Brett grinned.

Both Annie's and Sam's cards were facedown, while Brett, the dealer, had one card showing—the ten of hearts. Feeling more than a tad intimidated, Sam pulled his cards tight to his chest and peeked at them—eight of spades, seven of diamonds. Not quite seventeen. Great. If he asked for a card, there were too many that might put him over twenty-one.

Annie only lifted the tips of her cards.

"Hit me." Sam slid his cards back down and Brett dealt him a four. Whew, nineteen. "Stay."

"Stay," Annie said.

Brett flipped over his other card—ace of clubs. "Twenty-one." He indicated Sam should flip over his cards.

"I had nineteen," Sam said.

"Twenty." Annie tossed two tens toward her father.

"What's the count?" Brett asked, sweeping the cards played out of sight, and dealing more.

"Minus three," Annie replied without hesitation.

Before Sam could ask what they were talking about, something rustled near his elbow. "Can I play?" Maddy's curls tickled Sam's arm and he stiffened.

"Look at me," Annie commanded Sam. She gripped

his chin to make sure she had his full attention. With her other hand she drew Maddy into her lap, never breaking eye contact with Sam. "This is an adult game, pumpkin. You can watch."

Maddy protested. Sam concentrated on blue eyes floating over yellow curls.

Cards snapped down on the table. "Let's play," Brett said.

Trying to be a little cooler this time, Sam released Annie's gaze to peek at the upper corner of his cards— two sixes. He needed anything but a ten or face card. "Hit."

A six. Eighteen. "Stay." Breathing came easier now that no one was talking.

Annie flicked her fingers and Brett tossed her a five. She shook her head and Brett flipped over his other card so both were showing—a nine and a queen.

Well, that sucked. "I had eighteen." Sam tossed his cards into the center of the table facedown.

"Wait a minute." Brett turned over all Sam's cards.

"What does it matter?" Sam said. "I lost."

"She's got to count," Brett explained, shaking his head.

"Ooh, counting. I want to count." Maddy clapped her little hands.

"No, you don't." Annie sounded tense, looked at her dad. "She never counts anything."

Brett laughed. "She counts all the time. She could be great. Better than you."

Sam gritted his teeth, willing himself to stay upright. "What is she counting?"

"The cards. Why do you think they call it card counting?" Brett laughed again. He seemed happier than Sam had ever seen him.

"Dad, don't even think about it." There was an edge to Annie's reply.

"Mommy has two fives and a ten."

Sam's rifle. Trained on a child. "I never really thought about it." To hell with figuring out what these two were up to. He had to get out of here. He staggered to his feet.

"What's the count, Annie?" Brett demanded.

"In a minute, Dad. Maddy, wait here."

"I want some fives. I'm five."

The doorknob was cool against Sam's fingers. He had to focus on moving, just as he had that day in Iraq.

"Not in a minute. Now, Annie."

"I need more cards, Grandpa."

"I can't think about it now." Sam felt Annie's hands. Their touch was familiar. One covered his and helped him turn the knob. The other supported his arm. How could such a small woman hold him up?

"You've lost count." Brett swore. Then swore again. "How could you do this to me?"

"I didn't lose count. It's plus one." Annie sounded as if she was guessing.

"*No*. It's zero. *Zero!* You didn't…you didn't count my hand."

Someone's cell phone rang. The door opened. Warm desert air brushed over Sam's clammy skin. His feet were moving closer to the top of the stairs. He started to shrug Annie's hand off…

"Goodbye, mister," Maddy said in a singsong voice as she closed the door.

…and stumbled.

With unexpected strength, Annie righted Sam. Her curves were pressed against his side. His arm hung over her shoulder and his hand rested on the fullness of her hip.

"Easy, big fella. Grab that handrail and we'll take it one step at a time. Here comes the first step. That's right. You're doing great." Annie spoke to him as if he was a baby.

"I have walked before, you know."

"I've seen you walk." Somehow, Annie's fingers had tangled around his waistband. "I've seen you fall. I much prefer you upright."

"I'll keep your preferences in mind."

They neared his truck. Sam wasn't shaking anymore, but he didn't let go of Annie. In fact, his fingers had started tracing circles on her hip, and much as he wanted to release her and walk on alone, his body wasn't responding to that message.

Use your brain.

"So card counting is about…counting cards."

"Yes."

Sam slowed his pace. His hand drifted down to the hem of her shirt—all on its own, of course. "And you count…"

"Basic counting is high-low." Her thumb touched the bare skin above his hip. "The cards from two to six are each worth one. The face cards, tens and aces are negative one. And the seven, eight and nine are neutral."

Sam's hand inched up under her hem. "Okay, but

casinos and your dad play with more than one deck. You'd have to get in on the game after the shuffle and think of nothing else." Her thigh felt warm—no, hot. "That's impossible."

"Nothing's impossible." Beneath his polo shirt her hand slid across his back, leaving a tempting trail of warmth before she put distance between them. "Just difficult."

"But you lost track after only two hands." Sam leaned against his truck fender and stared at her.

"I haven't played in a long time." She hugged herself. "If you really want to know how to count cards, let's go back upstairs and I'll teach you."

"Not here. Maybe at Tiny's." Or maybe at my...

"You've really got to get over this kryptonite thing. You have to see your nieces sometime."

"I will. When they're in their teens." Sam reached into his pants pocket for his truck keys, never taking his eyes off her. "Can't say it hasn't been fun."

"Every gambler has a tell. And every superhero a weakness. Yours appears to be young children."

"So?"

"Seeing as how I've got all this time on my hands, being unemployed and all, I've got to wonder." She stared up at him with an endearingly sweet smile that should have promised homemade meat loaf and choco-late cake made from scratch. Instead, Annie's smile sent a chill down Sam's spine. "What would Carl over at Slotto think about this overreaction of yours? He's got young girls, too."

Annie Raye could never be a ho-hum, run-of-the-mill soccer mom. She was too unpredictable for that. Sam suddenly dragged her against him, leaned farther back against the truck so her body was on top of his, and kissed her the way a man did just before he had sex with a woman who was as wild and impulsive in bed as she was out of it.

CHAPTER NINE

"OH, MY." Annie pulled her head back to suck in much-needed air. "I've never wanted to… Not like this."

"Aren't you full of surprises?" Sam said, his voice husky.

Light-headed, Annie was still sprawled across Sam at nearly a forty-five degree angle. She didn't protest when he tugged her tighter against him for another kiss. And when he tilted his hips against hers she pushed back against his strength. "Oh, yes." Oh, yes, and more.

She'd never been with someone like Sam. He was emotionally scarred. He didn't have a proper job and didn't even try very hard at what he had. He was the furthest thing from father material she'd ever come across.

Maddy.

Ignoring her body's throbbing protests, Annie scrambled off him and put some distance between them.

Wearing a devilish grin, Sam held out his hand. "This isn't one-sided."

"Maybe not…but I'm not obsessed with you. I don't imagine what you'd look like in bed." She didn't have to. His size was imprinted on her belly. "I'm…I'm respectable." She could use the forty dollars Sam had given her as a stake, and play for Chauncey—just this one time—and then return to a normal lifestyle and reliable income.

"I respect you." A lock of hair fell across his forehead. Like heck he did. "Prove it."

His smile got broader. "Come with me."

"Give me that job at Slotto."

Just like that, the warmth and danger were gone. Well, the danger of Annie going to bed with Sam, at least. He closed the distance between them, his expression menacing. "Are you saying you'll have sex with me if I get you that job?"

No. She wanted a gesture, a show of faith. She wasn't really going to sleep with him. "Yes."

"Slotto opens at eight. Be at my place at seven forty-five."

Annie wasn't sure how long she'd been standing on the sidewalk before another car pulled into the space he had vacated.

She could get the job at Slotto if she slept with Sam. She'd have a steady paycheck and be able to afford a place to live in a nice neighborhood. She'd have money to help Chauncey.

It was what she wanted, right?

"LANA AND I GOT Aldo Patrizio to agree to a rematch." Ernie sounded breathless, as if he'd just run down a flight of stairs.

Forget Brett's *how dare you* and *what the hell were you thinking* first reactions. "She can't do it." Keeping an eye on Maddy, who was playing cards at the table, Brett whispered into his cell phone in the kitchen. "She's lost it."

"She was good," Ernie said. "Talent doesn't forget."

"She was a kid." His daughter had lost the skill. Brett couldn't believe it.

"If she had the knack for it once, she can pick it up again. Work with her. I don't like being constantly on the lookout for that P.I. And Aldo's putting up enough money to cover six months worth of treatments for Chauncey. She has to play."

"He'll only be disappointed and demand his money back." Or worse. There was no alternative. "I'll have to play him."

"You? We made a deal for Annie, not you."

"Listen to what I'm saying. I won't let her play." Brett wanted to wring Ernie's neck. "I'm telling you, Annie has no skill!"

Annie closed the front door behind her with a click. Her cheeks were red. She'd certainly overheard that last part.

"Maddy, it's time for bed." Without another word, Annie retreated into the bedroom.

Breaking the connection, Brett sank into a chair and covered his face with his hands. He'd blown it again.

NOT EVEN THE JETS of the air conditioner could cool Sam off. What was he to Annie? She was so desperate for that stinking job at Slotto she'd sleep with him for it? She didn't fit in there. Sam should know. The place was as devoid of life as a mortuary.

Was it wrong to sleep with Annie and get her that job?

Hell, yes. That didn't mean he didn't want to sleep with her. But he wasn't going to.

Right?

By the time he got back to his apartment, Sam was too wired to sleep. He should call Annie and tell her he'd been bluffing. But what if she was bluffing, too? Damn it.

His cell chirped, but it wasn't Annie calling to clear the air. It was his sister. Rubbing the back of his neck with one hand, he let Theresa's call go to voice mail.

In desperation, Sam turned on the coffeepot and booted up his computer. He'd get through those personnel files he'd let slide. Then early tomorrow morning he'd go out to Lake Mead and forget all about Mr. Patrizio's card counters and a diminutive blonde who was nothing but trouble.

Annie had expectations. She wanted things from him he couldn't possibly give. Respectability for one, although he considered her respectable enough as is. A partner in raising Maddy, for another. How hard could it be to imagine what would happen if Sam showed up at one of Maddy's soccer games? He had no future as a family man. He should just give Annie what she wanted and move on.

He blew out a sigh. Then he made the mistake of checking his e-mail.

Director finance position filled. Ignore Ray Ashton file. Carl.

Great. As usual, Carl was on hyperdrive. How desperately did Slotto need a finance director? So now Sam couldn't help Annie get the job even if he wanted to.

WAITING FOR seven forty-five, Annie stood near her car in front of Sam's garage apartment and considered her options.

She could back out and retreat to her father's place with her tail between her legs.

Or, she could knock on Sam's door, tell him she was a big coward and wouldn't sleep with him, but would he pretty-please call Carl and clear her for the job?

Or…she could sleep with Sam, because she really wanted to, and accept his help in getting the job at Slotto, because Maddy had to eat and Chauncey needed to live.

Annie had been unable to sleep much last night. Not because of Sam's kiss—just the memory of that kicked her pulse into high gear. Nope. It was overhearing her father's phone conversation that had kept her eyes glued to the ceiling. It sounded as if someone wanted her to play. She didn't want to believe her father had set up the game before he'd seen her play again, but it was so like him to manipulate her. She'd believed him when he said he was willing to sacrifice himself for Chauncey, but he was setting her up. What a fool she was.

Even worse of a fool because what hurt more than her dad lying to her was the realization that he didn't believe in her. No matter their differences, he'd always had confidence in her abilities, whether it was graduating early from high school and college or taking on some of the toughest blackjack players in town.

Like a coward, Annie had hid in the bedroom until her father got in the shower, and then she'd left Maddy, still sleeping, in his care without even asking if it was okay. She'd never felt more like a failure than this morning.

She should be used to it. Frank had always put her down. She hadn't been a good enough cook. She hadn't progressed quickly enough through the corporate ranks. She hadn't given him a son. And sex…well, he'd bought her a book once, but she'd been too self-conscious to use any of the techniques.

Annie wished she were someone else, someone without such an embarrassing past, someone just like everyone else. She tugged at the pearl necklace—why was it always so tight?—then smoothed the wrinkles out of her skirt.

With a sigh, she climbed the steps to Sam's apartment, resolved that she was too cowardly to sleep with him, even though she needed the job because she couldn't afford to be around her father any longer.

There was no doorbell. Annie rapped three times on the wood door, then three more times when Sam didn't answer.

THE HAJJIS WERE SMILING and singing as they danced in the rutted Baghdad street. Sam hummed along, trying to ignore the heat beneath his flak jacket. It was Vince's first day with the unit, his first day in the country.

"Gun! Shooter!" Vince had them in his sights, but froze. A rookie's mistake.

Sam lifted his M16. But before he could get a shot off they started firing.

"Sam?"

They fired again. Short bursts.

Something was wrong. Where was the shooter?

"Sam? Are you okay?" Annie's voice. And then her touch. Soft. Comforting.

Sam clawed his way out of Baghdad and into his bed in Vegas, opening his eyes to see Annie, the sun glistening on her golden hair from the window at her back. Annie. Safe.

"Thank God. You didn't see…" Sam wrapped his arms around her and held her tight. She wasn't on that street in Baghdad. Gradually, he became aware of her hand stroking his hair, of the soothing sounds she made as she rocked him like a frightened child.

Frightened child.

Sam pushed her away. "You'd better go."

"Sam—"

"Leave. Please." Why did she always see him when he was weak?

"Sam—"

"Go away!"

"No." Annie stood and paced the room, stopping to point at him. "You have a problem."

"Tell me something I don't know."

"You tell me. Tell me what this is all about. Look at this place. It looks like a cheap hotel room. Nobody *lives* here. You don't talk to your sister. You eat like crap. And you faint at the sight of children."

"And those are just my good points." He shouldn't look at her. He shouldn't.

There was no contempt in her expression, only misplaced anger. "You need to talk to someone."

"A shrink? Not me. In case you hadn't realized, I want to be alone." He gestured toward the door.

She ignored him and paced some more, probably trying to think of ways to use this latest revelation about him to her advantage. "Sure. I have a lot of friends who pass out at the sound of Maddy's voice."

"Breaking and entering is a crime. Leave before I call the cops."

"The door wasn't locked."

"You came here this morning with a purpose. Well, it's wasted on me." And then Sam blurted the words he knew would get rid of her. "The job at Slotto went to someone else."

Her mouth made a small *O*.

"You can leave."

It took Annie a moment to realize she'd lost one of her bargaining chips. "You still need to get those cardsharps, don't you?" There was a glint in Annie's eye.

"I can do it without you. I've got some leads. It's only a matter of time."

"I can find them today."

"How much clearer can I be? I don't want your help." He had nothing to offer.

Her forehead creased. "You may not want it, but you need it. Now, quit acting crazy and let's get to work."

Sam leaped out of bed and landed in front of her, in her face. "I'm *not* crazy. I'm all here. You have no idea what my problem is—none!" He clenched his hands at his sides so he wouldn't reach for her.

"Oh, Sam." Annie still didn't realize he was dangerous. He could tell by the softness in her gaze. She cradled his face in her hands. "You think because you shot someone as a soldier that you're a killer? That you're less of a man? That you have to keep yourself apart from everyone, including your sister?"

"I didn't just kill *someone*." Sam pushed her hands away, which was unnecessary, since she'd have removed them once she knew the truth. "I killed a child."

Now would be a good time to speak.

Sam backed away, waiting for Annie to say something, his unwavering stare challenging her. But she didn't know what to say. She was still wrapping her head around Sam's confession, but he wasn't waiting for her to catch up.

"That's why I can't be around Maddy or my nieces. I'm dangerous." His deep voice cracked.

"That's ridiculous. You don't want to hurt Maddy. You recoil every time you see her. She…she reminds you of what happened. You're afraid of kids because you…" Annie swallowed. "You killed a little girl. Oh, dear God, Sam."

He stood rigidly, in the same way he did right before he passed out, as if steeling himself for the worst to happen. Well, it wasn't going to this time.

"You didn't mean to." He couldn't have. Annie had heard about soldiers riding through towns waving at children with one hand, all the while keeping them in their gun sights for their own protection. "It was an accident."

Sam shook his head slightly, the movement barely perceptible. A muscle in his jaw ticked.

No. Something inside Annie threatened to break, and she realized with a start that she cared about Sam, perhaps too much. At the moment, she didn't care that she'd lost the Slotto job. Easing Sam's suffering was more important. "You didn't mean to," she repeated.

"I was trained to kill. Any threat. Regardless of age." Sam's eyes reflected the regret he was trying to suppress. "Or gender."

That didn't mean he was evil. Annie reached for him, but he stepped back.

"They came at us with toddlers strapped to their chests."

She didn't want to hear this, but Sam needed someone to listen.

"It was hot. They were singing, celebrating the an-niversary of the coup of the Iraqi Communist Party, a group that was later banned by the Baathists."

The need to hold him was overwhelming. Annie edged closer.

"When I saw the nearest gunman, I registered the fact that there was a girl in the way. I told him to stop firing. He hit the Iraqi police squad first, but he was trying to get to us. I told him…" Sam's apparent calm slipped.

Annie inched forward. Sam didn't seem to notice.

"But he kept firing. I tried for a head shot, but it wasn't clean." Sam's gaze dropped to the floor.

"You don't have to go through life like this." She'd figure out a way to help him. "You did the right thing."

"How do you know?" His gaze honed in on her.

"Because you care too much about people to have taken a life if there was any other option." Annie was certain this was true, and was determined to make him realize it, too. "You could have said ugly things to Maddy when you were suffering. You could have lied to me about the job at Slotto this morning and tried to sleep with me. At any time this week, you could have humiliated me and blown me off."

"I did humiliate you."

"You're no good at it, Sam." This time when Annie cradled his face in her hands, he didn't push her away. "You did your job. What you did saved lives. Including yours."

"Maybe my life isn't worth saving."

As gently as she could, Annie kissed him, determined to prove to him how vitally important his life was…to her.

ANNIE'S KISS TASTED like disaster. Sam, who was used to disaster, considered pulling back. This was Annie.

She made attempts to be bad like other women tried to be good. Falling into bed with him flew in the face of her true nature. This was just a pity kiss…one deep, soul-wrenching pity kiss.

Her mouth hot and wet, she made her way down his neck and back up again to his hungry, waiting lips.

"You should—" Sam began, full of good intentions.

And then Annie arched against him.

"—touch me like this." He guided her hand from his face down below his waistband, because she had it all wrong. He wasn't a decent guy. "I've been dying for you to touch me—"

Annie's hand broke free of his and slid beneath the band of his boxers.

"—there." He eased her back onto the bed so that they lay side by side. He cupped her full breast. If they were getting to know each other's body parts, Sam didn't want to be left behind. He kept his eyes shut because if he opened them he knew he'd wake up alone in bed. Besides, if this wasn't a dream, Annie was going to call a halt to this any moment.

Annie's fingers had him hard and throbbing. Sam groaned, and felt her smile against his mouth.

"Not fair," he murmured. He was all wrong for her. She deserved to be loved by someone…better.

Annie's mischievous hand stopped torturing him and her fingers laced with his on her breast. Some lucky son of a bitch was going to marry her and spend the rest of his life cradled by the hottest, most welcoming body on the planet. She'd have more kids and, eventually, bake cookies for a ton of grandkids. And all that time, Sam would remember this one October morning dream, when Annie had held him and copped a feel.

She nipped his lip. Sam's eyes flew open. Hers were the most startling dark blue, hypnotic with need.

"I'm going to burn up if you don't touch me." Her voice dropped to a whisper. She piloted his hand down beneath her short skirt, between her legs. "Here."

"We wouldn't want you to go up in flames…" there was only so much chivalry a man could draw on before his first cup of coffee "…without me."

FINALLY, THAT BOOK Frank had made Annie read paid off. Sam had seemed exceedingly pleased with a few of her moves.

"Tell me about your father," she said, lying on top of Sam with her clothes askew. With a private smile, she stroked the back of his hand where Maddy had "fixed" him last night. If she let herself, she could fall in love with Sam. He was refreshingly honest, with a compelling dignity that he clung to even as he fought his traumatic flashbacks.

"You want to know about my dad?"

Annie loved the way his voice rumbled against her chest. "Yes. My dad said he was a P.I." Her cheek was nestled against his neck and her hands tangled in his hair.

Despite losing the Slotto job, Annie knew that everything was going to be okay. She'd go back to her dad's place and start looking for another job. She and Sam would continue to see each other. She had no doubt that she could help him heal. It was time she let herself fall a little bit in love, and her heart had chosen Sam.

"My dad was amazing. He started out as a Phoenix cop, but what he really wanted to do was help people, not track down criminals. He got to be pretty good at finding runaways."

"Teenagers?"

"Yeah. He took on cases even if people couldn't pay. I worked for him ever since I can remember. First in the office and then later in the field, as a decoy. We were based in Phoenix, but we chased a lot of cases this way. He developed an amazing network of people on the street, and seemed to know where the runaways would go."

"I'd love to meet him."

"He died about six years ago." Sam's hands stopped roaming across her back. She would have protested if she hadn't wanted to know more about him. "We had an argument right before he died. I never got to apologize."

Annie placed a soft kiss on the side of his mouth. "I'm so sorry."

"It was unexpected. A heart attack. Too much junk food over too many years on the road."

Like father, like son. Sam stared at the ceiling, so she settled back down and let him speak. "I didn't know what to do with myself after that. I never went to college, and here I was at twenty-four, being asked by my mom if I wanted to take over my dad's practice. I couldn't do it. So I joined the army."

"It's funny the expectations parents lay on kids, isn't it?" Annie nuzzled his neck. They had more in common than she'd thought. They'd both escaped family pressures by moving away, and had unresolved issues with their dads. They were a lot alike. In his arms she didn't feel like a failure.

"I think my mom was relieved I didn't want to carry on in Dad's footsteps. She sold his practice to one of his junior partners. End of story." Sam had these incredibly long arms that enabled him to reach around to her private places. "Time to talk of other things, like why we didn't get all your clothes off the first time."

Heat pooled low in her belly, and Annie pressed her hips against him. In no time, he was sheathed in a condom and all hers.

"That was incredible," Sam whispered later. His eyes were closed, his hand making a lazy exploration of her curves. He sighed heavily, as if preparing for something unpleasant. "Definitely worth the price of admission."

"The price?" Annie sat up in bed, pulling the sheet up over her breasts.

"You know—my breakdown, your pity kiss. If you were trying to make me feel better, you succeeded."

"You think…? And you still…?" Annie couldn't get her clothes on fast enough.

CHAPTER TEN

"IT SEEMS I INTERRUPTED something." Vince stepped into the room in his thousand-dollar suit, making Sam look like a homeless man in his ratty old boxers.

"Can I help you, Vince?"

Annie slipped into her flip-flops as she gripped the chair back. She appeared ready to sprint for the door, as Sam had known she would once she came to her senses. He'd just helped her along. Best not to drag out her mistake. Sam ran a hand through his hair.

"I need your little lady to move her car." Vince crossed the room and offered his hand to Annie. "I'm Vince Patrizio, owner of the Sicilian. And you are…?"

"Leaving," she squeaked, edging around the kitchen table and practically running out.

Sam fell back on the bed. He'd never see her again. He rolled his head to one side and swore when he caught sight of Annie's pearls on his nightstand.

"We've got to talk about your technique, buddy. Look at you. You've got Mickey Mouse Band-Aids on your hands. No wonder she ran out of here." Vince walked over to the window and watched Annie drive away. "Who is she?"

Sam didn't answer; he just fingered her pearls.

"She looks like someone who could make you forget…." Vince glanced over his shoulder at Sam and then back out the window. "Who *is* she?" The question came out sharper this time. Vince wasn't letting this go.

"She applied for the financial director position at Slotto, but that didn't work out."

"What's her name? I might have a position open."

"Yeah, right." Vince's position would be horizontal and involve satin sheets and monogrammed pillows. Annie might get a weeks' worth of dates, some nice gifts, maybe even a condo in town for her and Maddy— none of which Sam could provide even if Annie wanted to see him again.

"Seriously. If she's done with you, and Slotto doesn't want her, the Sicilian might have a job for her. What's her name?"

"You're such an asshole." Not at all what Annie deserved, but anything was a step up from Sam.

"Yeah, but I pay you to put up with me. Her name?"

"WHAT HAVE YOU DONE, Lana?" Chauncey dragged himself to his full height, willing himself to ignore the way the room swam.

Lana begged him to understand. "Aldo Patrizio will pay to play Brett's daughter. She doesn't even have to win."

Chauncey swore. "Where are my shoes?" He'd let others take care of him for too long.

She fluttered about in her silk dressing gown. "The doctor said you shouldn't exert yourself."

"He's only keeping me alive so he can continue to collect your money—yours and Brett's and Ernie's and whoever else you've conned into this." His cherry loafers in the corner were dusty from disuse. Chauncey edged around the bed, using the wall for support, until he reached them. He stepped out of his slippers and into his shoes, taking an excruciating amount of time. In his youth he'd wanted to take his time and enjoy life. Now that Chauncey had no speed other than slow, it annoyed him.

"Ernie thought it was a brilliant idea."

Chauncey took in his reflection—bald head, rumpled pants and shirt, black circles under his eyes. He wasn't going to waste his energy dressing up better than this. It was a damn sight better than him in his pajamas, but not by much.

He tucked his wallet in his back pocket. "Ernie would jump off the London Bridge if you asked him." Ernie loved Lana that much. Hell, the three friends had all loved Lana. Chauncey had just been lucky enough to come off a winning streak and be the first to dazzle her with a huge diamond.

"Where are you going?"

"Out to earn my own money." There were a couple of casinos on their list a bus ride away.

"I won't let you." She plastered herself against the door.

Chauncey smiled, closing the distance between

them at his slow pace without breaking eye contact. Cradling her face in his hands, he kissed her deeply. When he drew back he noted the soft, triumphant look in her eye.

"I had no idea you were up to full strength, Chauncey." She squeezed his hand, slipping past him with a swing of her hips as she tried to entice him back to bed.

Chauncey held his ground, kissed the back of her hand and then opened the door. The rock-and-roll music that played nonstop in the strip club blared into the room. "I'm sorry. I've lost so much, Lana. I can't lose my manhood as well."

"I'VE GOT NEWS FOR YOU." Vince had dropped in unexpectedly during Aldo's lunch in his suite. Instead of sitting, Vince stood with his hands on a chair back. Waiting.

With deliberate care, his grandfather dabbed his mouth with the cloth napkin before acknowledging him. He had news of his own to share. He was going to play Annie Raye again, returning to the point when his life had started falling apart.

But Vince didn't give Aldo a chance. "I've found her, the girl who beat you years ago. It's only a matter of time until I strike a deal." He made it sound as if arranging a rematch was something Aldo would fear— and Vince took great pride in.

"A deal?"

"To play you again. To show you how easy to beat you are." Vince laughed as he turned to go.

The sucker punch rattled at the tenuous hold Aldo had on hope. Anger took its place.

"Others have beaten me, Vince. Just not you." He knew his grandson heard him by the way he slammed the door behind him. It took Aldo several minutes to calm down, several more to remind himself that all he had was hope and he couldn't let Vince steal that from him.

Aldo wasn't the fool he'd been fourteen years ago. He would cancel the game he'd arranged and see what Vince had up his sleeve. But he wouldn't walk into a game Vince set up as blindly as he had back then. There had to be a way to turn things to his advantage. Yes, the odds were slim, but so was the probability that Rosalie would wake up and return to him as she was before.

The Picasso stared down at Aldo, a symbol of enduring love. With a great work like that on his side, Aldo couldn't give up.

ANNIE WATCHED the Lucky Horse dealer shuffle the decks and load them into the plastic shoe. She'd been compelled to come here, perhaps because this was where she'd put one over on Sam. She'd watched other people gamble, watched the dealers' reactions. Then she stepped up and bought twenty dollars worth of chips. Fresh deck. Smiling dealer. Annie was back in the game.

Maybe she should have gone back to her dad's apartment after running out on Sam but she hadn't wanted to face Brett and hear him tell her she couldn't help

Chauncey. All these years, she'd known she was good at counting cards. That foundation of confidence had allowed her to push herself in school and, later, in her financial career. Now her insecurities were running roughshod, along with her hormones, and if she wasn't careful, she'd be afraid of her own shadow.

Or climb back into bed with Sam, which would definitely rank down there with her other major mistakes— such as staying with Frank five years too many. She'd confused Sam's attentions with real feelings, and now she was just another notch on his bedpost.

Applying for the Slotto job had been a mistake. She was more suited to a career playing cards. Her money would run out soon, and Annie needed a way to support Maddy. Blackjack was the only way to go now, at least in the short-term. Her first task would be to win a sizable contribution for Chauncey's medical fund.

Don't Smile as You Win. Don't Cry as You Lose. Only the Cards Matter and Next Time the Cards Will Offer a New Chance. That was her dad's motto, and it seemed to apply to Annie's life right now.

Even though she won a few hands, she felt soft. She'd become as bad as a tourist, with all sorts of baggage that got in the way of her concentration. Was she at plus four or five? Her stomach churned. What would Sam think of her if he knew she was trying to make money gambling?

Don't think of Sam now.

"Busted." Annie flipped over her cards, beaten by

the dealer for the second time in a row. With a five dollar minimum bet, she was already out ten bucks. Her father had always told her to play for the long haul. Of course, that was when Annie had been a winner, and people would spot them money to play.

The count was plus eight. She hoped. The high cards were due, but Annie didn't have much more money to gamble with. She'd bought into the game with one of Sam's twenties. She planned to use the second twenty to win money for a new start with Maddy.

So Annie only bet five when she should have bet much more. The dealer gave her two tens, with a seven showing on the dealer's hand. Annie had no choice but to split the tens, up her bet with her last five and play two hands. The dealer gave her a nine and an ace—nineteen and twenty-one. If the dealer had a ten, both of Annie's hands would win.

The dealer didn't have a ten. She had a five and dealt herself a nine—twenty-one. Only one of Annie's hands won. So she still had her ten dollars. Taking the other player's hands into consideration, the count was now down to plus four. Not as good odds as the last hand.

With a prayer to whatever higher power blessed gamblers, Annie settled in to play.

SAM SLOWLY SCANNED the blackjack tables at the Lucky Horse Casino, home of his best lead, looking for aging card players and tinted glasses, but his mind was on Annie. Sam couldn't help but regret letting her drive off, or giving her cell number to Vince—who'd laughed when Sam told him her name. Yeah, he'd felt that way, too, before Annie bulldozed her way into his life. Everywhere Sam looked he saw blondes, which made his work this morning that much harder.

Case in point: two tables up a petite blonde sat with her back to him. It couldn't be Annie. She was most likely on her way to a job interview with Vince. And yet, the way her hair fell in unruly curls was so like hers that Sam halted midstep. He had it bad. He got his legs moving, but couldn't resist one last glance as he passed the blonde's table.

Annie slid off the stool and stared at her empty hands dejectedly.

"Annie." Too late, Sam realized she might not want to see him.

It took a moment for her to recognize him. And then she greeted him coolly. "What are you doing here?" she asked suspiciously.

Annie wasn't a gambler. She had no job and was sharing a rat hole with her dad. "Did Vince hire you? Are you looking for the card counters?" Sam asked. It would be just like Vince to offer her a job. His job. And just like her to accept.

"Vince? No."

Why didn't he believe her? Sam swore. "Did you spot me first and then bust on purpose?" He towed her toward the exit, refusing to let her put one over on him. "This is my turf. You're not getting my job or my apartment. I don't care what Vince told you. I'm going to find those cardsharps first."

Annie started to struggle, then glanced up at a video camera and stopped. "Vince hasn't called me. Trust me. I wouldn't work for any of the Patrizios."

"Trust you?" Sam tried to ignore the fact that his hand was on the bare skin of her arm. Unlike this morning, touching Annie now was not about lust and need. "What have you done to earn it?"

"This is the thanks I get for saving your butt at Tiny's, picking you up off the ground when you fall and..." She didn't have to complete the part about rocking his socks off in bed.

"You've been scamming me from the beginning. I don't know what your game is, but I'm not playing into your hands."

The fight seemed to have drained out of Annie. "I don't have a game. I'm no good to anyone."

Sam wouldn't let the despair in her voice get to him. They walked out of the dark casino into the bright morning sunlight.

"Do yourself a favor. Stay away from the casinos." Sam had to swallow before he added, "And stay away from me."

"You were right." Annie flopped onto the couch next to Maddy. "I lost."

Brett looked up from the racing section of the newspaper. Annie's cheeks were pale. "You look like you lost your best friend." That damn P.I. Brett was this close to hunting him down and whacking him upside the head.

"What did you lose, Mommy?" Maddy snuggled close to her, with one eye on the cartoon on television.

"I lost my self-respect." Annie covered her eyes. "I can't get a decent job and now I can't even win a couple hands of blackjack."

Her trying to gamble at all would have made Brett happy, because that opened the door to a closer relationship. If only Annie didn't look so glum. If only he knew what to do about the game with Aldo— cancel or propose he play the old man himself. "How much did you lose?"

"Forty dollars."

"Forty bucks is chicken feed." Brett snorted and picked up his newspaper, pretending not to care, but he couldn't remember which race he'd been interested in. She'd tried to play. If Annie got her groove back they could play every house in town. They'd have Chauncey's money before anyone knew what hit them, and they could cancel the game with Aldo.

"I didn't have more than that to gamble."

"And that's exactly why you lost it." But that wasn't the real issue. Her concentration was. Dying to see her face, Brett continued to hide behind the sports page. "Did you lose count?"

"What does it matter?"

"If you don't know, I have nothing further to say." There was so much Brett wanted to tell her, so many strategies of the game she might have forgotten. He didn't want to hope, but he couldn't help himself.

"That's rich. The one time I want you to speak up, you won't."

He lowered the newspaper. "You keep telling me you want nothing to do with cards. What is it you want me to say?"

Annie slouched down farther. Maddy put her hands over her ears, but kept watching her program.

"Forget it," Annie mumbled. With a glance at her daughter, she retreated toward the bedroom.

Brett forced himself to remain seated. "The cards are as demanding as they are unforgiving. You've got to play smart every time." He tapped his temple. "You can't have it both ways, Annie. You either choose a life of cards or not."

"The cards..." With a hand on the doorknob, Annie hung her head. "Look. I don't know what to do. No, that's not right. I know what I need to do—find a job with a regular paycheck, medical and dental coverage."

"You were never happy as a cubicle jockey." He'd seen it in her face the one time he'd driven out to visit her in California.

"I don't think I know how to be happy." Annie shut the door.

Maddy was curled into a ball, her hands still over her ears. Brett shifted to the couch and lifted his granddaughter into his lap.

"I want her to be happy, puddin'."

"Me, too." Maddy nestled in his arms. "Does she need fixin'?"

"Not just yet. Sometimes you need time alone so you can figure out what needs fixin'." It had taken Brett years to realize that he had to be patient and wait for the right opportunity to repair his relationship with his daughter. He could be patient awhile longer.

CLACK-CLACK.

Startled, Annie nearly fell out of bed at the sound of gunshots. Her eyes flew open.

"I'm dancing, Mommy," Maddy said as she twirled across the room, then hit the heels of her princess shoes together. *Clack-clack.*

"He's got me imagining things now," Annie mumbled. Just thinking about Sam brought back unwanted memories—of his sly humor, his protective nature and his magic touch. Of course, he had his weak points. She just couldn't think what they were right now.

Clack-clack. "Look at me, Mommy."

"You're the prettiest princess in all the land," Annie said, glancing at the clock. Her brief nap hadn't made her feel any better.

Her cell phone rang. It was too much to hope that it was good news. "Go away."

It rang again. Irrationally, she wanted it to be Sam calling her. That's what finally motivated her to answer.

"Annie, this is Vince Patrizio."

She almost dropped the phone. "Ye-ye-yes."

"I was wondering if you could join me for dinner tonight."

A date? "Don't you know who…'?" *Stupid.*

"Who you are?" he finished for her. "Yes. You're the one who took my grandfather for more than half a mil. I thought it would be nice to talk about old times."

He couldn't be serious. Annie wanted to throw up. "They weren't good times."

"I'm sorry to hear that. I have a proposition for you. Win or lose, it's a very attractive offer."

"No." She should just hang up the phone, load Maddy into the car and drive until their money ran out. Except they were in the middle of the desert. They might get stranded on the highway and be worse off than this. If it could get worse than this.

"Wait until you hear me out. Over dinner. Tonight. At the Sicilian."

"*No.*"

"You aren't the least bit curious about my offer?"

She needed money. Chauncey needed money. And Vince was the only one offering. "No…yes…I'll meet you, but not at the Sicilian." Annie mentioned an Italian restaurant she and her father used to go to sometimes, far off the beaten path. She'd seen yesterday that it was still in business. "Six o'clock."

She disconnected and collapsed on the bed. What had she done?

IT WAS A SCAR THIS TIME. Long and silvery, it traced one cheekbone. The large, flashy rings adorning each finger were different, but the dark, oversize tortoiseshell glasses were a dead giveaway. The Lucky Horse was turning out to be full of good fortune for Sam.

He sat at a booth across from the card counter in the bar. He'd hung around drinking sparkling water all day, keeping an eye on the middle-aged female dealers, but distracted with thoughts of Annie and Maddy and Iraq. Until this tall, thin man had come along, with a swerving step that made Sam think he was drunk. He'd let him play a few hands before closing in.

"How many of you are there? I've seen three."

The man watched the keno girl cross the smoky bar. It was hard to tell what color his eyes were behind the dark glasses, but he was old, his shoulders permanently bent and he wasn't drunk. Upon closer inspection, he appeared to be alarmingly thin, with a sallow complexion.

"I've been hired to track you all down, but I've got no beef against you, personally. In fact," Sam offered, feeling inspired, "if you stop harassing the local casinos, I won't even ask for your name."

Liver-spotted fingers spun a tequila sunrise in a slow circle. The old man had yet to take a drink.

"Or I could call casino security, who'd hold you in a small back room until they get their answers."

"I've done nothing wrong." His voice creaked, as if he didn't use it much, or was a heavy smoker.

"No, but that doesn't mean the casinos can't photograph your face—minus the glasses and scar—distribute it to all the casinos in town and ban you from entry for a year."

The gambler didn't even flinch. Sam was willing to bet the man was already on such a list.

He smiled. "The scar is real."

So he'd been a badass in his youth. Right now he was nothing more than a pain in Sam's.

"Tell me what's going on, and you can just walk away." Sam followed his hunch. "I know Brett Raye's involved…and his daughter, Annie."

The cardsharp chuckled, but his glass turned slower, a confirmation of her guilt.

Sam should have been relieved that Annie was one of them. If she was a professional gambler, she was good at deception. She'd no doubt get over his rejection quickly. He'd be easy to forget. Sam tried to laugh, emitting a pathetic, hollow sound as he recalled how Tiny was familiar with Annie's name. Why should anything about Annie Raye surprise him?

And yet he stubbornly refused to believe it. Perhaps it was the dichotomy of image versus expectation—her string of pearls and conservative suits, versus the fashionable visual of a low-cut evening gown and jewels of a gambler. He needed confirmation. He needed…to concentrate on the man in front of him, not Annie's betrayal.

Sam unclenched his jaw. "How about I tell you who hired me?" It was time to cut through the bullshit. "Aldo Patrizio."

The glass didn't stop spinning. The gambler knew that already. But how?

Of course. *Annie.* How many more secrets had she kept from him?

Sam shoved his drink away. "You know Mr. Patrizio doesn't give up easily." And neither did Sam.

That got a rise out of the guy—a taut scowl. "Young man, do I look like I have enough time left to be intimidated?"

"No, sir." He looked like death warmed over.

The gambler laughed, but his laughter soon turned into a deep cough that shook his entire body. "Damn smokers," he said, wiping at his eyes when he'd regained his breath.

"Why don't you call it a day?"

The old geezer shook his head almost imperceptibly. "Haven't reached my quota yet. Wouldn't want to appear weak to the others."

Sam had stared down many a man in the military, but this gambler didn't even flinch. What was Sam going to do now? Turn this guy in to security? The shock would probably kill him. Sam wasn't even sure he had been counting cards.

Annie would have known.

He should turn them all in to Mr. Patrizio. And Sam would, as soon as he figured out why they had a quota. And why Annie had covered up her involvement. If she wasn't in too deep, maybe he wouldn't have to say anything to Mr. Patrizio about her.

With a curse, Sam stood.

"So, you've decided I'm not worth the effort, eh?"

"Don't tempt me."

The gambler just started laughing again, which sent him into another spasm of coughing.

CHAPTER ELEVEN

"I DON'T LIKE THIS." Annie's father stared at the deck of cards in the middle of the table.

"Just run through the drill," Annie said, trying to ignore the huge butterflies taking wing in her stomach. If she was going to play again, she didn't want to disappoint anyone, most of all herself.

"I won't help you do this."

"Vince knows my name." Sam had probably had a good laugh about the whole thing when Vince told him who she was. "You know how the Patrizios are. If Vince wants me to play, eventually he'll find a way to make me. At least he seems open to paying me up front."

"Aldo wants a rematch. Ernie set it up. So why would Vince call you, unless…"

"He doesn't know Ernie approached Aldo. What a messed-up family." Now she was calling the kettle black.

Her dad wisely opted not to point that out. "They weren't always that way. The game screwed us all."

"Don't cut them any slack. They almost killed you." Annie wouldn't let him get beat up again. If the Patrizios wanted to play her, she'd go alone.

"They had cause to be angry." Her father was looking at the cards, but not picking them up.

"It was just a game. They knew the stakes coming in. There's always a chance you'll lose." And in her case, a distinct possibility. "Let's do this."

Still he refused to pick up the deck. The expression in his eyes was the same hopeless one he'd had when discussing Chauncey's predicament last night. "I don't want you to play."

Because he knew she'd lose. Annie pushed the cards closer to him. "He'll be upset if I don't deliver a challenging game."

Brett swore under his breath, with a worried look in Maddy's direction. She sat on the floor at the coffee table, preoccupied with her own cards. "Don't do this."

"What choice do we have?" Annie tried to smile. "Besides, after I play I'll have enough money for Maddy and me, as well as some for Chauncey."

For a long time her father didn't move. Then, with a heavy sigh, he picked up the deck. "Running total. Don't think about anything other than the cards. And try to loosen up. You used to win because you thought playing cards was fun."

"Counting is work." Her hands were clammy.

"And mistakes happen at work all the time because it's drudgery. You've got to love what you do."

There was too much fear for Annie to feel the love.

Her father sighed. "Your count should be at zero after the last card."

"I know. Start flipping."

He turned over an eight.

"Zero."

King. "Minus one."

Three. "Zero."

Three. "Plus one. You can go faster."

Her father made a disparaging noise. Behind Annie, Maddy laughed. When Annie was a kid she used to laugh like that when she knew she'd frustrated him.

Six. "Plus two." Two. "Plus three." Seven. "Plus three."

Brett's pace quickened. Annie saw only the values of the cards, calling out the running total until she reached plus one.

"That was the last card."

She should have been at zero. Annie didn't need to register the look of disappointment on her father's face; she could hear it in his voice. She rubbed her temples. "Shuffle and let's go again. I've got a few hours before I have to meet Vince." She was going to need every minute.

"I want to play," Maddy declared.

"No, pumpkin. This is an adult game."

"But I love counting." Maddy's lower lip popped out.

"Let her learn. That's how you got started. You wanted to be part of the game when my friends came over."

"I don't want her to be part of the game." Annie's jaw threatened to lock up.

"Mommy." Maddy stretched across the table and

cocked her head in Annie's direction with a pleading smile. "Please."

"It wouldn't be called a game if people didn't have fun. Remember that weekend you first learned how to count? We went out fishing at Lake Mead and the fish got away with our pole because we were laughing so hard." Her father's smile was contagious as he set the deck in the middle of the table. "Let's cut cards. High card decides if Maddy stays."

"Me, too?" Maddy asked.

"You can take a card, too, puddin'." He chucked her under the chin.

Two against one. "The odds are against me," Annie said.

"That's when it's the most fun to get in the game."

"MEET ME OUTSIDE." Sam hung up before he started yelling at Annie. He'd followed the scar-faced gambler to Tassels Galore, when all he'd wanted to do was find Annie and confront her about her involvement with the card-counting ring. His temper flaring, he'd been unable to think through the implications of the old man going into the strip club.

Sam pulled into a parking spot in front of Brett's apartment and rammed the gearshift into Park as the afternoon sun beat down into the truck cab. He couldn't trust Annie. But he wanted her. It was killing him.

Annie took her own sweet time coming down the stairs. Sam was able to appreciate the sleek lines of her bare legs beneath her shorts, and the way the black

T-shirt with a pirate flag clung to her breasts. *Pirates.*
How appropriate.

She nodded at a woman unloading groceries from a
car next to him. Annie looked more composed than
when he'd seen her in the casino this morning. That
only fueled his temper.

Keeping his hands tight on the wheel, he stared
straight ahead as she got into his truck. "I found another
card counter today. I know you're a part of this," he
snapped. How easily he'd been played.

"And you believed him?" Annie's laughter seemed
forced.

"Why wouldn't I? You said you knew the guy with
the birthmark."

"I did."

Sam had to strain to hear her reply, strain to keep
from branding her once more with kisses. "So you
don't deny it."

"There's nothing to deny." Annie turned those big
blue eyes his way. "Until I met you I hadn't played
blackjack in a while. Both times I've played this week
you've been in the casino with me. If you have evidence
that I'm with these card counters, give it to me."

Give it to me. "I'll look the fool when I tell Mr.
Patrizio about you."

"I suppose that depends on what you tell him."
Without warning she spun to face Sam. "I'm sure
you've already detailed everything to Vince. Why else
would he have called this afternoon and asked me to
dinner?"

That son of a bitch. He probably thought he was going to get lucky tonight.

Over my dead body.

"GO AHEAD. Say it." Sam was scowling so fiercely that Annie was unable to wait any longer. "You knew from the beginning that I wasn't what I seemed. All you needed was confirmation, which I'm sure Vince was more than willing to give you."

When Sam still didn't say anything, she grasped the door handle, but he reached his long arm across and stopped her.

"Wait." It was the hint of pain in his eyes that held her immobile. Sam drew back slowly, ready to pounce if she tried to leave again. He opened the center console and lifted out a string of pearls. "You left this at my place."

Instead of handing it to her, he fastened the pearls around her neck, his fingers electric against her skin. Despite his betrayal, her heart pounded with wanting. When he pulled away again, Annie almost followed him.

"Don't go to dinner with Vince."

"You left me no choice. Vince knows who I am. I can't turn him down." Annie was dying to learn how Sam had reacted to the news that he'd slept with the girl who'd cleaned out Aldo Patrizio. Her hands were shaking, so she slid them beneath her thighs.

"Vince may seem like he has his shit together, but—"

"He's just a puppet."

"Then why go with him?"

"Self-preservation." She had to find out what game Vince was playing before she faced Aldo.

"Annie!" Her dad had the apartment door open and was pointing to his watch.

"I've got to go." She hopped out of the truck before Sam could protest. The butterflies swooped back into her stomach.

Sam touched her arm. "Annie—"

"I'm having dinner with Vince. I can't be late." It was best to be brutal. Sam had made it clear they had no future together, and being with him was torture. "Have a nice life, Sam."

When he didn't argue, she closed the door without looking back.

WATCHING ANNIE CLIMB those rickety steps, Sam wished he hadn't saved Vince's ass in Iraq. If his pal hadn't asked Annie out…

Sam pinched the bridge of his nose.

Have a nice life, Sam.

So polite. The ultimate brush-off. And her regret just made it that much more painful to watch her go. He'd disappointed Annie. If he wasn't such a shell of a man he could have fought for the right to take care of her, so she'd never have to associate with gamblers or Vince again.

The urge to charge up those stairs and make her forget all about the young, rich heir to the Sicilian was strong. If he was lucky, Maddy would be in the bathroom and he wouldn't pass out.

The woman who'd struggled with her groceries earlier came back out to her car. Her shoes were held together with duct tape, and she didn't even look up as a passenger jet thundered past. Her car started with a shudder and a backfiring burst of smoke, reminding him of Annie's car.

Who was Sam to hold Annie back when she was trying to escape this life? He wished he could just walk away, but he'd been hired to do a job and it wasn't yet finished.

"YOU LOOK LOVELY." Vince was waiting when Annie came in the restaurant door.

She murmured her thanks, even though the compliment was insincere. She wore an old sheath dress that had fit her two years ago, before her life fell apart. Now it hung off her shoulders like a sack, while her pearls were too tight. Vince, on the other hand, in a black suit and tie, looked as if he'd stepped off the pages of *GQ*. Definitely out of place in this run-of-the-mill restaurant.

"Relax. You look as if you could shatter," Vince said after they were seated in a dark booth and he'd requested wine.

"I'm not the little girl who beat everyone she played. Not anymore." Best to get that out in the open early.

"You can say that again." His gaze roamed over her, but it was a clinical scan, and lacked Sam's heat.

"I just want to be clear."

"Me, too. I'll give you twenty thousand dollars and you can keep whatever you win. That's a good offer for someone who has trouble passing a security check." Some of Vince's smooth demeanor dropped away and his dark eyes flashed. "We'll go to the Sicilian after dinner tonight and you can play."

"So soon?" Never mind that his offer was much less than she'd made the first time she'd taken on Aldo. Annie wasn't ready to play tonight.

"Oh, I get it." Vince laughed. "You're trying to leverage a higher ante. Okay. Thirty thousand dollars."

Annie shivered. "You expect me to win."

"Forty. Slotto was stupid not to hire you. Jeez, you strike a tough bargain." Whereas Vince was a simpleton when it came to negotiations. "I can't match what you got before. How much did you win last time? A million? Two?"

"Is that what Aldo told people?"

Vince fiddled with his fork. The restaurant was poorly lit and his face was shadowed. "I just figured it was heavy, since he was so upset about it."

"He had my father beaten to within inches of his life," Annie whispered as the waitress returned with two glasses of red wine.

Vince tasted the wine, grimaced. "Is that the best you have?"

The waitress assured him it was.

"Maybe it'll taste better with food. What shall we order? Linguine with clam sauce?"

"I'm not very hungry."

Vince ignored her. "We'll have two salads with the house dressing, and the linguine."

"My father?" Annie reminded him, when the waitress had gone. She wasn't going to say a word about Maddy.

"It's very important to me that you win, but no one's going to get hurt when that happens," Vince said.

Annie gave him what she hoped was her most cold, disbelieving stare.

"My father is the one prone to…" Vince reached for the wineglass, thought better of it and took a drink of water. "I won't let anything like that happen this time."

Annie's wine sat untouched. "What assurances do I have that my family won't get hurt?"

"You have my word."

Raising her eyebrows, Annie held Vince's gaze.

He shrugged. "Bring a bodyguard."

"I don't have—"

"Knight would be perfect."

Sam was perfect, but not hers. "He works for you."

"Yeah, but he has a thing for you."

"Leave Sam out of this." If she did this, she wanted to do it alone.

"Your call." Vince gazed around the restaurant. "My grandfather will be expecting me around eight."

"I haven't agreed to anything."

"Yes, but you won't walk away from my money, will you? After your ten-thousand-dollar buy in you'll have thirty thousand dollars. That'll go a long way to feeding your little girl until you find a job."

He was right. Much as Annie wanted to leave, she couldn't.

"I'm GOING WITH YOU," Brett insisted when Annie returned from her dinner with Vince. While she was out he'd come to the conclusion that he couldn't let her play.

"Why don't we take Maddy, too?" Annie asked sarcastically, sprawled on the couch with her arm curled around her daughter. She was in no shape to play, not that Brett believed she stood a chance against Aldo, anyway. "We can't leave her home alone."

"Go where?" Maddy stretched. "It's dark outside."

"Back to visit your princess, puddin'." Brett checked his watch. "It's seven-thirty. We need to leave now if we want to get you there by eight o'clock."

Maddy sat up, her hair a wild mess of yellow curls. "I want to go."

Annie didn't budge. "I'm going to show up alone."

Stubborn. Annie was so damn stubborn. "Okay, fine. At least let me drive you over to the Sicilian and wait downstairs."

"Dad—"

"We'll drop off Maddy with Chauncey and then go over together. I won't take no for an answer."

CHAPTER TWELVE

"RICK! RICK SABATINNI!" Sam had been watching the back door at Tassels Galore for more than an hour, but already felt as if he'd struck pay dirt.

The AWOL gambler turned beneath the glow of the neon stripper sign. Dressed in his trademark black from head to toe, including silver wing-tipped cowboy boots that mirrored the silver at his temples, Sabatinni frowned. "What are you doing here?"

"I think you better answer that question yourself." What other surprises did Tassels have in store for Sam? "I was told you'd help me find a group of card counters. Looks like you found them first."

Shaking his head, Sabatinni glanced away.

"Unfortunately for you, I've had a really crappy day. My tolerance for bullshit is over the legal limit. I'd appreciate it if you'd consider telling me the truth the first time around."

"Sam—"

"Or if you want we can swing over to the Sicilian and talk to Mr. Patrizio. He knows you've been gambling." Mr. Patrizio owned Tassels. The old gambler had come here. Sam was missing something and needed Sabatinni to talk.

A muscle in Sabatinni's jaw ticked. "I don't know what you know or think you know about what's going on—but it's not my place to tell you. All I can say is that I had to do this. If you want to know more you'll need to go inside and ask. When you know the truth you can decide what to tell Mr. Patrizio." Sabatinni walked away.

Sam turned back to study the strip club. Front door or back? He decided on the front.

"You wanted to see me?" Lana Tisdale leaned against the bar and smiled at Sam. When he got close, the dim lights couldn't hide Lana's worry.

Sam didn't waste any time, pitching his voice above Mötley Crüe singing "Girls, Girls, Girls." "I think you know who I am. I've identified several card counters working the casinos. One of them I followed back here. A few minutes ago I saw another one leave. Considering Aldo Patrizio owns the place and he hired me to find these players, I think you owe me an explanation."

"How…awkward." Without another word she led Sam behind the stage down the hall and into a back room.

Brett Raye. He and a short, fat man in a blue silk bowling shirt leaned over someone in a recliner. When they straightened, Sam recognized the sickly older gambler with the scar he'd found in the Lucky Horse earlier that day.

"We don't have time for him right now," Brett said,

scowling at Lana as he took a few steps forward. Without Maddy to cloud his vision, Sam noticed the slight limp right away. Brett was the gambler he and Annie had followed to the Sicilian.

"What was I supposed to do?" Lana closed the door behind Sam.

"Stall him until we were gone," Brett said.

"Sam?" Annie stepped out from behind an Oriental screen. She wore a black dress that hid her curves but showed enough leg to make up for it. "What are you doing here?"

"Somebody needs to tell me what's going on." He willed Annie to speak.

Brett returned to the recliner, where the man in the bowling shirt was helping the emaciated gambler out of the chair. "Fine. You stay here with Annie and she'll explain everything."

"What are you doing?" Lana fluttered around the men like a moth. "Chauncey's too weak to go anywhere."

"Lana, let it be." The thin man leaned heavily on the arms of his friends. "We started this all those years ago. We'll finish it."

Sam felt as if he'd come into a movie midreel.

"Dad, put Chauncey back in his chair. Nobody's going anywhere except me." Annie stepped between the threesome and the door, where Sam was rooted.

"I need to go," the man in the bowling shirt said. "I set up the game without asking you, Annie, and I'm sorry."

"Ernie, you set up *one* game." Annie pointed at the man in the bowling shirt, not budging. "I set up another."

With a sinking feeling, Sam realized they weren't talking about basketball. He'd hoped he'd been wrong about Annie.

"There's no need for anyone to go. Rick brought in enough to pay for Chauncey's treatments," Lana said.

"For this month," Brett countered, swaying under Chauncey's weight before finding his footing.

"We gave Aldo our word, Lana," Ernie said.

"Your word that *I'd* play Aldo, not you." The curls on the back of Annie's head shook.

"Wait a minute." Things were finally falling into place for Sam. "One of you is going to play Aldo Patrizio?"

There was a chorus of "I am" followed by an encore of frowns. Annie threw Sam a disgusted look over her shoulder. Mr. Patrizio was rumored to be one of the best gamblers in town, and Annie thought she stood a chance in a game against him? Sam was starting to agree with Brett.

"Ernie, head out the back door." Brett must have decided Annie was too formidable to get past. They did a slow shuffle turn and veered toward a door next to a row of glittery costumes. "The car keys are hanging on the wall out there."

Annie darted past them and into a well-lit garage. Sam followed, because someone had to talk some sense into her. Let the old men go lose their money.

It was the antithesis of Vince's garage. Peg-Board lined one wall above a greasy, dusty workbench. Cobwebs hung from the rafters. And a large piece of cardboard sat under the nose of a familiar, beat-up red car. Only the air was the same—warm, stuffy.

"This is for your own good," Brett said as the door behind Sam creaked.

"Mommy, I'm driving!" Maddy popped her head out of the driver's window and waved exuberantly.

Not now. Annie was trying to get back to the door, but Sam's knees buckled, sending him to the ground directly in her path.

The door swung shut behind them and a bolt slid home. A heartbeat later Annie tripped over Sam, and he heard a sickening thud.

ALDO HELD ROSALIE'S HAND. "Something's wrong, *cara mia.* I fear Vince is up to no good."

The sky was dark and the lights of the Strip promised their evening of excitement.

He stroked his wife's white hair. Just this morning he'd had the beautician wash and style it in the loose waves Rosalie preferred.

"Do you remember how proud we were of Vince when he graduated from high school?" A feat Aldo had never mastered. "Or the day he signed up for the army?" There was nothing more noble than a man willing to serve his country. "I wish I was wrong about him, but he's become so bitter." So like Nick.

The Bellagio fountain began its majestic dance, the strains of the music barely audible above the machines that pumped air into Rosalie's lungs. Aldo recognized the pattern as one of his wife's favorites.

"Someday, you will enjoy the fountain again. I promise." Until then, Aldo would keep his lonely vigil and pray for Rosalie's return.

"ANNIE!" Sam crawled across the cool concrete to get to her, ignoring Maddy's panicked shrieks.

Annie didn't move or respond.

"Mommy!" By the sound of things, the little girl was having trouble opening the car door.

"Be careful, Maddy." The last thing he needed was the child hurt as well.

Annie lay in a crumpled heap in front of the door. There was a pool of blood beneath her temple, but her breathing was steady. Still on all fours, Sam gently slipped two fingers beneath her head to inspect the gash, then looked up to see what she'd hit her head on. The doorknob had a squared, rather than round, edge, and seemed the most likely culprit.

"Annie, honey, wake up." In that moment Sam knew he'd go to the ends of the earth for this woman if she'd only open her eyes and look at him.

Her eyelids didn't so much as flutter. Sam knew better than to try to move her until she regained consciousness, in case she had a neck injury.

Small sandaled feet came to a stop behind him. Sam's stomach roiled and his head started to pound. He couldn't afford to lose it now. Maddy would freak out if both adults in the room were out cold.

"Mommy?" Maddy crooned in a thin voice. "Is she…dead?"

Sam probed Annie's wound with the utmost care. The sickle-shaped cut seemed to have already started to close. Blood barely oozed out of it now. "She's not dead and she's not going to die. But she's hurt. We need to get her to a doctor."

"We'll be locked in here until we're dead, too." Out of the corner of his eye Sam saw Maddy crouch and start to rock, her hands pressed against her ears. She kept sniffing as if trying not to cry.

Breathe. Sam focused on Annie's angelic face. "Maddy, I need you to help us get out of here."

"I'm just a baby." More sniffles.

Sam didn't blame her for falling apart. He was used to his own breakdowns by now; tired of them, too. But Sam needed to hang in there and so did she.

Maddy started sobbing. Sam wanted to close his fingers around Brett's neck.

Think. Think. Maddy needed a distraction from her mom's condition, the same way Sam needed a distraction from the sight of the small child. It had been so long since he'd seen his nieces he couldn't remember how he'd diverted their attention. What was it that Maddy was interested in?

"Can you…" Sweat popped out on Sam's brow. "Can you count the money in my wallet?"

"Why?"

"We need money to call 911." It was as good a reason as any. He'd left his cell phone in his truck's cup holder, and Annie's purse didn't seem to be anywhere nearby.

"Okay." The little girl sniffed once more.

Risking his equilibrium, Sam sat back on his haunches. Then he handed Maddy his wallet. She took it, but almost immediately it landed back in his lap. "There's just one dollar."

She was right. Damn it. He was practically broke.

"Wait. How many eights are on that bill?" The serial numbers on a bill went on forever.

Maddy took the wallet back and began to count. "One, two…three…four, five eights. Ask me another one."

"I will as soon as you look around for the keys. Your grandpa said they were hanging on the wall." Car keys or door keys. Sam would be incredibly grateful for either.

"How could Grandpa lock me in here? I'm just a baby." Her voice wavered.

"He thought he was keeping us safe." It was the best Sam could come up with. Personally, he'd like to give Brett more than a piece of his mind. Annie's injury may have been an accident, but the old man had no right to scare Maddy. "Have you ever wanted to be a hero? I have a plan, but it will take two heroes."

"Is someone going to shoot me?"

"No."

"Okay." With a swish of her skirt she scuttled closer to him.

"WHERE'S ANNIE?" Vince demanded as Brett, Ernie and Chauncey staggered into the foyer of the Sicilian at seven fifty-eight, after Lana dropped them off at the main entrance.

The patrons flowing around them were a diverse mix, wearing everything from tuxedos to basketball shorts and T-shirts. Brett half expected Annie to come charging up behind them at any moment, followed closely by Knight. Someday they'd understand that he'd locked them up for their own good. It was never wise to give a Patrizio what he wanted on first request.

"Did Annie get cold feet?" Vince asked.

"Food poisoning," Brett replied. "We're here…to play…in her place." Chauncey didn't weigh that much, but he was tall. Brett panted from the effort it took to keep him upright.

"That wasn't our deal. And he's half-dead." Vince tossed his head in Chauncey's direction. "I wanted a worthy opponent."

"Three…for the price…of one." Brett tried to grin, but all his panting had made his mouth dry, and his lips were stuck to his teeth.

Ernie, who wasn't looking so good, either, spotted a bench seat and headed for it. Vince trailed behind them.

Brett took a moment to wipe the perspiration from his forehead. "We'll be more than happy to reschedule. We've been busy playing Vegas all week." It seemed necessary to remind Vince that they were good enough to attract Aldo's attention.

The younger man's eyes narrowed. "He won't be happy to see you."

Handwritten annotation at top: "514 2220   12.30 PM   me drive"

"Probably not."

"The game's not worth as much to me. It's more the look on his face that I'll relish."

"We'll be happy with five grand." Out of the corner of his eye Brett saw Ernie flinch.

The young Patrizio laughed. "More like one."

"Two and a half."

"Tell you what." Vince leaned one arm against the pale gold wall above Brett's shoulder. "I'll give you a thousand just to come upstairs. If he agrees to play one or all of you, I'll give you another grand."

Since Brett doubted Aldo would agree to play any of them, it was a fair price for an elevator ride. Vince escorted them through the private corridors of the Sicilian and into a wood-paneled elevator. He inserted a key and pressed the button for the penthouse.

"You know," Brett said, seeing his chance, "I never expected to honor that bet. You were too young, and I thought I'd scare you away by challenging you to commit half a million."

Vince didn't immediately answer. He watched the red floor numbers flash across the display on the control panel. "I worshipped my grandfather back then. No amount of money was too high. I'd never seen him lose."

Brett realized that seeing his grandfather lose now was all Vince wanted.

The elevator made no other stops. The doors slid open at the penthouse floor. Chauncey wasn't looking so good, which was to be expected, since he'd already taken one field trip today. Ernie's face was pale. Brett had no explanation for that.

"Here we are." Vince used a magnetic key to open the penthouse door, and stepped aside with a flourish to let them enter, as cordial as any good host.

"MADDY, YOU LOOK FOR THE keys on the workbench. I'm going to see if I can open one of these doors." Sam staggered to his feet and tested the door next to Annie, first to make sure it was locked, and then with his shoulder. Both the door and the lock were solid and didn't budge.

Keeping the child in his peripheral vision, he walked around the other side of the car to examine the large garage door. It was padlocked from the inside. Surely that was a fire hazard.

Something jingled behind him. "I found keys!"

Sam grinned. "You're a superstar!"

"I'd rather be a princess." Maddy sniffed. "But not one that locks family up."

Out of the corner of his eye, Sam saw her skip over to him, waving her skirt with each step. She stopped at his feet and pressed the keys into his hand. Then she tugged on his pant leg. "Come down here."

With one hand on the rear bumper, Sam crouched, carefully keeping his eyes averted from Maddy's face. But the little girl had other ideas. She put her tiny hands on each of Sam's cheeks until he had no choice but to look at her.

Her luminous blue eyes held more than a hint of

fear. "You don't need fixin', do you? You took off your Band-Aids."

Sam held his breath, but nothing happened. His vision didn't tunnel. The world didn't spin. He was... normal.

He wrapped the child in a careful hug. "You are the bravest little girl I know."

"Mommy says I'm the only little girl you know," Maddy whispered.

She was just like her mother. Sam chuckled as he took Maddy by the shoulders and held her in front of him. He had to be sure this wasn't a fluke.

"You're a beautiful thing, aren't you?" He'd never really gotten a good look at her before. She had Annie's delicate features and coloring.

Maddy started to cry again. "I can't fix Mommy."

"But I know someone who can." Sam wiped away Maddy's tears and kissed her forehead. "Let's see what these keys open."

CHAPTER THIRTEEN

"WAIT HERE," Vince instructed, leaving them standing on the gold-and-white-marble entry before an elaborate mosaic of the waterways of Venice.

The penthouse was large and lavishly furnished. Butter-yellow leather couches, black club chairs and matching accent tables stood out against the warm yellow walls. Windows overlooked the Strip. There was a Monet water lily painting hung at one end of the room and what looked to be a Picasso at the other, and in between was a six-player card table covered in black felt.

"I think this was a mistake," Ernie said, taking a step back.

"Welcome to the Sicilian." A burly man of about their age, with white hair and thick glasses, stepped between them and freedom. His voice rumbled deep in his throat, emphasizing his Italian accent. "I'm Paulo. Can I get you a drink?"

"We won't be staying long enough for a drink," Chauncey said.

"Damn straight," Ernie echoed.

"Water," Brett croaked.

Vince came back through another door and closed it behind him, punching buttons on one of those fancy cell phones. "I told my grandfather I was here. He doesn't know I've brought the rest of you."

Paulo set Brett's water down on a coaster at the table and then retreated to stand by the door. No one spoke. Brett wished they'd never come.

A door opened. Everyone turned to look across the room.

"Vince, what have we here? This is our blackjack night, no?" Aldo Patrizio's slightly accented voice sent shivers down Brett's spine. The older man hadn't aged well. He took halting steps and wore thick Coke-bottle glasses.

"We're doing things a little differently." Vince strutted across the room and placed his hands on a black leather chair back at the card table. His smile oozed a self-confidence that Brett was far from feeling.

"Really?" Aldo studied him and his friends with those cold black eyes that still gave Brett nightmares. Age had curled the Italian's spine and stolen the color from his hair, but the eyes hadn't changed. They seemed more menacing distorted behind his eye-glasses.

"This is Brett Raye. You remember him, don't you?" Vince's gaze didn't leave his grandfather's face. "His daughter was the one who humiliated you so long ago. She broke the bank. Your bank. In front of all your friends."

"And these must be the rest of his cardsharps. The ones I hired Sam Knight to find." Aldo closed the distance between them so that he could get a better look.

How had he known? Ernie sent Brett a panicky glance, a silent communiqué to make a run for it. But Brett wasn't one to cut and run, and he wouldn't have been able to move his feet if he tried, so he shook his head.

"Hold steady," Chauncey whispered, although Brett wasn't sure if he meant they needed to keep holding him up, or to hold their ground against Aldo.

"I hear you've become quite successful. You must have invested my money wisely." The Sicilian founder continued his shuffling approach. "Where is your daughter?"

"I didn't ask to play you," Brett said, unable to contain the compulsion to explain. "And I don't want Annie to play you again, either."

Aldo smiled. He looked almost…regretful. "I wondered, but in the end it was Vince and your friend here that wanted to arrange this. I see that now. Since you're here, perhaps we'll find out why this game is so important to them."

"Chauncey's got medical bills," Ernie said.

"That explains *your* actions." Aldo turned to Vince expectantly.

"MADDY," Annie whispered as she became aware of her surroundings—hard floor, something wet on her face.

She cracked open her eyes and immediately shut them against the bright light.

"These are car keys. Was there another set of keys, Maddy?" Sam's voice had an odd echo.

"Just those ones."

Annie brought one hand up to shield her eyes, and risked opening them again. Sam was standing at the workbench. Maddy sat on the counter next to him. Annie pushed herself into a sitting position, which caused her head to throb like a bass drum.

Sam noticed Annie first. He lifted Maddy down, then knelt in front of Annie. "Hey. I don't think you should be sitting up. Are you okay? You hit your head." He ran his hands over her shoulders and neck.

A bundle of energy in calico and lace climbed into her lap. "Mommy, Grandpa has been very bad. He locked us in."

"What?" The last thing she remembered was driving with her father to a strip club.

Sam frowned. "Where does it hurt?"

"Just my head. It feels funny."

"We're getting you to a hospital," Sam said. He scooped her up and carried her to the car. "Open the door, Maddy."

The child scampered to do it and when she was out of the way, Sam set Annie carefully in the backseat.

"Help your mother put her seat belt on, Maddy. This is going to be a bumpy ride." Sam climbed into the driver's seat. "I hope Mr. Patrizio has decent insurance on this place."

"Why?" Annie collapsed against the seat, letting Maddy buckle her in.

"We couldn't find the keys to the garage door. We're going to have to bust through."

Just like in the movies. Annie didn't feel scared or nervous. Just proud. Sam was taking charge and getting them all to safety. A real hero.

"Hurry, Sam," Maddy said in a stuffy voice, as if she'd been crying. Poor baby. When her daughter had her seat belt on, Annie held her hand tightly.

The car sputtered to life. "Hang on," Sam warned.

The vehicle whined and shuddered with increasing intensity until Sam sent it leaping backward. They slammed through the locked door with a scream of metal—accompanied by a scream or two from the backseat. And then they screeched to a halt.

"And I thought my mommy drove crazy," Maddy said.

Sam spared a glance back at them. "I guess that means you're okay."

"Can we get a doctor for Mommy now?"

"One doctor, coming right up."

"I'm WELL AWARE OF MY grandson's schemes." Aldo mirrored Vince's stance and leaned on a chair back across from him, squeezing the cushion when his hands started to shake. "He doesn't realize everything I've done has been for him."

"Now I know you've lost your mind," Vince said through gritted teeth.

"No." If anything, the past twenty-four hours of waiting had cleared Aldo's mind. "About eight months ago, I realized I'd lost your respect. You became surly and questioned every decision I made."

"Some of your decisions needed to be questioned," Vince retorted.

"Did they? I've spent many hours thinking about what to do with you." Aldo shook his head, searching for any trace of the grandson he loved in the bitter man across from him. "Then one day, after beating you in blackjack and having you throw a long-forgotten loss in my face, you gave me the answer. I was just too blinded by my love for you to act on it. Until now."

SAM BROUGHT LANA'S CAR to a screeching halt beneath the emergency room portico. He turned off the engine and it coughed its way to a reluctant death.

"Head injury. We need a stretcher!" He yelled to the attendant as he hopped out of the car and ran around to Annie's side.

The young medic took off to get help.

Sam poked his head in Annie's window. "Are you okay?"

"This is so unnecessary. I've just got a little bump is all." But the earnestness of Sam's attention warmed her heart.

"Mommy doesn't like your driving, either," Maddy said. "You ran four red lights."

"The lights were yellow, and I was afraid if I stopped, the engine would die." Sam winked at Maddy.

For some reason that seemed unusual, but Annie couldn't quite put her finger on why.

"Sam, I'm fine." Even as she said it she lost the battle with her heavy eyelids. All she wanted to do was sleep.

"Annie." Sam's voice was urgent. "Annie, stay with us. Get that stretcher over here!"

"Mommy?" Maddy tugged on her hand. "Mommy?"

"In a minute, baby." Annie just needed to close her eyes for a minute.

"HIS DAUGHTER *BEAT* YOU," Vince stated, reemphasizing exactly what Brett didn't want him to. "She humiliated you."

"Yes, she did." Aldo looked at Brett without even a hint of threat in his dark eyes. Of the two Patrizios, he seemed the most reasonable, and the safer bet to get Brett and his friends out of here. "But you were the one who didn't think before acting. You've done the same thing tonight."

Vince scoffed.

"You lack honor, Vince. Perhaps your grandmother and I were too lax in your upbringing. I don't know." Aldo shook his gray-haired head. "I've lost my patience."

Vince's face grew red.

"This is my final offer before I wash my hands of you. I want *you* to play Miss Raye. As before, she'll start with her fifty thousand dollars, and I'll front you the same amount."

"I'm not playing her."

Brett switched to rooting for Vince. "Annie doesn't want to play."

"They'll play," Aldo said coldly. "And Vince is going to play in front of a roomful of witnesses, just as I did. And he'll place a side bet. This time with me. When you lose, Vince, you're going to find a job elsewhere."

The younger Patrizio muttered something under his breath. "And if I win?"

"You won't." Aldo's confidence was more than a little scary, it was downright terrifying. He was so determined to put his grandson in his place. What if Annie couldn't do it?

"I *could* win."

Brett had to agree with Vince, but he still didn't like the way the younger man smiled.

"Hmm. On the slight chance that you do, you'll get what you always wanted." Aldo's expression was cold and detached. "I'll move to Florida and leave you the Sicilian."

The room was absolutely silent. Brett could practically feel the electricity between the two men as they stared at each other. "I'll hold you to that." Vince's dark gaze bored into Brett. "Where is she?"

"You and I are too much alike, you see," Aldo said quietly, not moving. "At least, we would have been had I not been so cocky as to play a young girl."

"We are nothing alike!" Vince shouted, his face contorted with rage. "I would never pay someone to run down my wife!"

In that moment, everything changed. Aldo's calm demeanor dissipated.

"How could you accuse me of such a thing? Rosalie is my life. I am nothing without her. I would have been nothing without her. She alone believed in me. I would just as soon have run Rosalie over as myself."

"Nonna stood in the way of your *mistress*." Vince pointed at the Picasso. "*Le Rêve*. Picasso's mistress. Why else would you choose to display this painting in your house but to flaunt it in Nonna's face?"

"They're going to kill each other," Chauncey muttered.

Ernie's eyes were as wide as saucers. "Better each other than us."

"From what I hear this is pretty much par for the course," Brett whispered, unable to quit feeling as if he was somehow to blame for their animosity. If only he hadn't taken that bet with Vince all those years ago… "This would be as good a time as any to make our exit."

"It is a work of art I've admired for many years." Aldo fisted his hands and raised his bent arms. "Steve Wynn knew I loved it, and lent it to me to enjoy for a time. You always look for the worst in a person."

They all heard a high-pitched sound in the other room. The two Patrizios fell silent.

"What's that ringing?" Ernie asked. "Is it a fire alarm?"

A nurse ran from one side of the suite to the other, going into the room Aldo had come from.

"No." Aldo started to follow her, but his knees buckled. "No!"

The doorman was immediately at his side, helping him walk. Vince raced past his grandfather.

"Stay here," Brett said, slipping out from under Chauncey's arm to follow Vince in case they needed help.

The ringing came from the bedroom. A hospital ventilator was making a horrible racket. Mrs. Patrizio's skin was blue.

"She's not breathing." The nurse picked up the phone. "We need an ambulance right away." Then she started CPR.

"Don't leave me, *cara mia*." Aldo collapsed over his wife.

Vince hovered helplessly at the foot of the bed.

"Save her, please. She cannot breathe on her own," Aldo rasped, sounding none too good himself.

CHAPTER FOURTEEN

ALDO FOLLOWED ROSALIE'S stretcher out to the lobby, where he watched the paramedics take her away. He and Vince couldn't fit with them and had to wait for the elevator to return. The three card counters had disappeared.

"This never would have happened if you hadn't taken a mistress." Vince gave his grandfather a disgusted once-over, as if he were yesterday's trash. "That woman at Tassels isn't worth it."

"Vince, please. She is *not* my mistress," he protested, after taking a moment to figure out who Vince meant. "I have never betrayed my wedding vows."

"Why did you have to buy Tassels, then? You've done nothing with it since."

"I bought the entire block with my personal funds to keep the press out of my business before all sales were completed. I was going to expand the Sicilian," Aldo said. "The project has been on hold since Rosalie…" *His grandson had thought for months that Aldo would try to kill his love.* He swallowed thickly.

Vince had been studying him. "You're serious. That Tisdale woman means nothing to you."

"Less than nothing." Aldo was such a *jamook*. So this was why his grandson had come to hate him so intensely. It seemed incredible that someone he loved so much could believe he, Aldo, was capable of such a betrayal.

Vince appeared shaken and spoke haltingly. "You and Nonna had that fight. You never explained anything. I tried to put two and two together. I was afraid you'd get rid of me, send me away like you did my father."

Aldo's heart nearly stopped beating. "Why would you think that?"

"Because I'm a failure. My dad knew it—tried to beat it out of me. I place all the wrong bets. When I was in uniform I couldn't even shoot insurgents when they aimed a gun at me. And if you asked me to run someone down or beat someone up, I couldn't do that, either."

A cold thread wound its way through Aldo's veins. "Why would you think I'd ask that of you?" What kind of man did Vince think he was?

"You were in the Mafia. You controlled Dad. A man like that uses brute strength and expects it from others."

His grandson didn't know him at all, just as Nick hadn't known him.

"A powerful man controls others with his wits." Vince must not have seen Nick and his hoodlum friends beating Brett Raye.

The problem was Nick's cruelty had clearly hurt his grandson more than Aldo had ever understood—in ways he couldn't fathom. There was a lesson to be learned here, but the learning would be no less painful than the feuds of the past few months.

"Vince?" Sam lifted Maddy off his lap and steered her toward the activity table in the emergency waiting room. He would still be glued to Annie's side if Maddy hadn't fallen apart earlier. "What are you doing here?"

"My grandmother stopped breathing."

"Oh, my God."

"She's stable now. They're going to run more tests." Hunching down in a chair, Vince looked undone. He'd just tossed his jacket over a chair back, his tie was loosened and his hair hung in his face. Sam hadn't seen him so disheveled since Iraq.

"And your grandfather?"

Vince closed his eyes. "It's hard to believe he's such a wreck. Usually nothing gets to him."

"Give the guy a break. And pull yourself together. He needs you."

"He doesn't need anyone but my grandmother." Vince glanced at Maddy, who was busy with a puzzle, before adding in a low voice, "He sure as hell doesn't need me."

"Families aren't easy." Sam was no Dr. Phil. But Vince sounded too much like the runaway kid he must have been fourteen years ago. "I've told you about my dad, haven't I?"

"Yeah."

"He knew people and he was honest about his

feelings." Sam gazed at the paneled ceiling. "My mom would get so mad at him sometimes for stupid stuff like the trash overflowing. He'd let her rant until she ran out of steam. Then he'd wrap his arms around her, tell her how sorry he was and that he loved her." Sam was struck with a sudden longing to do the same to Annie, to hold her and tell her everything was going to be all right. "I think that's how love is supposed to be. You have to be there for each other through all the everyday crap, whether it's your grandfather or your lover." *Whether they want you there or not.*

"One, two, three, four…" Maddy counted the puzzle pieces, eliciting a smile from Sam.

"When I lived with my parents, they yelled at each other and…me. Sometimes there was more than yelling." Vince, turning the large flashy wedding ring on his finger, confirmed what Sam had always suspected about his past. "My grandfather finally paid them to move to Florida. I've been waiting for him to do the same to me. Guess I don't have to wait any longer. He was very clear."

"He needs you." Sam had the strongest suspicion that he himself might need Annie.

"Hardly." Vince was every bit as stubborn as his grandfather. "He wants me to play her. Do you think Annie will agree? She wasn't so willing when I asked her."

Sam clenched a hand as something hot and danger-ous coursed through him. "What do you mean? You didn't *force* her to do anything, did you?"

"It was a straight-up deal. I swear." Vince held up his palms.

Far from reassured, Sam felt like hitting someone, preferably Vince. "If I hear you've pulled something—"

"If it'll make you feel better, come to the game, be there for her."

"Annie doesn't want me there." Annie didn't want him, period. And just like that, Sam felt drained.

With a shout of laughter, Vince slapped him on the back. "Let me tell you about love according to the Patrizios. Staying power. That's what it's all about. He who takes the most hits is the best loved."

"That's a little too masochistic for me," Sam muttered. But perhaps his friend was on the right track. Sam hadn't known about the pressure Annie had been under, with the card counters helping Chauncey.

"Can you explain something to me, Vince? Why is playing Annie such a big deal?"

Vince started to laugh. "Oh, man. I thought you knew."

IT WAS AFTER TEN and Emergency was starting to fill up. Waiting for word on Annie's condition, and for Brett to show up to take Maddy home, Sam sat in the waiting room long after Vince had gone to check on his grandmother. Lounging in the plastic chair, he stewed about the situation until he was ready to flay somebody— Annie for hiding the truth, Brett for taking advantage of Annie, Vince for trying to use the Raye family against his grandfather, himself for being so blind. Sam felt as if he'd been duped by Annie and Brett and the rest of Las Vegas! He didn't like being taken for a fool.

He had heard the stories about the little girl who'd fleeced Aldo Patrizio, but he'd thought they were exaggerated. Since he'd misread her from the start, it was as if he was learning who Annie was for the first time. The woman he'd slept with wasn't this modern day myth. She was...too down-to-earth.

Annie should have told Sam the truth. He would have acted differently if she had. Exactly what he would have done differently wasn't clear.

"You've got a hell of a lot of nerve," Sam said as he transferred a sleeping Maddy from his arms to Brett's when the older man finally showed up.

"I had to make sure Annie didn't go to the Sicilian. I'm sorry Maddy got scared and Annie bumped her head." Brett looked repentant as he placed a kiss on Maddy's blond curls. Then he chuckled. "You tore quite a hole through—"

"You knew the Patrizios wanted Annie to play. Why didn't you send her away, or take her out of Vegas before it came to this?" Fathers were supposed to protect their daughters, not exploit them. Annie must have had one hell of a childhood.

"That's none of your business." Brett kept his voice low, turning to carry Maddy out into the hallway.

"Hell, you even tried to hone Annie's skills. Cut the bull. You didn't want her to gamble just for Chauncey, did you? There had to be something in it for you."

Brett stopped and faced him. "I did it all for her. You

don't understand what Annie's been through. She's lost all confidence in herself and all faith in me." He paused, looking suddenly confused. "Oh, she pretends everything is okay. She's good at that. But Annie needs people around who care about her."

"You've got a fine way of showing it."

Brett's jaw worked and he closed his faded blue eyes. When he opened them again, all the fight had drained out of him. "I'm taking Maddy home. Tell Annie I'll be by later to check on her."

Robbed of a good argument, Sam stewed some more in the stiff, stained waiting room chair. Questions he couldn't answer taunted him. Why *had* Annie seemed so lost whenever she played cards in the casino? Had she laughed behind his back, knowing she had him bamboozled? And how could Sam ever live up to the expectations of a woman who'd done something so amazing by age twelve?

"Raye? Annie Raye?" A nurse stood in the entrance to the waiting room. "Family for Annie Raye."

Sam rushed over. "Yes. That's me." At the moment, he was all she had.

"We've taken her up to a room. You can see her now."

"Is she all right?"

"We're keeping her overnight for observation. She's got a concussion and a couple of stitches, but everything else checks out."

At present, just hearing that Annie would be all right seemed enough.

When Sam finally found her room, Annie was

sleeping. Her thick lashes were dark against her pale skin. Beneath the bandage he saw a purple bruise, and the black ends of the thread that held her cut together. She looked worn-out and in need of some tender loving care.

What she did not need was some burned-out, lonely private investigator demanding answers. He could wait until tomorrow for that, he decided. Though it would have been a hell of a lot easier if he could stop the questions from burning a circular track in his brain.

An hour later, Annie stirred.

Sam watched with a mix of longing and frustration as she licked her dry, chapped lips and opened her eyes, smiling when she saw him. He lifted the cup of water from her bedside table and placed the straw to her mouth. He could hold his tongue until morning. He could—

"You lied to me," Sam blurted, inwardly cursing.

Annie pulled her head back, and Sam returned the cup to the table. "Maybe you could come up with a new gripe? One that has some teeth to it."

"You're a frickin' local legend." Yeah, he was angry. Still, a guy had to be proud of the fact that his almost-girlfriend was the Vegas equivalent of Wonder Woman, didn't he?

"That's not a lie, Sam. That's *private* history," Annie said ruefully.

"You beat Aldo Patrizio out of a million dollars! How did you blow that? Vince thinks your dad spent it." She'd just been through hell, but Sam couldn't seem to control himself.

"First off, it was nowhere near a million dollars." Annie inched up into a sitting position, shrugging off his help. "Second…it's none of your business what happened to me fourteen years ago."

None of his…? "Like it was none of your business what happened to me in the war?"

She bit her lip and glanced away, but then turned back full force, giving him a glimpse of the take-no-prisoners woman she went to such pains to hide. "Are you here to console me with pity sex? Is that why you waited around?"

"No!" Sam scowled. Talk about the past returning to bite you in the butt. He leaned back in his chair and studied her. Why *had* he stayed around? "What I'm trying to say… What I came here for…" He was at a loss for words.

Annie slumped against the pillows, once more the vulnerable woman who comforted him during his dark episodes. "I'm human. I've made mistakes just like everyone else. I'm trying to start over. I thought we had that in common, but it's obvious that you're not rebuilding your life. You want to keep on being a lonely idiot who manipulates women into having sex with him, and then moves on."

"Is that what you think of me?"

"What matters is what you think of *me*. I'm happy to be a disappointment to you. That means I won't wonder if it's you knocking on the door." She took a deep breath, letting her gaze drift to the doorway. "And I never have to sleep with you again."

"YOU DON'T HAVE TO WORRY about Chauncey's care anymore," he said. Sam's eyes had that haunted look she'd noticed the first day they'd met. Or maybe she'd been bumped on the head too hard and was imagining things.

Annie clung to the bars on the side of the bed. "Did they play? Is my dad all right?"

"Brett is fine. He took Maddy home. Said he'd be back later."

Relief washed through her, and Annie relaxed her grip on the bars. "So they won." They hadn't needed her, after all. So why did Annie feel an embarrassing sense of frustration?

"They never played." Sam explained what had happened with Mrs. Patrizio.

Annie started to frown, but the action pulled the skin around her stitches, "Then where did the money come from?"

"Vince said he'd take care of it."

"You told him." Annie's throat tightened when Sam nodded. He could be so sweet. She couldn't take her eyes off him.

"I don't suppose…I mean, it seems rude to ask, but would you mind…" Sam trailed off and sat there staring back at her.

"What?"

"Could you tell me what happened? With Aldo?"

Hell. "No. Ask Vince."

"He said he wasn't allowed inside the room where you played." Sam gave her a lopsided smile. "I think it might do you good. You were freaked out even thinking about going inside the Sicilian the other day."

"Didn't Vince go into the details?" It was hard to breathe. Sam was acting as if she should have been— and should be—open about her past. But she'd done her best to hide it for so long that it didn't seem right.

"You know how guys are. He said it was you in pigtails and Aldo losing a million bucks." Unexpectedly, Sam reached for her hand. "Has it really been fourteen years?"

Again with the flattery. "You have no problem imagining me in pigtails?"

"I'm not much for flowery words," Sam admitted, his grin widening. "I know you think I'm a pathetic idiot who was lucky enough to have twelve-point sex on a ten-point scale this morning."

"I didn't say you were pathetic." Annie had to give him something since he'd given her such a rave review.

He raised a dark eyebrow, and places that had no right to heat up in a hospital started percolating.

"Why do you want to know?"

Sam covered their clasped hands with his free one. "I've shared more with you in the past few days than I ever have with anyone, other than my dad. On some level, hearing you say what I did and not pronounce me Lucifer changed something. I'm not saying you waved your magic wand and now I'm healed, but I feel… I think I owe you one."

His humility and the huskiness of his voice were her undoing. "I'm not sure where to start."

"We'll go slow." He rubbed her hand with his. "How did you come to play Aldo?"

An easy question. The pressure in her chest eased up. "I think Aldo asked. He'd probably heard I was winning matches, and he fancied himself quite the player."

"Weren't you intimidated?"

"He was just another grown-up to me. I was twelve. I thought I could beat anybody." She stared at their joined hands.

Sam had strong masculine hands. Annie dragged her gaze away. "Ask me another question."

"Where did you play?"

"One of the VIP rooms downstairs at the Sicilian. They had all this food laid out—shrimp, caviar, champagne. All I wanted was a McDonald's cheeseburger and fries."

Sam squeezed her hand as he laughed.

"The strangest thing was Aldo. He was the dealer."

"He was the house?"

"Yes. I'd always played the house against other people. It made me nervous, but in the end I had fewer cards to count, so I think the counting process was easier." But Aldo had scowled at her the entire eight hours they'd played. Annie sucked on her bottom lip. "You want to know how much I won."

"It wasn't a million?" Sam sounded disappointed.

"Our stake was fifty thousand dollars." That was all the money they'd had, including what Chauncey and Ernie chipped in. "Aldo put up the same."

"My bullshit meter is rising. The story goes—"

"It's true. I swear. I won." The rest of the tale came tumbling out. "People had been watching, but after the game, more came into the room, especially after Aldo and his son, Vince's dad, left. Before I knew what was happening, Aldo's son came back in yelling in Italian and pointing to my dad. I didn't understand what was going on. And then…they held me in a chair while these men took turns hitting my dad, kicking him when he fell." Again and again until her father's head had fallen back, and she'd thought he was dead. Annie couldn't quite catch her breath, remembering.

"I thought I was next, but Aldo came back in and they carried my dad down to a back door, loaded us into a taxi and let us go." Annie didn't realize she was crying until Sam wiped away a tear on her cheek with his thumb.

"Fifty thousand dollars is nothing to Aldo. He's worth billions." Sam looked up as a nurse walked past. "It would have been nothing to him fourteen years ago. And why was it his son, Nick, who went ballistic?"

"Pride?"

"It had to be something else."

"You're on good terms with Vince. Why don't you ask him?" Wiping her other cheek, Annie felt as if a load had been lifted from her shoulders. "The next day, Aldo came to visit us in the hospital with a suitcase full of money. He said something to my dad about a misunderstanding." That was the closest he'd come to an apology.

"That's where the million dollars came from."

"*No*. My dad said it was about five hundred thousand.

We bought a house and put the rest in a trust fund." Blood money. She hadn't questioned the amount or wanted to know more.

"Which your ex-husband probably made short work of."

"Could you be a little less astute? Now you know my private history. Satisfied?" Annie should have felt empty, but instead felt content.

"Wow." A smile curled one side of Sam's mouth. "You really are a wunderkind of blackjack."

"Was." She forced herself to look away, not ready to be teased about it.

Sam touched her chin lightly, turning her face to his. "I think you're whoever you want to be."

She should have laughed off his silly pep talk. Instead, she found herself compelled closer by the slightest pressure of his fingertips, and then his lips reclaimed hers.

SOMETIME LATER, a man appeared in the doorway, his face in shadow.

When he entered with halting steps, Sam snapped wide-awake. He'd been holding Annie's hand while he dozed in the chair next to her bed. "Mr. Patrizio."

Fear caused Annie's heart to pound with almost the same intensity as the throbbing in her head. "What are you doing here?"

"My wife had an episode. She's on another floor." Aldo moved close enough for Annie to see his face— lined, pale, his dark eyes hidden behind thick glasses.

He seemed old and tired, a shell of the man he'd once been.

Annie murmured her best wishes for his wife's recovery.

Aldo waved her off. "My grandson said you were supposed to play me tonight, but fell ill. Why did you agree to such a thing?"

"I needed the money," she admitted, lifting her chin. "I'm not proud of it."

"Annie had the misfortune to marry a man who later became an embezzler," Sam explained. "She's a finance whiz. But the history of her ex makes it hard to get a job."

"Too much information," Annie said under her breath. The less Aldo Patrizio knew about her, the better.

The elderly Italian took Annie's measure. "Two parties requested a rematch."

She sent Sam an I-told-you-so look.

"I'm sure Vince meant well," Sam said, trying to support his friend.

"I'm sure he did not," Aldo countered, his frown lines deepening. "How much money did Vince offer you?"

With effort, Annie held Aldo's penetrating stare. "Forty thousand dollars."

Sam whistled and Annie's cheeks heated. She knew she looked like a money grubber. "I was going to give half of it to my father's friend Chauncey."

Aldo's lips compressed into a thin line. "I had no idea Vince wanted to humiliate me that badly." He clasped and unclasped his hands, never taking his eyes off his plain wedding band. "So, you're in need of a job, Miss Raye?"

"Yes, she is." Sam put his hand on Annie's. Though she knew she should shrug him off, its sturdy weight settled her nerves.

"I believe the Sicilian has a job opening in our finance department."

No-no-no. She couldn't work for Aldo. "Why would you do that?"

"You're qualified." He clasped his hands again.

"And the terms?" Sam asked.

Aldo's eyes settled back on Annie. "I'll front you fifty thousand dollars and you may keep what you win from Vince."

Holding her breath, Annie waited, knowing what Aldo would say next.

The old man turned his head toward the hallway. "You will beat Vince. And when you do, the job will be yours."

Sam shifted. "But Vince—"

"This is for his own good." Aldo's black eyes bored into Annie.

She couldn't breathe. Her past had caught up to her yet again.

"I'M JUST SAYING I think you should consider Aldo's request," Sam repeated. The old man's offer had sent Annie into a tailspin.

She had called her father as soon as Aldo had left. Sam would have preferred she turn to him.

"Guys like Aldo don't make requests. He told me what he wanted to have happen."

"So? He's backed you into a corner. If you lose, you'll walk away with fifty thousand dollars. And if you win you'll walk away with more. What happened to the confident way you claimed you were going to beat me?"

"You don't understand the game. It would've been easy to clean *you* out." She said it too dismissively for Sam's taste.

"I just saw Aldo in the lobby," Annie's father said breathlessly as he hurried into the room with his uneven gait. "He told me not to worry about any hospital bills. He's taking care of everything."

"I don't want the Patrizios' charity. Where's Maddy?"

"I left her with Ernie. Wait until you get a bill for a five-hundred-dollar aspirin before you reject Aldo's offer." Brett winked. He turned to Sam with a smile, as if they'd never argued a few hours ago. "Here's Maddy's hero. From what I hear, you could have had a great career in NASCAR."

"I'm a much better driver without someone bleeding in the backseat."

Brett turned to his daughter. "Where's the fire?"

"Aldo came here." Annie's voice shook. "He still wants me to play."

"This isn't about you giving Aldo an opportunity for revenge, Annie." Brett sat at the foot of her bed. "This is an all-out war between Vince and Aldo."

"I want no part of it," she said.

"I agree." He patted his daughter's foot.

"Well, I don't. Here's a chance for you to earn some seed money." Sam came to his feet. Maybe they wouldn't be so quick to discount his opinion if he was standing. "Fifty thousand dollars is nothing to sneeze at. You can get a nice place, make sure Maddy has what she needs."

"With all due respect, Knight, you don't know what you're talking about," Brett stated.

Annie nodded in agreement.

"I've seen them argue. They go at it like two hungry dogs fighting over a bone, but that's just the way they are. They'd never hurt…" Sam's gaze fell to Brett's legs.

Brett took pity on him. "They might not lose control, but no amount of money is worth the anguish Annie would have to go through wondering if they might."

He had a point, and made Sam look as if he cared more for the money than Annie's feelings. "I was only trying to watch out for her." Sam sank back into the chair.

"We appreciate that," Brett said sincerely.

"Thanks for everything you did tonight, Sam," Annie said softly. "Why don't you go home? My dad can sit with me now."

She might just as well have told him to have a nice life.

CHAPTER FIFTEEN

"MOMMY, WHY ARE YOU sleeping in your dress?"

Annie cracked her eyes open and sat up. Her head ached and her breath was atrocious. Instead of waiting for morning to leave the hospital, she had asked her dad to take her home after Sam left. She couldn't bear the possibility of Aldo walking in on her while she was sleeping.

When they got back to the apartment, she'd barely had the energy to crawl into bed.

"Did the doctor make you better?" Without waiting for an answer, Maddy climbed into Annie's lap. "Did you like how Sam broke us out of that place? It was just like Mr. Toad's Wild Ride."

Sleep lost its hold completely, and Annie tucked Maddy closer in her lap, wrapping her baby in the folds of the thin blanket. "I'm sorry you were so scared."

"I was only scared when you fell down. I cried," Maddy said in a small voice. "But Sam took good care of me. And cr-r-rash! We were free."

"It might be time to think about leaving." They'd move somewhere safe and far away from Vegas, like

Wisconsin. Annie would never have to worry about Aldo Patrizio again. Or private investigators with expressive green eyes who butted into everyone else's business. She still couldn't get over the way Sam had taken Aldo's side.

"Grandpa said he was sorry last night, and I believed him. I want to stay here."

Choosing to ignore that remark, Annie rubbed her little darling's back.

Quick as a snap, Maddy shifted gears. "There's nothing to do here. I want to play cards. I like playing cards. Don't you like playing cards?"

Annie would like to laugh with Maddy over a game of cards. She'd like to be that carefree again. Life used to be as simple as eating, sleeping and doing the two things she loved most—playing cards and laughing with her dad. Annie closed her eyes. Was it that simple?

No. Her emotions weren't governed by a light switch. This would take time.

"Can we, Mommy?"

"We can play when we get home." Home. That was it. They'd collect their things and then go to the house in Henderson. Wisconsin could wait. Annie needed to find herself, and to do that she needed to go back to the beginning, back to the place where life had been simpler.

"I want to play every day," Maddy said dreamily.

"Me, too." Admitting it brought a smile to Annie's lips.

Her daughter sat up and reached for something on

the bedside table. "Mommy, did you bring these?" She fanned out the plastic strips. "One-two-three-four-five-six. When Grandpa wakes up we need to fix him, too." Band-Aids in hand, Maddy collapsed against her chest, clearly content.

Annie touched two of the Band-Aids. Her father must have brought them in after she'd fallen asleep. "I could use some of those myself."

With a solemn look, Maddy got right to fixing Annie. If only fixing her life was that easy. So much of it depended on Annie fixing herself first.

At least now she knew where to start.

THEY WERE GONE.

Midmorning, after showering and putting on the best of his shorts and polo shirts—his wardrobe needed updating—Sam had gone to the hospital, to find Annie's bed already occupied by another patient. He'd hurried over to Brett's apartment, only to find someone cleaning it for the next tenant.

Sam stood for a moment in the living room, looking for the decks of cards and piles of newspaper, but there was no trace of the Raye family, only the furniture that came with the place.

"What's the word on that game?" Sam asked Vince when he got him on his cell phone.

"Next week. I may not make it that long. My grandfather came to a planning meeting this morning and one of my staff quit."

"Hang in there." Sam, who'd been afraid Vince

would say it had been canceled, was instead relieved. Annie was going to play. She hadn't left town. Now all he had to do was find her.

She'd mentioned something about a house she and her father had bought. Was it too much to ask that Brett might still own it?

Back at his apartment, Sam booted up his computer and began to search for Brett Raye's home address. A smarter man might have let Annie move on without him, hoping that his life would return to an even keel without her constant surprises, but Sam had always been a glutton for punishment.

"THIS IS IT." Annie pulled into the driveway of the house in Henderson with Maddy. "Look at those colors."

The house had been painted soft white with red trim. The roof tiles were black. Her father had brought in mounds of rock and a gray fountain where they'd once had grass, giving the place a minimalistic, yet oddly welcoming appearance.

Maddy clapped her hands and giggled. "It looks like cards."

"Yes, it does." Annie rubbed one of the Band-Aids on the back of her hand. "I wonder what he did to the inside."

Her dad had the garage door open. Annie hurried to unbuckle Maddy and bring in their few things. Only then did she allow herself to explore her old home.

"Three bedrooms," Maddy said quietly. She gazed longingly at the bedroom that had been Annie's. "Did a princess live here?"

Annie swung her daughter into her arms and went to sit on the dusty canopy bed. "If we clean this up, a princess could live here."

Maddy stiffened. "Who?"

"I meant you, silly." Annie kissed her nose. "We can live here for a while." Annie wasn't sure she could live across the valley from Sam without seeking him out, and that would be emotional suicide. He just didn't understand her.

"Me," Maddy breathed, before climbing out of Annie's lap and reaching up to finger one dusty ruffle. "Can I go to school? I miss Mrs. Guichard."

If Annie had been sure they were staying, she'd have put Maddy in school that day. The pressure in her chest increased. "We have a lot of decisions to make."

Her daughter's face scrunched up. "I like school. Don't forget about school."

"I won't. Tell you what. Let's clean this room until it's sparkling and fit for a princess. And then we'll go to the store and buy you a Popsicle."

Maddy scrambled to the floor.

True to his word, her dad had kept the house in good shape and tastefully decorated, just not all that clean. Quality window treatments kept out the hot summer sun. For now, Annie opened the blinds to enjoy the sun, and flung open the windows to let in the fresh October breeze. She almost felt as if she was home.

At least, that's what she told herself later in the day when, sprawled on the floor with Maddy, next to a large poker table, she heard a truck rumble by. It might have been her imagination, but the truck sounded an awful lot like Sam's. But it couldn't have been, because it didn't stop.

Annie buried her face in her hands.

Brett walked into the room. "Are you okay?"

"I'm going to be fine." She tried to sound convincing without taking her hands from her face. "It's not like him to give up."

He pulled her to her feet, drew her into his arms and patted her head awkwardly.

"I'm not crying," Annie said, not ready to relinquish him yet. She could feel Maddy's curious gaze on her.

"Of course not." Her dad's voice was gruff, as if he was trying not to cry, too. "Want to tell me what's behind all this?"

Annie squeezed her eyes shut. She would not cry.

The doorbell rang.

"I better get that. You never know when someone might be running a good door-to-door deal on carpet cleaning." Her dad turned the handle and swung the door open on silent hinges. *"You?"*

Sam walked right past him to Annie.

"Sam!" Maddy popped up from her cards on the floor.

He reached down to touch Maddy's golden curls, never breaking eye contact with her mom.

"When did you get over the *flu?*" Annie demanded. "Or was that an act?"

Sam shook his head. "It was no act. We did kind of a Vulcan mind-meld last night, and Maddy cured me."

"She's a trooper," Annie's father said, a grin spreading across his face. "Come into the kitchen, puddin', and we'll have a Popsicle."

"Can Sam take me for a drive after?" Maddy hadn't stopped grinning up at her idol. "Vroom, vroom!"

"No." Annie barely had enough breath to answer. Sam wouldn't stop staring at her.

"How 'bout if Grandpa takes me to Tassels?"

"Double no." Annie got up and took several much-needed steps away from Sam. "I'm a bad mother."

"You're an excellent mom," Sam said.

"Maddy will be fine. Look how good you turned out." Her father's smile was so bright, it hurt to look at him.

The emotional roller coaster Annie had been on the past few days hit a corkscrew twist that short-circuited something inside her. In a shower of sparks, her fears came shooting out. "I'm not fine. I'm a failure. I peaked at age twelve and got conned by the first man who showed interest in me. I've been tossed in jail. Maddy's been taken to foster care. I had to move back in with my dad because I can't get a job. I'm being black-mailed into the only job prospect I have. And the sad part of it is that finance bores me. I can see my future stretching out before me—year after year of dull, predictable routine calculations!"

Two men and a little girl stared at her for several long moments.

"Well? Say something." Not that she wanted them to say anything. She'd much rather sink into the floor now that her insecurities were out in the open.

"What's so bad about the old ways?" Her father was so predictable.

"Have you ever considered that playing cards is what you were meant to do?" Sam ventured, his gaze dropping to Maddy when Annie scowled.

"There's no future in cards. A child needs an adult with regular job benefits so they can go to the doctor and get braces and have a mother home to cook dinner."

"I know a lot of dealers, pit bosses and casino owners who would disagree with that," Sam pointed out.

"And card counters," Brett added.

"And little girls," Maddy breathed.

Annie shook her head. No one understood. "I can't decide on a future until I know who I am. I'm not like everyone else. I'm not normal, and Maddy deserves better than that."

"Maybe you are normal and everyone else is odd." Sam's voice was gentle, magnetic. "You've buried yourself, hoping to fit in. Clearly, that's not working. Why are you so afraid to be yourself?"

"You want me to add to the list?"

"No. I want you to start living your life to the fullest."

"That's rich, coming from you."

Sam ignored her. "Don't be afraid to step up—"

"You don't even like the real me."

He shook his head. "I might just be able to love you. I've been drifting through life waiting for someone to fix me. Then you and Maddy came along and gave me what I needed."

Annie couldn't move. He had not just said—

"We accept your proposal." Annie's dad inched closer to her. "Don't let him get away."

And Sam had accused her of a pity kiss? Reality came crashing back in. This was Sam. A guy who wouldn't even talk to his sister. "Dad, he wasn't proposing. Sam's more the one-night stand type." Annie couldn't take another one of his rejections. "From the moment we met he had his own interests at heart."

Sam's eyebrows dropped and he looked ready for battle. "How do you figure?"

Her father pointed to the door. "If you need more privacy, you'll have to take it outside."

"You knew I needed that Slotto job, and after everything I told you last night, all you could think about was money," Annie said, more than willing to spell it out for Sam. "When I fall in love, it's going to be with someone who's home every night at dinnertime, a man who mows the lawn and remembers my birthday."

"June twentieth." As her eyes widened, Sam shrugged. "I did your background check. And don't try to say we're all wrong for each other. You just said you hate boring and predictable."

"You're twisting my words."

"You're doing a good job of it all on your own." He glared at her. "We've only known each other a few days. I'm trying to figure out what's best for all of us."

Annie forced herself to look Sam in the eye, hoping that if she did, he'd realize how unfair the relationship he was proposing was to her. "I need more than guesses. Besides, you can't even take care of yourself, much less someone as messed up as me.".

Sam tossed his hands in the air. "Call me when you shake this *flu* and admit what you want isn't what you've been telling yourself all these years."

Annie stared miserably at the door long after he'd gone, wondering if she'd made the right decision.

"ANNIE," HER FATHER SAID softly as he slipped into her bedroom later that night. "Why didn't you tell me this sooner?"

"What?" She had dumped far too much tonight to sort through what he was talking about. She sat up in bed and turned the light on.

"That you were unhappy. That you've been unhappy for a long time."

"Frank was an embezzler." And a terrible husband and father. He hadn't tried to call Maddy once since he'd been arrested.

"But you were unhappy before that."

Annie nodded.

"You were unhappy after you beat Aldo."

Annie nodded again. "After that it was hard to be a kid. The other seventh graders all seemed so…stupid. They worried about what they wore and if they were chewing the right gum. I couldn't blend in. My father had almost been killed."

"That wasn't your fault."

"You know, you've been saying that for years, but I'm the one who played. You were just my driver."

His eyebrows knitted a line across his forehead. "It was entirely my fault. I took a side bet with Vince."

"He was barely older than me. I had no idea you'd hit such lows."

Brett's sad smile seemed to say he agreed with her. "He was a pain in the ass who wouldn't leave me alone. He was confident his grandfather would win. I kept increasing the bet, hoping to scare him off, but he was determined."

If her dad thought this would make Annie feel better, he was mistaken. "*Vince was a kid.* You had no right to take that bet. What would you have done if I'd lost?"

"Skipped town. Laid low. Who would have held me to it if you lost?"

"His dad certainly took the bet seriously."

"Unfortunately." Brett shifted his feet, as if remembering the blows, and Annie's anger melted away. "I think he took it out on me rather than on Vince. In that respect, it was the least I could do for the kid. And Aldo did honor the bet, plus pay my medical expenses and his fifty thousand dollars. I figure he lost more than six hundred thousand bucks."

"I never questioned how I had so much in my trust fund after buying the house." Annie frowned. "Why didn't you tell me this before?"

"Would you have understood? Would you have forgiven Vince's father?"

"No." On both counts. "I'm not sure I can ever forgive him, or any of the rest of his family."

"That's not a good way to live, puddin'. Anger eats you up."

Annie nodded. "Is that why I feel so empty? I don't know if I have anything left." For Maddy. For herself. And now Sam was gone.

"Puddin'..." Brett sat on the edge of her bed and held out his right hand.

Annie carefully moved over next to him and leaned into his embrace. They'd each made mistakes, but forgiveness was part of being a family.

IN THE HOPE THAT ANNIE would come to her senses and want to see him, Sam caught up on all pending background checks, helped Vince locate the owner of a property on the edge of town, and went shopping for clothes during daylight hours. He felt as if he were a recovering vampire.

Sam steered clear of families, but didn't pass out or otherwise make a fool of himself. Still, he looked over his shoulder a lot, expecting to see Annie, but she was no longer following him. How could he miss her so much?

"She's still going to play you, right?" Sam demanded of Vince at the end of another long day without her. There were only three days left until the game.

Vince loosened his tie as he climbed the stairs to Sam's apartment. They'd become like two old geezers, keeping each other company at night in front of the television while they nursed a beer. They'd both lost their taste for Tassels. "If you want to see Annie, go find her."

"I already have." He'd driven by Brett's house in Henderson again this afternoon, caught sight of Annie inside the living room, and nearly stood on the brakes. Instead, he'd come back here, buried his head in his pillow and tried to smell strawberries. "If she wants to see me, she knows where I am."

"Oh, that's mature." Vince grabbed a beer from the fridge. "Why don't you put a note in her school locker and ask her to go steady?"

Annie needed time to make some key decisions about her life. Only how would Sam know what progress she was making if he didn't ask her?

The game seemed too far away. "Vince, when you play, you've got to lose," he told him. Annie's fragile ego would never survive a loss.

"I'm starting to question your sanity. You do realize if I lose I have to leave the Sicilian, which means you're out of a job, too?"

It didn't matter to Sam. He'd find something else, and Vince could easily land a job in casino management. "She needs this more than you do. You don't have a kid to feed."

"Marry her and you can support her kid. That way we all win." Vince turned on the television. "What games are on tonight?"

Marriage. Sam nodded, not freaked out about the idea as he would have been a few weeks ago. Vince was right. This way everyone would win. "Raising a kid is tough alone. My sister has two girls."

Grabbing his shoulder with a viselike grip, Vince

shook Sam. "In three days, I'm going to play to win. And when I do, you're going to get your second chance with Annie."

"But she's better than you," Sam said with absolute certainty. "There's no way you can win. It would be better to call off the game."

Vince swore and sat on the couch. "You know nothing about my grandfather, do you?"

CHAPTER SIXTEEN

"MOMMY, WHY DO YOU HAVE all the chips?" Maddy whined. "I counted just like Grandpa said."

Annie exchanged a smile with her dad, who'd been playing the role of dealer. They'd been home several days and each day Annie grew stronger. Surprisingly, so did her peace of mind, despite the blackjack game with Vince looming on the horizon, and the longing she suffered at night lying in bed thinking about Sam.

"What did Grandpa say about holding?" Brett asked his youngest protégé.

"Don't take cards at seventeen," Maddy said solemnly.

"So why did you ask for a card? You had seventeen," Annie pointed out.

"'Cause the highest number should win! I wanted more cards." Maddy popped out of her chair in a huff and collapsed on the carpet, but not before snatching the remote control and strategically placing herself in front of the television. "Stupid game. I don't want to play anymore."

Annie collected their cards and passed them to her father. "I guess it's time to make dinner."

He tapped her shoulder when she walked past. "You're back in the groove."

"I fleeced a five-year-old. That hardly puts me on top of my game."

He didn't disagree. "Why don't I make some phone calls? I think you're ready for the next level."

"I'm not going to a casino." Annie gently disengaged herself and went to find something to cook. "I know I have to play this game, but I'm not taking his money or his job."

"I told you I'd give you money."

"I'm not going to lose your money." There wasn't much in the refrigerator except hamburger. The milk barely covered the bottom of the plastic gallon container.

Brett followed Annie and leaned on the counter that separated the family room from the kitchen. "What if I told you most of the money I have is yours?"

"Is this like a will or something?" There was one can of soup in the cupboard. How many days had it been since she'd gone to the grocery store? Annie frowned, trying to remember how much money she had left in her purse.

"No, I..." He climbed onto a bar stool. "You know how I made a side bet with Vince?"

"Yes." Soon she'd have to face reality and go out and find a job.

"That wasn't the only side bet I made."

That got Annie's complete attention. "What are you saying?"

"I'd been making side bets on your games for years. They just got larger the summer you turned twelve." He was trying to reassure her, but he couldn't quite manage a smile.

"How much larger?"

"Large enough."

"Large enough that you would have had enough to pay off Vince?" Something cold churned in her belly. They'd lived hand-to-mouth, watching every dime, while her father squirreled away money?

"No."

Annie sagged with relief against the kitchen counter.

"But I made enough to invest and generate a modest income. And then after that summer I didn't feel so boxed in when I played, so worried that every dollar I lost should have gone to feed you." He scratched his ear. "Financial freedom can do a lot to clear your mind. And a clear mind is damn hard to beat."

"I wouldn't know anything about that." Having been counting pennies since the police had shown up at her door and frozen her bank accounts in their quest to nail Frank.

"But you did. As a kid it was all just a game, something you enjoyed doing. You were competitive and you won for the joy of winning. If you'd known I was risking our nest egg every time you played, you would have lost. And now you're broke and you can't win because you need the money. If you play Vince it'll end in disaster."

"Thanks for the confidence." Annie drew herself up. Wisconsin beckoned.

"I do have faith in you," her dad said. "I screwed up and robbed you of your childhood. I want to make up for that. Don't worry about money. I have enough. You can stay here with Maddy until you figure out what you want."

When had he turned into a model parent?

"It's what you want, isn't it?" he prompted when she didn't answer.

Was it wrong to let her dad do this? He did owe it to her, but it seemed an awful lot like mooching.

"Then it's settled. Come here and give your old man a hug, puddin'."

Neither one of them mentioned the upcoming game. Annie was in a position to back out of it now. But she was her father's daughter, and some small part of her didn't want to.

"YOU WANTED TO SEE ME?" Aldo sat in the chair Paulo had helped him into when Sam Knight had shown up requesting a meeting.

"Yes." The tall man came down the foyer steps to shake his hand with a strength of youth Aldo envied. "How is your wife?"

"She's the same." It could have been far, far worse. Unfortunately, Aldo couldn't shake the feeling of loss. The episode had taken any hope he'd had of his wife's recovery, or of Vince's.

"I'm sorry." Sam sat with a heaviness that made Aldo believe he truly was sorry.

"What can I do for you?" If the old Italian had to

guess, he'd say something had gone wrong with Sam's plans for Miss Raye. Aldo had seen the way the younger man looked at her in the hospital.

"This blackjack game between Annie and Vince...I want you to cancel it."

He should tell him to get out. "How well do you know my grandson?"

"I've pieced together enough to know he needs you as much as you need him."

"You're not wealthy?"

"No, sir."

"And yet you've never gone hungry. There was always something on the dinner table."

Sam frowned. "What does this have to do with Vince?"

"Struggling for survival breeds character. You tend to trust those you've gone through hell with." He and Rosalie. He'd thought he and Vince, too, but now he knew better.

"In the war—"

"Vince trusts you. He told me he couldn't fire a gun. You protected Vince. How else would he have made it home alive?" Aldo owed this man a tremendous debt if he had honor.

"Only that first day—"

Aldo leaned forward. "Did he pay for your loyalty?"

"No." The private investigator was firm. "I watched out for him because he's a good man."

"You still watch out for him or else you wouldn't be here." It was as Aldo suspected. Sam would understand. "Your father tracked runaways. You know that sometimes a night on the street is enough to scare the fragile ones into reaching out for help or realizing a truth about their situation. My Vince…" Aldo swallowed. "He was gone only a few hours before being found. He's never struggled. You and I have made sure of that. We meant well. But we were wrong. He's never asked for help, has never acknowledged he lacks the skills to make a name for himself, and yet…"

When Sam said nothing, Aldo sighed. "You know I speak the truth. What Vince needs is to build his life from nothing. On his own."

Sam sat forward. "And yet you still hope he'll come around without having to cast him out." The private investigator was too good at reading people.

"Even when hope was slim. I will not cancel the game."

"Vince doesn't want to disappoint you."

"I set these conditions to build Vince's character. What he thinks of me no longer matters." Aldo's gaze drifted out the window.

"If you force Vince to go through with this, you may never get him back."

"I'm used to losing people," Aldo murmured.

"Maybe you don't have to be." And that's when Sam offered an interesting side bet.

ANNIE SAT IN A CHAIR by the window while she smoothed Maddy's hair, her child asleep in her arms. Earlier, Maddy had woken from a nightmare about evil princesses and guns. Annie needed to add Band-Aids to the shopping list, as this was the second night her baby had awakened in a panic since they'd moved to Henderson.

The moon was vying with the lights from the Strip. Annie preferred the moonlight. She was drawn to the quiet.

Her head rolled back. Who was she kidding? She missed the energy of the casinos. She missed the crowds. And, yes, she missed Sam.

Just thinking about him brought a smile to her lips. The image of him scrunching into her car, the surprise on his face when she'd confronted him at the 7-Eleven, the way he'd looked at her when he'd walked into this house… She yearned to talk to him.

She wouldn't think about his intense lovemaking, how he'd held her tenderly while kissing her so possessively it took her breath away.

Annie glanced over at her purse for her cell phone, just as Maddy stirred.

No, it was better to focus on her family and herself now, tucking away memories of Sam where they belonged—with other lost dreams.

IN THE LAST GOLDEN RAYS of sunlight, Annie wheeled the trash can out to the curb, with Maddy skipping around her. After she'd deposited the can, she held her little girl by the arms and whirled her around in a helicopter ride. Their laughter, a bittersweet sound, reached Sam, despite the fact that he was parked six houses down. Annie and Maddy seemed so carefree.

He was happy for them, and yet he wished he could paint himself into the picture. It was hard to be patient.

And then there was the dilemma of the card game. Much as Sam didn't want to agree with Mr. Patrizio, he did. Vince had issues that needed resolution. Some might call it tough love, but not when your grandson was twenty-seven. Still, Mr. Patrizio needed family, and Sam had a compromise in mind. If only Annie would agree.

His phone rang. Sam glanced at the display and answered the call. "What's up, sis?"

"You're kidding! You actually picked up the phone?" Theresa wasn't about to cut him a break, and Sam expected no less. "It's about time. I was almost ready to drive up to Las Vegas and find you."

His sister could do it, too. Sam wasn't the only one their dad had trained how to find people.

"I talked to your assistant a week ago, and she said you'd call," Theresa added. "Didn't you get any of my messages?"

"Don't blame Annie. I've been an ass. I'm sure you can come up with more imaginative names. I deserve the lecture." Sam had nothing better to do while he sat and watched over Annie. He relaxed back into the truck seat. "Why don't you tell me about the girls and your plans for Christmas? What day do you want me there?"

"Why do I have a suspicion this is all a dream?"

He ignored her. "You probably need something fixed around the house. Go ahead and make a list."

"Who are you and what have you done with my brother?"

A car pulled up in front of Brett's house and a slightly overweight man in a bowling shirt got out, along with a very tall, very thin man. Rings glinted in the fading sunset. The cardsharps were paying a visit the night before the game?

"I've got to go."

"But we haven't talked about—"

"Later." Sam wasn't much for skulking in the bushes, but he was going to find out what was up.

"ERNIE, REMIND ME TO GET you some decent cologne for Christmas." Annie waved her cards in front of her nose. That, combined with his new fondness for cigars, made her father's friend quite aromatic.

"The ladies like me just the way I am." He smoothed down the collar of his bowling shirt.

"I think he smells wonderful," Maddy said, blinking up at him.

"See?" Ernie gave Annie a superior look.

Maddy giggled, kicking her feet beneath the table. "Just like a skunk."

Everyone laughed as Ernie said, "Charming child. Let's play."

"I like skunks. And pretty rings." Maddy eyed Chauncey's bejeweled fingers. "This one looks like a perfect princess ring." Maddy tapped a silver one with a jeweled crest on Chauncey's pinky. It might have been Annie's imagination, but Chauncey didn't look quite so haggard tonight.

"That's a man's ring, honey, and the only skunk

you've seen is on television." Annie wanted to soften Maddy's comments. Ernie and Chauncey were like beloved uncles to her. Playing with the old men gave Annie a sense of belonging she hadn't experienced in years. Their stories made her laugh, and their banter included Maddy, too. And they'd been willing to come to her rescue with Aldo. If only Annie could get paid for being with them, life would be good.

They'd been playing for nearly an hour. Annie kept slipping Maddy chips when she wasn't looking, so her daughter could stay in the game. Her little cardsharp had been unable to shake her fixation with accumulating cards. Finally, they let her keep the dealt cards in a pile, in an effort to keep Maddy happy.

Something out the front window caught Annie's eye. But it was dark outside and she couldn't see a thing beyond the glass. It must have been a passing car. She stayed alert anyway, winning a hand and calling out the count while her father dished out chips.

This time she saw more than a shadow, jerking when she recognized the face that had haunted her for the past week.

"Gentlemen, it's break time." Annie pushed away from the table.

"What does that mean?" Maddy asked.

"Time to go to the bathroom and get something to eat or drink, puddin'," her father explained with an inquisitive look Annie's way.

While the men and Maddy drifted toward the kitchen,

Annie slipped out the front door, her heart leaping as it hadn't for nearly a week. "Get out of those bushes, buster."

The bushes beneath the living room windows quivered.

"Sam, I know you're out there." She couldn't be wrong, could she? What silly hope she'd had shrank in the silence.

Until a tall body emerged from the greenery.

"Sam!" That sounded desperate. She tried again, with authority. "Sam." Better. "What are you doing here?"

"I was following the cardsharps to make sure they weren't harassing anyone else." He twisted, squeezing out from between the house and the shrubbery.

Annie didn't believe him, but was willing to let it slide just to be near him again. As Sam came to stand before her, she had to stop herself from grinning like a lovestruck idiot. Time apart had taken away none of his appeal.

"How are you?" he asked when she didn't say anything else.

"Better, I think."

"Have you decided what you're going to do?"

"Kind of. Not really." She laughed self-consciously. "I'm taking a father-sponsored sabbatical from work until I decide where I go next."

"Good for you."

She wished Sam wouldn't smile like that, as if she'd

given the correct answer and he was moving her to the head of the class.

"About the blackjack game tomorrow... If you win, you know Aldo's going to toss Vince out."

"I know." Why were they talking about the game? She wanted to kiss him. It was a stupid impulse that would definitely lead to stupider things.

"Vince is nervous."

And Sam didn't think Annie was?

"Vince doesn't count cards. He's at a disadvantage and he...he needs this more than you do."

The reason for Sam's visit sank in with a bone-jarring thud. No. She'd backed into the wall and hit her head. "You want me to lose."

"I just want you to know what's at stake. It doesn't sound as if you need Aldo's job." Sam took a step closer. "You're a better player. There'll be other games. If you could just..."

"You want me to lose," Annie repeated. In all the scenarios she'd played out in her mind if she saw Sam again, this wasn't even close. She wouldn't even give him points for believing she could win. How could Sam ask her to lose? And yet it all made sense. He worked for Vince.

Sam reached for her. "Annie, you don't know—"

She batted his hands away. "I do know. I've had enough of the Patrizios and their selfishness. You can tell Vince I'm coming tomorrow, and I'm coming to win." Blinking back tears, Annie banged her way back inside, slamming the door behind her.

Four pairs of eyes turned her way.

Annie stomped over to the windows and closed the heavy drapes. "The count is plus two. Let's play."

CHAPTER SEVENTEEN

UNCOMFORTABLE IN THE LAP of luxury, Sam sat beneath a really ugly Picasso and waited for Annie to arrive. There was still time to fix this mess, if by some chance miracles happened. He'd blown it big-time with her, so much so he'd second-guessed coming at all tonight. He was only trying to protect both her and Vince, but she hadn't wanted to hear him out. His presence might piss Annie off and ruin her focus. Then again, she might beat Vince in a deadly, take-no-prisoners win. In the end, Sam needed to be here for Annie, regardless of the outcome.

Vince stood at the window, his dark suit matching his grim expression, staring out over the Strip as if it was the last time he'd get to see chance at such a spectacular view. Any attempts Sam made at conversation had been wasted after he tried again to get Vince to back out of the game.

The elder Patrizio was sitting with his wife. The only greeting he'd made was a nod of his head as he closed the bedroom door upon Sam's arrival. Once Mrs. Patrizio's vitals had stabilized, she'd returned to the Sicilian in the same comatose state she'd been in for months.

The doorbell rang and Paulo went to answer it,

moving with a stately grace for one so large. And then Annie entered, wearing a white halter dress with a pink ribbon beneath her breasts and pink polka-dot flip-flops. Her hair was tousled, as if she'd just climbed out of bed. Her lips were the chaste shade of deep pink roses. She was neither a soccer mom nor a pirate.

As far as Sam was concerned, she was perfect. He stood, as self-conscious in his new clothes as if it were prom night. "Hello." He raised the bag of food he'd picked up from McDonald's.

Annie stared down her nose at Sam from the raised marble landing, and then looked away. "Are you ready, Vince?"

Not the best of beginnings. Sam tossed the bag on the sleek coffee table.

"Of course. I'll get my grandfather."

Aldo must have been listening. He opened the door from his bedroom and walked in, his steps slow and careful. Sam suspected Vince's failure would crush the old man, but knew he'd stand by his word to banish his grandson.

"You don't have to go through with this," Sam said, taking a moment to look each of them in the eye, willing them to make the right choice.

"Miss Raye, you will be the dealer." Aldo's eyebrows met over his nose as he scowled.

Not to be outdone, Vince scowled, too. The Patrizio family resemblance was strongest when things didn't go their way. The dealer held the advantage, and Vince had been counting on that.

"I will not represent the house. Especially not the Sicilian." Annie breezily situated herself in a chair across from the dealer's shoe, and crossed her legs, a flip-flop dangling precariously from one slender foot.

"I knew there was a reason I liked you, Annie," Vince said. "Since this game is between the two of us, we should make the rules."

Aldo's brows dropped thunderously low.

"We'll play by *my* rules. Five-hundred-dollar chips and a four-deck shoe." Annie's chin was up, daring anyone to challenge her terms.

Despite the seriousness of the event, Sam couldn't help smiling. Come hell or high water, he'd win her back. He couldn't imagine life without Annie.

"You'll play with hundred-dollar chips and a double-deck shoe," Aldo said darkly, gripping the back of a club chair and holding it for support as he shuffled around to sit. "You will not give the dealer the advantage of so many decks."

"Your grandson is going to lose and lose quickly," Annie said. "I don't have all evening. My daughter is with a babysitter." And then she gave Aldo a familiar smile, the one she used on Sam right before she knew she was getting her way. "We'll compromise with five-hundred-dollar chips, a twenty-five-hundred-dollar maximum bet and a double deck…or I walk."

While Aldo looked as if he was going to pop a vein, Sam was lost in the jargon.

Vince took pity on him. "The fewer the decks, the

better the odds for the card counter. The higher the minimum bet, the quicker to a bust."

Okay, now Sam remembered that Brett had mentioned something about the number of decks and the odds. "If fewer decks are better, why don't you want the double deck?" Sam asked Annie, but she stacked her twenty chips as if she hadn't heard him.

"She's giving me back the advantage she takes away by the high minimum," Vince clarified. At least he was still acknowledging Sam's existence.

"That's my girl," Sam said. There was hope for this game yet.

"Where?" Annie looked over her shoulder. Her gaze bounced off Sam before she returned her attention to her chips.

Sam felt a decided chill.

ANNIE NEEDED SOMETHING with a kick—coffee, a shot of tequila—anything to take the edge off her anxiety. She'd even settle for one of those syrupy energy drinks. She'd taken her father's advice and picked out something new to wear that inspired confidence, but a great outfit took a girl only so far. The rest had to come from chutzpah.

Good thing she'd brought some. Annie had small, round, flesh-covered Band-Aids on the back of each hand. She rubbed her thumbs over them for luck. She'd come a long way in the past week. She liked playing cards again, enjoyed calculating the odds in her head, and took great pleasure in winning. Annie owned this table.

As long as she ignored Aldo's abominable mood and

Sam's distracting presence. What was he doing here? She was still furious at him for wanting her to throw the game.

Her gaze drifted back to Sam. He caught her looking, darn it. The dark green polo shirt he wore brought out the color in his eyes. She loved his eyes. They were so expressive. *Whoa.* Sam was on the side of the enemy.

Vince had finished shuffling, and loaded the shoe. Annie placed a chip out on the felt and the game began. She was dealt a stiff hand, a four and a ten. Vince had an eight showing. She had to take a hit, and received a six.

"I'll stay."

Vince flipped over a ten. "Eighteen."

Suppressing a whoop of joy, Annie turned over her cards. "Twenty. Pay up." A little cockiness would rattle her opponent.

The count was zero, since the positive from four and six were countered by the negatives of two tens, and Vince's eight was neutral. Vince was now down five hundred dollars of his ten-thousand-dollar stake, but the odds were even between the house and Annie at zero. She left a five-hundred-dollar chip out there.

Aldo didn't look quite as sour as a moment before. Vince wore a blank poker face. Annie only allowed herself to glance at Sam out of the corner of her eye, but every time he moved he incited a memory of a touch, a kiss. They made perfect sense physically.

How could she want to be with someone who didn't

have her best interests at heart? It was Frank all over again.

After over an hour of play, Annie was up seven thousand dollars and her back was stiff. With just the two of them, the rounds went fast, and the cards had to be shuffled frequently.

While Vince shuffled, Annie excused herself and went to the bathroom. It was next to Aldo's bedroom. She turned on the light and closed the door, but didn't flip on the fan. She didn't need to go, she'd just wanted to hear what Vince and Aldo thought of the game. It was an old trick of her father's.

"You will lose in the next few hands," Aldo said.

"I'm always willing to do whatever makes you happy."

"This is ridiculous." Sam's voice. "You need each other now more than—"

"I can fight my own battles, Sam," Vince said, cutting him off.

It was just like Sam to leap to the defense of the underdog. Annie would have smiled…if he was defending her.

"I could beat this girl. She's nothing anymore," Aldo said. "If she cracked a nail, she'd lose her concentration."

O-kay. She'd thought Aldo respected her talent, but his comments pretty much killed that notion. He really was a petty, lonely old man. The fear she'd had of him all these years ebbed.

"She's the same nothing who took you before. It doesn't look as if she's lost her touch. If you want to play her, step right in and play for me." Vince's voice shook with anger.

"Perhaps I will." There was an unexplained sadness in his tone.

"This is out of control." Sam again. "I say we end it here. Declare a truce. Forget the stakes."

Silence.

For a moment, Annie could believe Sam only wanted peace among all parties involved, that he'd been honest when he suggested she had the least to lose.

"Or you can play on until there's only one man standing," Sam added.

One man. If Sam thought she was going to lose, he had another thing coming. Vince Patrizio was going down. And then she'd call Aldo's bluff. Power surged through her veins. She would beat them both.

Annie came out of the bathroom with a purposeful *snap-snap* of her flip-flops. She sat down and put five chips on the table, the maximum bet. It was time to end this. "I'm ready for something more challenging. Are you?"

"Annie." Sam moved into a chair next to hers. "What are you doing?"

She wouldn't be hurt that he cared more for Vince than for her. "I'm a busy woman. I don't have time for these petty games." It was a stupid move. The deck was fresh and there was no count. The cards could go either way.

Vince dealt and flipped over a jack. Not good.

"Twenty-one." Annie had a natural, a ten and an ace.

A three brought Vince to a stiff thirteen. He had to take a card. He dealt himself a two. Fifteen. Aldo's grandson had to take another card. A seven. Busted.

Annie released a breath she hadn't known she was holding. Vince was left with only one chip. The count was negative one. The odds from the cards were ever so slightly in Vince's favor, but Annie could outlast him. She placed a chip on the table.

"Let's not draw this out," Vince said. "I don't care how much you've won or how much I've lost. It wasn't your money to begin with. Let's play all or nothing on this hand."

It was a gutsy play, but one Annie didn't have to accept. She had Vince in her sights. Aldo knew it and was smiling, but it was a sad smile of a man about to lose something precious.

Sam was right.

"WAIT." In desperation, Sam leaned closer to Annie. "I need to talk to you."

She stiffened. "No."

He grabbed Annie's arm and stood, dragging her all the way out to the penthouse lobby. He had to make her see the consequences of a win on everyone's long-term happiness. "You owe me."

"How do you figure?" Annie demanded, rounding on Sam as soon as he let her go and the suite door slammed shut behind them.

"I drove a car through a wall to get you to the hospital that night."

She crossed her arms and looked every bit the exasperating, stubborn blonde he'd been missing.

"I comforted Maddy when she was scared and thought you were dead."

Annie tapped her foot, adorned with pink polish and a silver toe ring.

"Forget about favors and who owes who. I'm between a rock and a hard place on this one. I want both of you to win." Sam reached for her hand, but Annie stepped back with a swish of her skirt. "Vince is difficult, sure, but he's the only one who stood by me when I needed a friend. And you. There are so many things I want to share with you, including a future with that wonderful daughter of yours."

She narrowed her eyes. "It's a game, Sam. There can only be one winner."

"So tell me…" Sam drew a deep breath "…why does it have to be you?"

She opened her mouth…and then closed it again. Annie was seldom speechless.

"I know you. You aren't going to take Mr. Patrizio's money or his job. You've already proved that you're back and better than ever. You've already won and I love you for it."

Her eyes widened.

"When you walked in that door tonight, I looked up and saw you. Just you—Annie. For the first time, you weren't hiding." Sam took her hands in his and kissed the back of each one, where she'd been fixed by Maddy. "You've got so much going for you, why do you need this? You've got your dad and Maddy and me. Mr. Patrizio is scared to lose Vince and Vince is scared of losing his grandfather. Neither one of them can say that to the other. If you win, they'll never get that chance."

Annie stared up at him with those baby blue eyes that were capable of showing incredible love and fiery anger. But now they were cold, assessing, as if she was weighing what to do next.

"I couldn't let you take that job at Slotto, because you would have died there. They would have sucked the life right out of you. I knew it wasn't the job for you when I first saw you in disguise, all buttoned up with those tacky pearls." Sam considered it a small victory that Annie hadn't pulled her hands away. He had to prove once and for all that he did know what was best for her. "You don't need this. You're here more to thumb your nose in my face than win this game." With effort, he let Annie go. "If you can't see that, then I guess you were right. I'm not the man for you and I never will be."

She stood frozen. Not a good sign. It meant she was overthinking, and when she did that, Sam lost.

He took a step back, then an agonizing two more. She didn't move to stop him. Nothing he'd said had proved he cared about her happiness. He'd failed.

"Goodbye, Annie." Sam reached for the elevator button. "Have a nice life."

It seemed an eternity passed.

"Sam," Annie whispered, as the elevator doors slid open.

But she didn't say more, so he backed into the elevator.

The doors began to close. This was it. He'd called her bluff and lost it all—Saturday nights in bed with Annie, Sunday mornings with the newspaper spread across the living-room floor, reading the comics with Maddy.

"Sam!" Annie stumbled forward when the doors had inches to go.

His arm shot between them and they jerked open. And then Annie was in his arms, kissing him as if she never wanted to stop. Her kiss was ripe with promise and Sam was sure he was smiling like a love-struck fool when they came up for air.

"You're right. I don't care about the game." She pulled back. "But how can I lose now? Aldo will be furious."

Sam shook his head. "I tried to tell you last night about a deal I made with Mr. Patrizio."

"A deal?" Annie retreated a step, but Sam didn't let her go.

"It was the only thing I could think of that would give those two space yet keep them together."

She narrowed her eyes. "What deal?"

"If there was no game—no winner—Mr. Patrizio would give Vince ten percent of the money he'd need to build a casino somewhere else."

"So little? How could Vince possibly make that work?"

"He'd have to stand on his own."

Comprehension dawned in Annie's eyes, and Sam took the opportunity to tug her closer.

"Wait." She splayed her hands against his chest. "I'll do this on two conditions. One, we do it my way. And two…" Her smile was positively wicked. "I'd like to go into business with you."

"You want to be a private eye?" He had something more personal in mind than a business deal. Marriage, babies…

"Not exactly. I want to create a security agency that specializes in protecting casinos from gamblers who swing the odds in their favor."

Sam tilted his head as he studied her to make sure it was Annie who was off-kilter, not him. "Like card counters? Aren't you selling out?"

"Not really." There was a glint in her eye that sent Sam's heart racing. "I want to learn how the pros do it first, then figure out how to even the odds back for the casinos. They'll pay for that."

"So, you'll be dabbling on the dark side but working for the good guys." That was so like Annie Sam had to laugh. "I'm flattered you'd want me to be your *partner*."

She ran her hands up his chest to fix the collar of his shirt. "If it doesn't work out, we can always resort to locating runaways. You have a knack for finding people. You're just not too stealthy when you find them."

He'd never live down the fact that he'd been caught

in her bushes. "Sometimes it's not stealth as much as the technique when you find them."

"You need to work on that, too." But her gaze was filled with tenderness.

She'd left him no choice but to seal their deal with another kiss on those clever lips of hers.

"I was miserable without you," Sam said, his arm draped over her shoulder as she rang the doorbell to Mr. Patrizio's penthouse.

"Don't let me chase you away again."

"Never. Is it too much to hope that you'll become the most predictable person in my life?"

"If there's one thing you can be sure of, it's that I'll always be one step ahead of you." But Annie turned when she said it and touched Sam's cheek.

When Paulo opened the door, Annie entered alone, as if she owned the place. Then she spun on a flip-flop and beckoned for Sam to follow.

"What's the holdup?" Mr. Patrizio demanded. Then he took in the grin on Sam's face and scoffed.

"Are you ready?" Vince didn't seem happy, either. He didn't look at Sam, probably assuming he'd lost his only ally at the table.

"Deal," Annie commanded, sitting down.

Sam's smile gave out at the same time as his knees. He dropped unceremoniously into his chair.

"My way." She dropped her chin and shot Sam a look that reminded him of their bargain. Vince dealt what Sam hoped would be the last hand, with the queen of hearts showing.

Cool as any professional at work, Annie slipped a peek at the corner of her cards. "Hit me," she said, asking for another card. It was a six. With a heavy sigh, she passed a hand over her cards.

What did she have? Sam barely stopped himself from snatching up her cards to find out.

Vince turned over his hole card slowly. A seven. He blew out a tense breath. "Dealer has to stay."

If Annie had eighteen or higher, she'd win.

"Busted. You win." Annie pushed her cards facedown into the center of the table. She was trying to look disappointed, but Sam caught that mischievous sparkle in her eye.

Mr. Patrizio made a frustrated noise, while Vince sat back and thrust his arms to the ceiling. "Yes!"

"Wait a minute," Mr. Patrizio said, leaning over to look at Annie's cards. "You had two tens and you took a hit? You would have won."

With a simpering smile on her face, Annie batted her eyelashes at the old man. "Is that what I did? I must have broken a nail and lost my concentration."

"You can't throw the game." Mr. Patrizio drew up short, as if realizing the implications of the situation.

Coming to her feet, Annie spoke to Vince, "I don't know about you, but I'm done playing his game. Neither one of us won at cards, but I think we won something more important." And then she headed toward the door.

Vince blinked, as if not yet aware of what had just happened.

"Remember our agreement," Sam said to Mr. Patrizio, before hurrying out the door so he could sweep Annie off her feet.

EPILOGUE

"DAD, MY HANDS ARE TOO small to palm the cards. I can't do it," Annie protested. Nearly six months after Annie had played Vince, a group of women had been working together to control their play at blackjack tables in Las Vegas, and the Knight-Raye Agency had been hired to stop them.

"Fine." Her dad gave in. His idea was to befriend and infiltrate the female group. "I'll have to send Ernie and Chauncey out to do it. They're used to wearing wigs."

"*Dad.* I don't think Chauncey could pull off a dress."

"He's got nice legs for a man his age," her dad grumbled. He retreated to the outer office, which was large enough to accommodate a poker table with a well-worn felt cover.

Annie and Sam had recruited her father and his friends because of their vast knowledge of card gaming, but sometimes their ideas were as old as their orthopedic shoes—or in her father's case, a pair of well-worn Birkenstocks.

Annie barely had time to glance out her window at the Vegas skyline before Sam and Maddy barreled into the office, full of smiles. Sam had chaperoned Maddy's kindergarten class on a trip to the Lied Discovery Children's Museum.

"Mommy, I went grocery shopping and built a sand dune and drove the space shuttle." Maddy was on a roll before she'd even passed through the door. "There was a room. It didn't have a princess bed. But I made the sun go up and down."

"That was really cool," Sam said. He had what looked like jelly fingerprints on the cuff of his shorts, and something suspiciously like chocolate on his shirt. He sank into one of Annie's leather office chairs.

She handed Sam his messages, one of which was from Vince, who was struggling to put together financing for his casino. He was still trying to get along with his grandfather on a strictly nonbusiness basis, but Sam was afraid it would take an act of congress to bring that about.

"A good day?" Annie asked, dropping a kiss on Maddy's crown when her darling hugged her.

"Oh, Daddy and I had a good day." Maddy had had no trouble adopting Sam. Frank—thank God—had approved Sam's adoption of Maddy, although it wasn't legal yet. Frank had three years left on his sentence and, in the middle of a hot and heavy correspondence with his former secretary, he was too busy to bother being a good father. Annie hadn't needed to try very hard to convince him.

"There were fifty-four kids on the bus. Have I ever counted to fifty-four before, Mommy? They didn't all have backpacks. I don't know how many backpacks they had." Maddy frowned.

"Maybe half had backpacks," Sam said, his eyes making a lazy scan of the V-neck of Annie's pirate T-shirt.

"Half." Maddy held up the index finger on her right hand. "One." Then the index finger on her left hand. "Two." Then the middle finger on her right. "Three… I can't count halves until I'm in the bigger grades."

"Wise child." Sam chucked her chin. "Why don't you go tell Grandpa about your day?"

Maddy scampered off.

Annie came around her desk and sat in Sam's lap. "You survived?"

He wrapped his arms around her and buried his face in her neck. "Fifty-four kids. It was a high volume day. I'm going to need extra-special treatment tonight." His lips did something naughty and wonderful to her neck.

"Poor baby. I'm sorry I forgot I had that doctor's appointment." Annie sighed and tilted her head just enough that her husband had better access to the sweet spot below her ear. "It's a good thing you married me last month because…oh, right there." There was something heavenly about his touch.

"Because…" Sam prompted, stopping.

"The doctor seems to think we're on the way to enlarging this family."

Sam's mouth stilled against her neck. He tipped his head sideways to see her face. "A baby?"

"Yes," Annie whispered. "Is it too soon?"

He settled her more firmly against him. "No."

"It's too soon."

Sam chuckled, the sound reverberating into her. "Is that why you wanted to put in an offer on that monstrosity of a house?"

"I said I wanted everything normal people have, including the lawn."

"When are you going to learn that you aren't normal?" Sam shifted and cradled her face in his hands. "You are the most special, exasperating woman I know, and I'm going to love you until my last breath. But just once—" he sighed "—just once I'd like to be a step ahead of you."

"Oh, honey, I wish that was possible, but I don't think it's meant to be." Annie leaned closer and whispered in his ear. "Twins."

"Twins?"

But Sam was grinning, and Annie knew she may not be counting cards but she could count on Sam's love no matter what hand they were dealt.

* * * * *

*Silhouette® Romantic Suspense
keeps getting hotter!
Turn the page for a sneak preview of
Wendy Rosnau's latest SPY GAMES title
SLEEPING WITH DANGER*

Available November 2007

*Silhouette® Romantic Suspense—
Sparked by Danger, Fueled by Passion!*

Melita had been expecting a chaste quick kiss of the generic variety. But this kiss with Sully was the kind that sparked a dying flame to life. The kind of kiss you can't plan for. The kind of kiss memories are built on.

The memory of her murdered lover, Nemo, came to her then and she made a starved little noise in the back of her throat. She raised her arms and threaded her fingers through Sully's hair, pulled him closer. Felt his body settle, then melt into her.

In that instant her hunger for him grew, and his for her. She pressed herself to him with more urgency, and he responded in kind.

Melita came out of her kiss-induced memory of

Nemo with a start. "Wait a minute." She pushed Sully away from her. "You bastard!"

She spit two nasty words at him in Greek, then wiped his kiss from her lips.

"I thought you deserved some solid proof that I'm still in one piece." He started for the door. "The clock's ticking, honey. Come on, let's get out of here."

"That's it? You sucker me into kissing you, and that's all you have to say?"

"I'm sorry. How's that?"

He didn't sound sorry in the least. "You're—"

"Getting out of this godforsaken prison cell. Stop whining and let's go."

"Not if I was being shot at sunrise. Go. You deserve whatever you get if you walk out that door."

He turned back. "Freedom is what I'm going to get."

"A second of freedom before the guards in the hall shoot you." She jammed her hands on her hips. "And to think I was worried about you."

"If you're staying behind, it's no skin off my ass."

"Wait! What about our deal?"

"You just said you're not coming. Make up your mind."

"Have you forgotten we need a boat?"

"How could I? You keep harping on it."

"I'm not going without a boat. And those guards out there aren't going to just let you walk out of here. You need me and we need a plan."

"I already have a plan. I'm getting out of here. That's the plan."

"I should have realized that you never intended to take me with you from the very beginning. You're a liar and a coward."

Of everything she had read, there was nothing in Sully Paxton's file that hinted he was a coward, but it was the one word that seemed to register in that one-track mind of his. The look he nailed her with a second later was pure venom.

He came at her so quickly she didn't have time to get out of his way. "You know I'm not a coward."

"Prove it. Give me until dawn. I need one more night to put everything in place before we leave the island."

"You're asking me to stay in this cell one more night...and trust you?"

"Yes."

He snorted. "Yesterday you knew they were planning to harm me, but instead of doing something about it you went to bed and never gave me a second thought. Suppose tonight you do the same. By tomorrow I might damn well be in my grave."

"Okay, I screwed up. I won't do it again." Melita sucked in a ragged breath. "I can't leave this minute. Dawn, Sully. Wait until dawn." When he looked as if he was about to say no, she pleaded, "Please wait for me."

"You're asking a lot. The door's open now. I would be a fool to hang around here and trust that you'll be back."

"What you can trust is that I want off this island as badly as you do, and you're my only hope."

"I must be crazy."

"Is that a yes?"

"Dammit!" He turned his back on her. Swore twice more.

"You won't be sorry."

He turned around. "I already am. How about we seal this new deal?"

He was staring at her lips. Suddenly Melita knew what he expected. "We already sealed it."

"One more. You enjoyed it. Admit it."

"I enjoyed it because I was kissing someone else."

He laughed. "That's a good one."

"It's true. It might have been your lips, but it wasn't you I was kissing."

"If that's your excuse for wanting to kiss me, then—"

"I was kissing Nemo."

"What's a nemo?"

Melita gave Sully a look that clearly told him that he was trespassing on sacred ground. She was about to enforce it with a warning when a voice in the hall jerked them both to attention.

She bolted away from the wall. "Get back in bed. Hurry. I'll be here before dawn."

She didn't reach the door before he snagged her arm, pulled her up against him and planted a kiss on her lips that took her completely by surprise.

When he released her, he said, "If you're confused about who just kissed you, the name's Sully. I'll be here waiting at dawn. Don't be late."

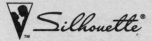

Silhouette®

Romantic
SUSPENSE

Sparked by Danger,
Fueled by Passion.

Onyxx agent Sully Paxton's only chance of
survival lies in the hands of his enemy's daughter
Melita Krizova. He doesn't know he's a pawn in the
beautiful island girl's own plan for escape. Can
they survive their ruses and their fiery attraction?

**Look for the next installment in the
Spy Games miniseries,**

Sleeping with Danger

by Wendy Rosnau

Available November 2007 wherever you buy books.

Cut from the soap opera that made her a star, America's
TV goddess Gloria Hart heads back to her childhood
home to regroup. But when a car crash maroons her in
small-town Mississippi, it's local housewife Jenny Miller
to the rescue. Soon these two very different women,
together with Gloria's sassy assistant, become fast friends,
realizing that they bring out a certain secret something
in each other that men find irresistible!

Look for

THE SECRET
GODDESS CODE

by

PEGGY WEBB

Available November wherever you buy books.

HARLEQUIN®

NeXt™

The Next Novel.com

HN88146

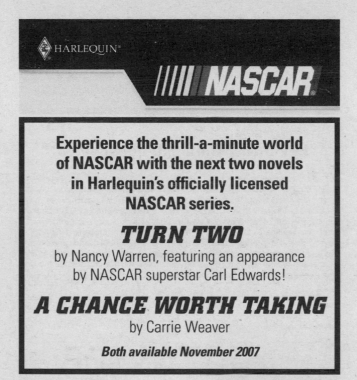

REQUEST YOUR FREE BOOKS!
2 FREE NOVELS PLUS 2 FREE GIFTS!

HARLEQUIN®

Super Romance®

Exciting, emotional, unexpected!

YES! Please send me 2 FREE Harlequin Superromance® novels and my 2 FREE gifts. After receiving them, if I don't wish to receive any more books, I can return the shipping statement marked "cancel." If I don't cancel, I will receive 6 brand-new novels every month and be billed just $4.69 per book in the U.S., or $5.24 per book in Canada, plus 25¢ shipping and handling per book and applicable taxes, if any*. That's a savings of close to 15% off the cover price! I understand that accepting the 2 free books and gifts places me under no obligation to buy anything. I can always return a shipment and cancel at any time. Even if I never buy another book from Harlequin, the two free books and gifts are mine to keep forever.

135 HDN EEX7   336 HDN EEYK

Name	(PLEASE PRINT)
Address	Apt.
City	State/Prov.	Zip/Postal Code

Signature (if under 18, a parent or guardian must sign)

Mail to the **Harlequin Reader Service®:**
IN U.S.A.: P.O. Box 1867, Buffalo, NY 14240-1867
IN CANADA: P.O. Box 609, Fort Erie, Ontario L2A 5X3

Not valid to current Harlequin Superromance subscribers.

Want to try two free books from another line?
Call 1-800-873-8635 or visit www.morefreebooks.com.

* Terms and prices subject to change without notice. NY residents add applicable sales tax. Canadian residents will be charged applicable provincial taxes and GST. This offer is limited to one order per household. All orders subject to approval. Credit or debit balances in a customer's account(s) may be offset by any other outstanding balance owed by or to the customer. Please allow 4 to 6 weeks for delivery.

Your Privacy: Harlequin is committed to protecting your privacy. Our Privacy Policy is available online at www.eHarlequin.com or upon request from the Reader Service. From time to time we make our lists of customers available to reputable firms who may have a product or service of interest to you. If you would prefer we not share your name and address, please check here. ☐

HSR07

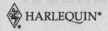

EVERLASTING LOVE ™

Every great love has a story to tell ™

Charlie fell in love with Rose Kaufman
before he even met her, through stories her
husband, Joe, used to tell. When Joe is killed
in the trenches, Charlie helps Rose through
her grief and they make a new life together.
But for Charlie, a question remains—can
love be as true the second time around?
Only one woman can answer that....

Look for

The Soldier and
the Rose

by
Linda Barrett

Available November wherever you buy books.

HARLEQUIN Romance.

New York Times bestselling author

DIANA PALMER

Handsome, eligible ranch owner Stuart York knew
Ivy Conley was too young for him, so he closed his heart
to her and sent her away—despite the fireworks between
them. Now, years later, Ivy is determined not to be
treated like a little girl anymore…but for some reason,
Stuart is always fighting her battles for her. And safe in
Stuart's arms makes Ivy feel like a woman…his woman.

Winter Roses

Available November.

HARLEQUIN Super Romance

COMING NEXT MONTH

#1452 BETTING ON SANTA • Debra Salonen
Texas Hold 'Em

When Tessa Jamison sets out to find the father of her sister's toddler, she doesn't expect to like anything about Cole Lawry, a carpenter with humble aspirations. Theirs is a secret-baby story with a twist. Because when it comes to love, the stakes are high....

#1453 A CHRISTMAS TO REMEMBER • Kay Stockham

A soldier wakes up in a hospital unable to remember anything. Before he can regain his memory, he runs into the woman he once betrayed. He can't believe that he could ever do anything to hurt someone, but there's no other explanation. Or is there?

#1454 SNOWBOUND • Janice Kay Johnson

Fiona MacPherson takes refuge from a raging blizzard in the lodge owned by John Fallon. John bought Thunder Mountain Lodge because he wanted to be by himself. Spending time with Fiona has him wondering if love might be something he wants more.

#1455 A TOWN CALLED CHRISTMAS • Carrie Alexander

A woman named Merry, a town called Christmas. Both could be just what a lonely Navy pilot who's the recipient of a Dear John letter needs. But Mike Kavanaugh isn't looking for a relationship that lasts beyond the holidays. And how can he ask that of Merry when she's expecting a little bundle in just a few months?

#1456 COMFORT AND JOY • Amy Frazier
Twins

Coming home for Christmas—to stay—is not what Gabriel Brant had in mind. Not when it means he and his twin sons have to live with his father. But Hurricane Katrina left him no choice. And now small-town do-gooder Olivia Marshall wants to heal him. Gabriel doesn't want pity. Love? That's a whole other story.

#1457 THE CHRISTMAS BABY • Eve Gaddy
The Brothers Kincaid

The Bachelor and the Baby could be the title of Brian Kincaid's life story. The perpetual playboy has just gotten custody of a baby boy. In desperation, he hires Faith McClain, a single mother of a baby girl, as his nanny. Could marriage and family life be the next chapter?

HSRCNM1007